LIKE CATS AND DOGS

Kate McMurray

sourcebooks
casablanca

Published by Sourcebooks Casablanca, an imprint of Sourcebooks
P.O. Box 4410, Naperville, Illinois 60567-4410
(630) 961-3900
sourcebooks.com

Library of Congress Cataloging-in-Publication Data

Names: McMurray, Kate, author.
Title: Like cats and dogs / Kate McMurray.
Description: Naperville, Illinois: Sourcebooks Casablanca, [2021] |
Series: Whitman Street Cat Café; 1
Identifiers: LCCN 2020054452 (print) | LCCN 2020054453 (ebook)
Subjects: GSAFD: Love stories.
Classification: LCC PS3613.C58555 L55 2021 (print) |
LCC PS3613.C58555 (ebook) | DDC 813/.6--dc23
LC record available at https://lccn.loc.gov/2020054452
LC ebook record available at https://lccn.loc.gov/2020054453

Printed and bound in the United States of America.
VP 10 9 8 7 6 5 4 3 2 1

CHAPTER 1

SADIE THE OFFICE MANAGER YOWLED.

"I hear ya," Lauren said absently as she leaned against the counter and looked at her phone. There was an unusually long line of people waiting for their morning coffee. Lauren was a bit of a spy in her own kingdom as she waited for her own coffee, letting customers go ahead of her as she kept an eye on her staff.

She glanced at her phone and refreshed the page one more time. The photos were still right there on top. Derek and Joanna's wedding. Derek smiling like he hadn't in years, Joanna looking ridiculously beautiful, and Lauren wondering how Derek was happy and married now when she was single and surrounded by cats.

Literally. Sadie walked up and rubbed against her leg. The little butterball of a cat had the loudest purr Lauren had ever heard, and she deployed it now, sounding like dice being rolled across a wooden table.

Lauren had read recently that cats likely purred not to display happiness but rather to lure prey into a false sense of security. She leaned down and pet Sadie's head anyway.

Evan walked into the Whitman Street Cat Café, pushing

through the second door and grinning at Lauren like he'd already had three cups of coffee.

"Derek got married this weekend," Lauren said by way of greeting.

"Aw, honey, I'm sorry," said Evan. "Anything I can do?"

"Drive to New Hampshire and punch him in the face?"

Evan tilted his head and seemed to consider doing just that. "As fun as that sounds, Derek is kind of a big guy. He might punch back, and I bruise like a peach."

Lauren laughed despite herself. She shoved her phone in her pocket. "I'm over it. So my ex got married? It's fine. I'm fine."

"Attagirl." Evan looked up at the menu like he didn't get coffee here nearly every morning.

"Not that I'm sad for the business," said Lauren, "but where did all these people come from?"

"Didn't you hear? The Star Café closed last week."

The Star Café was a great independent coffee shop that had, apparently until last week, been right across the street from the Cat Café. If it had closed, that explained all the people here, the last place that served coffee between Henry Street and the subway entrance on the next block.

"I'm devastated," Evan continued.

Lauren raised an eyebrow at him. "If anything, this is probably better for your health. There are only so many cups of coffee you can drink per day because you think the barista is cute before the caffeine gives you heart palpitations."

Evan sighed and leaned against the counter next to Lauren. "Pablo gave me heart palpitations."

"Any idea what he's up to now?"

"When I got my caramel vanilla latte on Friday, he told me he'd applied to work at that little indie bookstore a few doors down. Hope springs."

"Crazy idea, but you could, like, ask him out."

Evan gasped dramatically. "Where's the romance in that? We're performing an elaborate dance."

"Right." Lauren glanced behind the counter, where Monique looked panicked as she took another order. "Maybe I should hire him."

"He makes a mean caramel vanilla latte."

A bewildered man with light brown hair walked into the café then. Lauren had never seen him before, and she would have noticed. He was so handsome, Evan sucked in a sharp breath.

Lauren had sworn off men ever since Derek had announced his engagement, because she was tired of getting her heart stomped on, but that didn't mean she couldn't look. Because this man was pretty foxy. He was tall and fit with neatly trimmed hair, a square jaw, and blue eyes that sparkled even from behind the dark-rimmed glasses he wore.

"Hello," said Evan.

The man looked around. When Sadie trotted over to investigate him, he looked a little startled by her presence.

"Oh," he said, catching Lauren's eye. "I've heard about places like this, but I guess it didn't occur to me that the cats would just be...out."

"Only Sadie has free rein in the café," said Lauren. "She's in charge. She's also terrified of cars, so she doesn't try to escape. The rest of the cats are through that door." She pointed.

"Ah."

Lauren wasn't really sure what to say next. Evan elbowed her, though, so she said, "Did you want to see the cats, or—"

"I just need a cup of coffee for now. This place is hopping."

"Go on," Lauren said. "I'm not in line, and you look like you're in a hurry."

The man pulled a phone from his pocket and glanced at the time. "Yeah, a little." He slid forward. "Thank you."

"Are you new to the neighborhood?"

"Yeah. Just moved to Brooklyn a week ago, actually."

"Welcome!"

He shot her a bashful half smile and nodded. "Thanks."

Monique said, "Next!"

The brown-haired man nodded at Lauren and then walked to the register.

Victor, the other barista, must have noticed this guy was a little twitchy, probably with a job to get to—he was wearing a blue oxford shirt tucked into navy-blue slacks, the uniform of the Midtown office worker—so he grabbed the pot and poured a cup of coffee right away. Once the man paid, Victor handed him the cup and said, "Milk and sugar are at the end of the counter."

"Great." The man took his cup.

"The usual," Lauren said to Monique now that the line had dissipated. Then she walked over to the man as he shook a sugar packet. "I'm Lauren, by the way."

The man gave her a genuine smile this time. "Caleb. Maybe

I'll see you around, Lauren." Sadie meowed and sat at his feet. "And you, too, Sadie."

Handsome, and he liked the cats. No wedding ring. This had some potential.

Oh, except for the part where Lauren was not dating in order to concentrate on making a fulfilling life for herself without a man.

Caleb walked back outside.

"Girl," said Evan. "He was totally checking you out."

Warm excitement spread through Lauren's chest. It had been a while since she'd met anyone who made her pulse race like this. She wondered if Caleb would come back.

"Boss, your coffee's ready," said Monique.

Lauren took it gratefully. "All right. Do you have to work today, Ev, or do you want to meet our newest resident? We've got a gorgeous new calico named Lucy."

"I'm meeting a client at ten, so I gotta go, but you can tell me all about Miss Lucy and report back on that tall guy over drinks tonight."

"Pop at seven?"

"Perfect."

Monique handed Evan his coffee, which he took with a grin. He blew Lauren a kiss with his free hand and then walked out the door.

"Come on, Sadie," said Lauren. "Let's get to work."

———

Caleb walked out of the Cat Café, wondering what he'd just seen. For some reason, he hadn't expected actual cats. When his new boss had recommended it as a place to grab coffee, he'd expected beatniks or something. There was a bar on his block called the Salty Dog that contained zero dogs, after all. But, no, the Whitman Street Cat Café was a place people went to get coffee and pastries and hang out with *actual* cats.

The woman had been pretty nice to look at. Lauren, she'd said her name was. A little tall, with long, straight brown hair, a fringe of bangs across her forehead, and a dusting of freckles across her nose. Pretty smile. And, okay, he'd noticed her figure, too. After his recent and very messy divorce, it was nice to know that part of him hadn't died along with his belief in happily ever after.

She'd been so comfortable in the space that he figured she worked there or was at least a regular, so maybe he'd run into her again.

In the meantime, though, he had to cope with his first day at the new job. Caleb strolled all ten feet from the café door to the main entrance of the Whitman Street Veterinary Clinic. A little bell rang over the door, catching the attention of the cat perched on the lap of a woman sitting in the waiting area.

"Dr. Fitch!" said the vet tech at the reception desk as Caleb approached. He couldn't remember her name at first, but then noticed she had a name tag on her scrubs identifying her as Rachel. Olivia's weird insistence on name tags would pay off after all, because Caleb was terrible with names.

Although he'd remember Lauren.

No, not the time. He smiled at Rachel. "Good morning."

"I see you got coffee from the Cat Café," she said, pointing to his cup. "The Star Café made better lattes, but they're closed now."

Caleb took a sip of his coffee. It was pretty standard drip

coffee, stronger than the stuff those dumb little pods at his old job made, so he was happy enough with it.

"Welcome to Whitman Street," Rachel said. "Olivia's in her office. She told me to send you there when you came in."

"Right. And that is…"

"Oh!" Rachel hopped up and led Caleb to a swinging door that he remembered led to the exam rooms and administrative offices. She held the door open and said, "Go left here, then right at the end of the hall, and Olivia's office is right there."

"Thanks."

Olivia Ling was indeed in her office when Caleb found it. She seemed absorbed in something on her computer screen, so Caleb knocked on the doorframe. She looked up and seemed confused for a moment, but then recognition dawned. "Caleb! Please come in."

He'd already taken care of the new-hire paperwork, so the main thing would be to work out scheduling and procedures. Caleb would be the fifth veterinarian on staff at a fairly busy clinic, but he was happy to work in a big office. The clinic he'd come from had been run by two people and constantly felt short-staffed.

"I see you got coffee from the Cat Café."

"Oh. Yeah, you said it was the best coffee on the block." Also the only coffee on the block, from what he could tell.

"Did you talk to the manager?"

"No. I got coffee."

Olivia smiled. "Well, just so you know, we have a partnership. We're the official vet of the Cat Café, and they help us find forever homes for any cats who end up here."

That made sense. "Do they do pet adoptions?"

"Yeah, that's the Cat Café's secret mission. They lure people in with coffee and pastries in hopes the customers fall in love with one of the cats and take it home."

"Sneaky."

"Anyway, scheduling."

Olivia had already explained when she expected the vets in her clinic to work—including at least one overnight per week, because this was the only animal clinic in Brooklyn that kept emergency hours. A whiteboard on the wall showed which vets were scheduled on which days. Then she took him on a chatty tour through the exam rooms.

"Remind me where you worked before this?" she asked, sounding like she was trying to make conversation but probably gauging whether she could leave him alone with patients or if she needed to keep an eye on him until he adapted to her preferred procedures.

"The Animal Care Clinic on 110th Street in Morningside Heights. It closed a few weeks ago." Well, it closed because Kara had divorced Caleb, shut down the clinic, and moved to LA with her new boyfriend, but this was not information Olivia needed.

"Let's do the first patient together," Olivia said. She grabbed a chart from the plastic holder on the door to Exam Room 1, then popped her head into the waiting room and said, "Jingles?"

The woman, who'd been holding the cat in her lap when Caleb had walked in, kicked a cat carrier under the seat and carried her surprisingly placid-looking gray cat into the exam room.

All right, that was how this would play out. Caleb plastered his best animal-loving smile on his face and prepared to examine this cat under Olivia's watchful eye.

CHAPTER 2

LAUREN AND HER EVENTS MANAGER Paige sat at a table in the main part of the café, hammering out ideas for an adoption event. Lauren hoped all this extra business they'd been getting in the wake of the Star Café closing meant some of the cats would be adopted by the affluent animal lovers in this rapidly gentrifying neighborhood near downtown Brooklyn.

Lauren had gone for kind of a mod look when she'd decorated the main sitting area: bright colors, mid-century modern design, a Shag-esque retro mural on one wall that depicted cats drinking coffee. She loved this space. At first, she worried she'd grow to hate the bright colors, but there was so much visual interest in the room that she never tired of looking at it. There were, of course, structures for the cats to lounge on all over the space. She'd built some of them herself, with particleboard and some lime-green carpeting she'd gotten for a steep discount. There were also bins full of cat toys—Lauren was forever picking up little fur mice and balls with attached feathers from places where people might trip over them.

Diane breezed in with her customary cup of tea in her hand. She wore a pink caftan that flowed over her body and, without asking permission, sat at the table with Lauren and Paige.

Lauren didn't shoo her away. Diane owned the building and the Cat Café, after all.

"Good afternoon, Diane," Lauren said.

"Hello, dear. This place is hopping today."

"I know. I might have to start imposing limits on how many people can sit in here at a time. Too many people stress out the cats."

One of those cats, a tortie kitten named Chloe, hopped up on the table right then and began to investigate the half-eaten muffin on Lauren's plate. Lauren scooped her up and put her in her lap.

"Have you met the new vet yet?" Diane asked.

"New vet?"

"The clinic hired a new vet who started there a few days ago. He's a cutie."

Lauren laughed. Diane was pushing seventy and retired from some corporate job she didn't like to talk about. She had used her savings and the money her late partner had left her to buy this five-story apartment building with two storefronts on the first floor: the Cat Café and the Veterinary Clinic. Olivia Ling owned and operated the vet clinic, but the Cat Café had been Diane's idea, and she technically owned the business as well as the space. She was a hands-off owner, though, and she let Lauren run the café however she liked, as long as she ran financial decisions by her, and Diane could come in for a cup of tea and some time with the cats free of charge whenever it struck her fancy. Diane reminded Lauren a lot of her own mother, although Diane was far more eccentric. Today, her short bleached blond hair had been styled into soft waves around her face, and she'd completed the look with a full face of makeup and purple cat-eye glasses.

And she loved gossip.

"I haven't met the new vet," Lauren said.

"You should go introduce yourself! He's working today."

Lauren caught Paige rolling her eyes just outside of Diane's peripheral vision. Lauren had detected a bit of matchmaking fervor in Diane's tone but chose to ignore it. "If we ever have a slow moment again, I'll pop over and say hi."

Diane sipped her tea and looked at Lauren over the top of the cup, her eyes sparkling. "See that you do. I've got a feeling about this one."

Paige snorted. "The same way you had a feeling about that kid who works at the bookstore?"

Lauren sighed. Diane was hit-or-miss with the matchmaking.

"You don't have to marry him," Diane said. "Just go say hello. It's in the best interest of your business anyway, since you will very likely be working together."

Lauren raised an eyebrow. She could still detect a bit of mischief in Diane's enigmatic smile, but she said, "I will." She thought of the handsome guy who got coffee the other morning. Caleb. He was really cute, and Lauren wouldn't have minded flirting a little—no harm in that, after all—but he hadn't been back since, at least not while Lauren had been in the café.

"Is Mitch doing another one of those rescue events?" asked Diane as she leaned forward and peered at Lauren's notes.

Lauren glanced at her notes and then back at Diane. Mitch was an old friend of Lauren's, and he ran an organization that trapped feral cats and brought them to the Whitman Street Veterinary Clinic to be spayed or neutered before either organizing adoptions with Lauren or tagging and releasing the cats back into the feral colony that lived around the Brooklyn Museum. Some cats would not make good pets, but they could be prevented from making more cats. Mitch organized events to trap untagged cats about once a month in an attempt to humanely decrease the feral cat population in Brooklyn.

"They usually go out the third Thursday of the month," Lauren said, flipping through her notes to find the printout of her calendar. "Why, do you want to go?"

"No, but my niece is interested."

"Oh, great. I've got flyers behind the counter with all the information. Want me to get you one?"

"No, that's all right. I'll ask Monique on my way out. I'll also keep an eye on things here if you want to go see the new vet now. And, hello, nice to see you!" Diane reached down and pet the head of a tuxedo cat who was rubbing against her leg.

"We can go over the rest of this later," said Paige.

Traitor, Lauren mouthed to Paige. Then she stood. "Fine. I'll go say hi. Keep an eye on that stripy orange cat. His name is Houdini because he thinks he's an escape artist."

"I've got this," Diane said. "Go."

———————————

Caleb pet the head of a French bulldog named Howard, whose tongue lolled out in appreciation. "He'll be fine on the new diet," he told the anxious pet parents. "I'll write you a prescription for the new food. Rachel at the front desk can get you all set up with that."

"Thank you so much, Dr. Fitch," said the wife. "I appreciate that you helped him calm down so much. His old vet made him so nervous."

"My pleasure." With one last smile and nod, Caleb left Exam 1. Through the door to the waiting room, he heard Rachel say, "Hi, Lauren! Good to see you."

He peeked through the little window in the door. He could only see her in profile, but it was indeed Lauren from the Cat Café. She had on a boxy denim jacket that obscured her figure somewhat, with her long hair splayed out around her shoulders, and she wore a friendly smile on her face.

Before he knew what he was doing, Caleb pushed through the door. On the pretense of giving Rachel the prescription for Howard's new food, he pulled out his pad and scribbled down the patient's name and the food he needed. He handed the slip to Rachel without really looking at her and said, "Hello again," to Lauren.

Lauren looked a little startled. Her gaze traveled over him, probably taking in the white lab coat and the name tag. "You're the new vet."

"Uh, yes."

Rachel cleared her throat. "Lauren, this is Dr. Caleb Fitch. Caleb, this is Lauren."

Caleb couldn't take his eyes off Lauren. It was like he'd conjured her.

"Lauren manages the Cat Café," Rachel said.

She manages the café? "Oh," said Caleb.

"I came over to introduce myself to the new vet because we will inevitably end up working together. All cats who live in the café come through here first. I didn't realize *you* were the new vet."

Caleb didn't know how to interpret the way she'd said *you*, but he said, "Great. I look forward to working with you."

She smiled, which Caleb took to mean she was pleasantly surprised, so that was something. "I mean, if I'd known, I would have given you a discount on the coffee or something."

"It's fine, really."

"Let me make it up to you. Next time you get a break, come on over and I'll hook you up with a cup of coffee and a pastry. We have really good blueberry scones."

Caleb recognized this as an olive branch, not a date. Which was good, because he had no business dating so soon after the divorce. "Sure, I can do that."

"Great. I gotta go, I was just coming by to say hi. So, hi! I'll, uh, see you around, Caleb."

He and Lauren could potentially spend a lot of time together, depending on what kind of cat turnover the café had. "How long has the Cat Café been open?" he asked Rachel after Lauren left.

"About a year."

"Wow." That was impressive for something that seemed like a fly-by-night idea. "And it's popular?"

"Yeah. Pretty popular. She's got a good group of regular customers, mostly people who can't have pets at home for whatever reason but want to pet some cats. It's therapeutic."

"Sure." Caleb recognized the therapeutic value of animal companions, but he still found the idea of a cat café a little silly. If one liked spending time with cats, why not just...get a cat?

Caleb loved animals, though he didn't currently have pets because Kara had gotten their mixed breed rescue dog Jimmy in the divorce. Caleb still missed that dog.

And this was why he was never getting married again.

He cleared his throat as Howard led his owners back into the waiting room. "Howard here needs a bag of the Pro Diet SD formula," he said to Rachel. He gave his spiel about feeding routines and where they could order more food, and once they were gone, it hit him that, well, he had a coffee date with Lauren from the Cat Café. And he was kind of looking forward to it.

CHAPTER 3

LAUREN SIGNED THE DELIVERY SLIP for three dozen bagels she had delivered every morning from, in her opinion, the best bagel place in Brooklyn.

The café had a kitchen—the space had been a little Italian bistro before Diane had the idea for the Cat Café—but it wasn't currently in use. Instead, they ordered their array of pastries from several local bakeries and cafés. If they were going to keep all this business after some new coffee shop inevitably opened nearby, they'd need to enhance their offerings.

Something to mull over.

Sadie walked over and headbutted Lauren's leg, then sat down and meowed.

"You need something, pretty girl?" Lauren asked.

Sadie trotted over to the door that led to what staff referred to as the cat room, the main seating area of the café, and pawed at it. Lauren said goodbye to the delivery guy and walked over to let Sadie into the room. While she was there, she decided to check on the cats. Sadie hopped up on the sofa, where a calico named

Sunday was curled up, napping. Sadie then acted entirely out of character and snuggled up to Sunday. Lauren's pulse spiked; something was wrong with this cat.

Sunday had acted oddly the day before, and Lauren suspected it might be a mild cold, the kind of thing that blew over in twenty-four hours. Cats tended to get more affectionate when they didn't feel well, wanting comfort and snuggles just like people did.

Lauren knelt beside the sofa and pet Sunday's head. The little cat picked up her chin and started purring, so she was probably okay, but just in case, Lauren picked her up and carried her to the back room so that, if she was sick, it wouldn't spread to the other cats. She didn't want to bother whichever vet was on duty today in case it turned out to be nothing.

Although she did wonder if it would be Caleb. He still hadn't come by for his cup of coffee in the few days since she'd invited him, which she probably should have taken as a sign that he was just not that into her... Even though she didn't want him to be into her... Well, okay, she did... But, well, love was still off the table. And it seemed ill-advised to pursue a quick roll in the hay with a guy she'd likely have to work with in the future.

Sunday curled up in the cat bed. Lauren put a bowl of water and a bowl of kibble down for her. "I'll be back to check on you soon, okay?"

Sunday gave a disinterested snort, stood up, turned around, and lay back down.

Lauren got pulled into helping with the rush hour crush, mostly putting pastries in paper bags while her employees made lattes and rang people up. When things finally calmed down a couple of hours later, she checked on Sunday, who had wandered into the curtained-off back area where litter boxes and extra food were stashed. She hadn't touched the food but was presently squatting over a magazine that had fallen on the floor. But nothing came out. Classic sign of a UTI.

"Lauren, can you come out here?" called Monique. "I need help with something."

"Hang in there, Sunday. We'll go see the vet soon and get you some antibiotics to clear that right up."

There was finally a lull in the late afternoon, by which time Sunday seemed a bit droopy. She hadn't eaten anything, probably because she was in pain from the UTI. Lauren grabbed a carrier and loaded Sunday into it, then took her next door.

Caleb stood at the reception desk when Lauren walked in. He seemed to be chatting with Rachel, and no one else was in the waiting room. He was still as handsome as ever, his light brown hair a little disheveled today, his white lab coat fitting neatly over his shoulders.

"Hi," Caleb said, standing straight suddenly. He smiled.

"Hi. I've got a sick cat," said Lauren.

Rachel wheeled over to a filing cabinet and said, "Which one?"

"Sunday."

Rachel pulled out a file and handed it to Caleb. He said, "All right. Come on back."

Lauren followed Caleb into an exam room. He flipped through the file as Lauren took Sunday out of the carrier. Sunday was definitely sick, because she didn't put up a fight or try to dig her claws into the floor of the carrier, as was otherwise routine. Rather than put her on the cold metal table, Lauren cradled Sunday in her arms and pet her head.

"What are the symptoms?" asked Caleb.

"I think it's a UTI. She's been doing that thing where she randomly squats like she's going to pee, but nothing comes out."

Caleb looked up and met her gaze, and Lauren wondered how it was that she was talking about cat pee with a very handsome man. What wrong turn had she taken to end up here?

"Anything else?" he asked. "Is she eating? Drinking water?"

"No. I put water and food out for her in the back room at the café this morning, and both have been basically untouched all day."

Caleb put the file down. "Can I examine her?"

"Oh. Of course."

Slowly, Lauren put Sunday down on the table. Sunday let out a little mewl of protest when her paws hit the cold metal. Caleb pet her head as he looked her over. "Hi, little girl," he cooed. Sunday was putty. She started purring and leaning into his hand.

"I'd like to run some tests," he said.

"Is that really necessary? It's pretty clearly a UTI. Can't you just prescribe antibiotics?"

"She's also not eating or drinking water, so there may be another underlying problem."

"Or she's in pain from the infection. I don't want to traumatize her by putting her through a bunch of unnecessary tests."

Caleb gazed at Lauren over the top of his glasses. That was clearly a "Which one of us is the veterinarian again?" look. "Nothing invasive, just a urinalysis to confirm the UTI and a few blood tests to make sure nothing else is up." He leaned down toward the table and started examining Sunday more closely.

"I don't want to tell you how to do your job—"

"Then don't." Caleb glanced up at Lauren, then went back to examining Sunday.

"But I've worked with probably a hundred cats in my time at the Cat Café. This is a garden-variety UTI."

"You're probably right, but just to be safe, indulge me."

Did Caleb not get how this was supposed to work? If Olivia had been working, she would have written the scrip without all this drama. Urinary tract issues were common in cats, and Lauren had seen a dozen of them. She knew what this was.

"I know you're new here, but I don't think I can justify the expense of unnecessary tests."

"They aren't unnecessary. I'm trying to make sure there isn't a worse underlying problem. If it's not a UTI and Sunday gets sicker, then where will we be?"

Lauren let out a frustrated grunt.

Sunday let out another little mewl as Caleb ran his hand over her belly. He frowned. "This could be a blockage. Maybe I should do an ultrasound."

"Geez." It was like he was deliberately challenging her now. Lauren crossed her arms, wondering if she should prepare to do battle.

Caleb stood up straight again. "I mean, I only spent five years in veterinary school, and five in practice, but you run a café, so you must know better."

Lauren took a step back. She hadn't expected the sarcasm,

even though she knew she was poking him. Maybe he was right, but she hated to put Sunday through unnecessary tests, or to subject her bottom line at the café to a huge veterinary bill. She was willing to eat the cost for a real problem, but she could see the dollar bills floating in front of her, a lot of them, for what should have been a pretty standard course of treatment.

"I'm sorry," she said, "but—"

"Could you maybe trust me? Wouldn't you rather rule out any potential issues that could be causing this little cat worse problems that antibiotics won't cure? Cats have short memories. Drawing a little blood will be forgotten in an hour. And an ultrasound is not invasive but will tell me if she has a blockage or anything else unusual going on. Did she use the litter box at all today?"

"Not that I could tell."

"Well, then."

Caleb felt a little bad for snapping at Lauren, but not that much, because she was getting on his last nerve. On the other hand, she looked kind of adorable when she was all angry and befuddled.

Besides which, this cat probably had kidney or bladder stones and not just a "garden-variety UTI." UTIs were usually associated with frequent urination, not no urine at all. The fact that this little cat had stopped eating was a red flag to Caleb, an indication of a more serious problem.

Lauren furrowed her brow. "I'm not an idiot, you know. I've worked with a lot of cats over the years."

"I know. But I'm not an idiot either. Here, hold her on the table. Let me go get the portable ultrasound."

He could tell she was going to fight him. He was in the right here, though, and he didn't need some café manager telling him how to do his job. Because if the cat did have some kind of stones, she was likely in pain, and Caleb needed to know exactly what was wrong so he could provide the right treatment to stop that pain.

Maybe Lauren was right. But she could let him run a couple of damn tests.

He walked out of the exam room and stuck his head into the waiting room. "Hey, Rachel? Can you assist me? Exam 1."

"No prob! Be right there!"

He went back into the exam room and said to Lauren, "Why don't you wait in the waiting room?"

"Olivia usually lets me assist."

"She must have better insurance than I do."

"Caleb—"

"Do you have to fight me on everything? I've done these tests three times just this week. I know what I'm doing, and you can trust me. Please wait in the waiting room. This will take ten minutes, tops."

Lauren pursed her lips and looked at Sunday, uncertainty all over her face. But she nodded and left the room, passing Rachel on her way out.

Ten minutes later, Caleb had ascertained there was a bladder stone small enough to pass on its own, so there wasn't much he could do. Usually, the treatment he preferred was blasting the stone with lasers to break it up, but he could already hear Lauren objecting to surgery, and it wasn't necessary anyway. But antibiotics certainly wouldn't do anything, so he wasn't going to subject the cat to them.

"I better go give Lauren the good bad news," he said to Rachel, who smirked.

"She means well," Rachel said.

"I'm sure she does, but I don't enjoy people telling me what's wrong with their cats as if they have the veterinary degree and I don't."

Rachel filled a small bowl with water and put it on the table next to the cat, who lapped at it.

Caleb took a deep breath and walked back to the waiting room. "You can come back now."

Lauren had clearly spent the last ten minutes working up a good amount of resentment toward him, and now she scowled and set her shoulders forward before marching into the exam room.

"Good luck," said Rachel under her breath.

Back in the exam room, Caleb said, "She doesn't need antibiotics. It's a bladder stone. This one is pretty small and should pass on its own in a day or two and she'll be back to normal. Try to make her drink as much water as possible. If you notice blood in her urine, bring her back and we'll look into surgically removing the stone."

"Surgery?"

"It's a small stone, but it's just big enough to block part of her urinary tract, which is why her symptoms read like a UTI. I doubt surgery is necessary. Give it a day or two, and if she's not better, come back."

But rather than thank Caleb for figuring out what was wrong with her cat, Lauren continued to glare at him. "Your bedside manner leaves something to be desired."

He sighed. "What do you want from me? You marched in here and told me what you thought was wrong. I actually did the tests to find the problem. If I'd gone ahead and prescribed antibiotics without checking, she probably would have gotten better on her own, but you'd have to chase her around to shove a pill down her throat twice a day for no reason. I saved you from that. I'm the good guy here."

"Are you this charming with everyone?"

He watched her pet Sunday for a moment. Sunday flopped onto her side and presented her belly to Lauren, who gasped.

"Did you shave my cat?"

"I had to for the ultrasound. Which is how I saw the bladder stone, by the way."

Lauren grunted and rubbed the cat's belly.

"Are you...mad I was right?"

"We're not friends, you know."

"Okay."

"I mean, you don't need to be this frank with me. We're basically strangers, so you could be polite. The other vets here are far more friendly. Maybe you don't realize the vet clinic and the Cat Café have kind of a symbiotic relationship."

It felt like the moment when the sky suddenly got dark, minutes before the heavens opened and the thunderstorm began in earnest. Caleb spoke anyway.

"As you so aptly pointed out, I am new here, and I'm happy

there's a good relationship between the clinic and the café, but I'm also the actual veterinarian here, so I don't need you to barge in here and tell me how to treat my patients. And I hate to point this out again, but if I'd just done what you'd said without actually examining the patient, I would have needlessly prescribed antibiotics."

"Fine, but you don't have to be rude about it."

"I'm not, I'm…fine. Sorry. But still, you were arrogant enough to assume you knew what was best for your cat and tried to tell me what tests to run, so I'm not the only one who acted inappropriately here."

Lauren scowled again. She picked up Sunday and bundled her back into the carrier. "I misjudged you."

"How so?"

"First time we met, you were just this good-looking guy in my café who needed his morning coffee, and everyone who has met you so far says you're this great guy, but good looks are no measure of character, and you, sir, are an arrogant prick."

Caleb opened his mouth to respond but couldn't come up with anything to say. She thought he was good looking. She also thought he was an arrogant prick. She was probably right on both counts, although he didn't think he was arrogant so much as right.

"I apologize, I do," he said. "But I try to be passionless when evaluating a patient. I can't assume my knowledge of the animal is enough to make a diagnosis without doing a few tests to back up or refute what I think. And cats are cute and all, but I—"

"Let me guess. You're a dog person." Lauren rolled her eyes.

"I like cats fine, but if I had to pick one or the other to have as a pet, I'd rather have a big, friendly dog."

Lauren snatched the cat carrier off the table as if his admission to being a dog person was the last straw. She probably lived in an apartment that had a huge cat condo in the living room with cats draped all over. He still found Lauren very attractive, but maybe he'd dodged a bullet.

He walked toward the door and opened it for her. As she stormed through it, he said, "I'm sorry if I was rude, but you have to admit you could have let me do my job."

"Sure, fine. I shouldn't have assumed." The "I'm over this and you irritate me" was left unspoken. "I'll see you later, Rach. And I'll see you," Lauren turned and pointed toward Caleb. "Much later, hopefully." Then she turned on her heel and walked out of the clinic.

"You've got a way with the ladies," said Rachel.

"But she… No, you know what? It doesn't matter. Are there any appointments this afternoon?"

Rachel looked at the computer. "Nothing until seven."

"Great. I've got some charts to finish up. I'll be in the office. Holler if anyone comes in."

"Is this like a schoolyard thing?"

Caleb paused on his way toward the back. "What?"

"Did you yank on her pigtails because you like her?"

"I'm a grown man."

"Uh-huh." Rachel turned back to the computer and smirked like she knew something Caleb didn't.

Well, she could believe what she wanted. Caleb had no time for whatever flakey nonsense Lauren peddled in. Cats in cafés, and people coming to drink tea and pet them? What even was that?

He sighed and pushed through the door to the back part of the office. Okay, sure, he liked her, and he sure had enjoyed riling her up, but they clearly had nothing in common, and she would very likely never speak to him again. Right?

CHAPTER 4

"I HATE HIM."

Evan rolled his eyes. "You don't."

Lauren and Evan were at Pop, a bar on Whitman Street a few blocks from the Cat Café. It had become Lauren and Evan's favorite bar in the short eight months or so it had been open, despite its absurdity. It was trying to be an upscale Manhattan cocktail bar, but this part of gentrified Brooklyn was all hipsters and young families and trust fund kids—more of a flannel-and-jeans crowd than a sparkly-cocktail-dress crowd. However, the martini page of the drink menu had twelve different options. Lauren was currently drinking something called a Deep Blue Sea, and she had no idea what was in it, but it was a blue martini garnished with a gummy shark, shoved onto the rim of the glass like an errant lemon wedge, and it tasted like cotton candy.

"I *do* hate Caleb," said Lauren. "He's such a smarmy know-it-all."

"I hate to even point this out, but he *is* a veterinarian. He does know a lot."

"Whose side are you on?"

"Yours, girl, always yours, but you doth protest too much."

"He's a *dog* person."

Evan laughed and then covered his mouth, probably realizing Lauren didn't find this funny. Lauren glared at him and sipped her martini.

"So you're telling me," Evan said, "that this isn't some, like, love-slash-hate thing like in the movies, where you fight but only because you're secretly into each other? Like, uh, Heath Ledger and Julia Stiles in *10 Things I Hate About You?* Or Moira Kelly and...that guy in *The Cutting Edge.* Or Sandra Bullock and Ryan Reynolds in *The Proposal.* Or *Moonlighting.* Or—"

"I get it." Lauren rolled her eyes. "And please. The world doesn't work that way."

"I dunno. When I was twelve, I picked fights with this boy Tommy because I was madly in love with him and didn't know what to do."

"See, that's a dick move. You probably traumatized him."

"Nope." Evan plucked a strawberry from the rim of his glass and popped it in his mouth with a grin. "What I did was exchange blow jobs with him in the locker room after gym class in tenth grade."

"Men are the worst."

"What? He wasn't traumatized. He had a crush on me, too."

"I just mean, you think sex fixes everything."

Evan picked up the bar menu and started perusing the appetizers. He raised an eyebrow at Lauren. "Ah, I see what has you all riled up. He frustrates you. You say you hate him. But you still want to bang him."

Lauren sighed and looked around for the waitress so she could order another martini.

"I mean, I get it," said Evan. "He's foxy."

"He's not... That's not what I..."

Evan just grinned.

Okay, Lauren was attracted to Caleb, and he was quite foxy, but she was not in the habit of sleeping with people she found annoying—or sleeping with anybody, really, since it had been awhile—and it seemed like a bad idea to bang the guy who worked next door. They didn't exactly work together, but if things went wrong, which they totally would, she'd still have to see him.

Of course, he seemed to be avoiding her. He hadn't stopped in for coffee since that first day. He probably didn't have much fondness for her, either.

Whatever, it didn't matter. Caleb was an infuriating man. If Lauren slept with anyone, it would be with someone with whom she got along, someone she had mutual respect with.

Evan pursed his lips and gazed at the menu. "I want something salty. You want to share a bowl of their homemade potato chips?"

"Sure." But before Evan could flag down the waitress, she said, "You know, you're one to talk."

Evan scoffed. "I have no idea what you're talking about."

"If sex fixes everything, then why are you here with me and not with Pablo the barista?"

Evan shrugged. "I'm playing the long game. He did get a job at the bookstore, so I guess I'll have to catch up on my reading."

"Right."

"It's not the same thing."

Evan successfully got the waitress's attention, and after they ordered several appetizers and Lauren ordered two more martinis because happy hour was almost over, Evan said, "This doesn't have anything to do with Derek, does it?"

"Oh, for the love of—"

"I'm sorry, just the timing. I know you don't want to get back together with Derek, but his wedding photos have been all over my social media feeds, too, and I know that can't be easy."

"No, it has nothing to do with Derek. Well, not directly. I mean, yeah, seeing him all happy with his new wife is not exactly filling me with warm fuzzies, but that's not it. I've made a decision."

"Yeah?"

"Derek was… I mean, he's a great guy, but being with him didn't really make me happy, nor did the stupid rebound fling with Jason the Math Tutor. You know what I've decided? To find what makes me happy. Working at the café makes me happy. Rescuing cats makes me happy. Spending time with my friends makes me happy." She reached over and gave Evan a soft punch on the shoulder. "Even when they irritate me. So I've decided rather than pursue some relationship just for kicks and sexual gratification, especially with a guy I hate, who probably thinks I'm an idiot, I'm going to focus on the things that make me happy. I want to build a fulfilling life. If I happen to meet a nice man, great, but if not, that's okay, too. As long as I'm happy."

"All right."

"You think that's stupid, don't you?"

Evan shook his head. "I mean, you do you. I want you to be happy, too. But I couldn't go that long without sex."

"Are men lining up outside your apartment while you're playing the long game with Pablo, or..."

"Shut up." Evan scowled at her for a moment. Then he said, "Oh, speaking of, I ran into that girl Jen who used to work at Star Café. The really tall ginger? She works at the wings place in the Atlantic Center now."

"Sure, I remember her."

"She told me the reason it closed is there's some up-and-coming developer buying up buildings in the neighborhood and jacking up the rents. He thinks the proximity to the Barclays Center will bring in some big-money tenants."

Lauren grimaced. "Right. Because what this part of Brooklyn needs is more banks and cell phone stores."

"I know."

"One of the best parts of Whitman Street is that it's so cute and full of mom-and-pop stores. Did Jen know what the Star Café is going to become?"

"No, just that the new owner raised the rent well beyond what the café could afford. Should we place bets?"

"Chain coffee shop."

"Fast-food restaurant."

Lauren winced. "Ugh. What did that video store near your place become?"

"A chain fried chicken place. And the bodega at the end of my block became a Duane Reade."

"That tracks."

Evan sighed. "Your block is so gosh-darn cute that I'd hate to see it go big corporate."

"I think you'd have to pry the building from Diane's cold, dead hands."

"I can't see her selling, either, but stranger things have happened. Remember that guy, Charlie, I dated? He used to live off Flatbush Avenue, before we dated. When they built the Barclays Center, he had to move because of eminent domain. There was a little old lady in his building who refused to move and delayed construction."

"Oh, yeah, I remember that."

"If this real estate developer plans to buy up most of the block, he could want to put in a big-box store or a mall or something."

"Bad enough that the meat market gym is across the street."

"Don't knock the meat market. If I had a few hundred dollars to blow on a gym membership every month, I'd be trying to pick up rich jocks there."

Lauren laughed. "Well, let's hope the Star Café is the only casualty."

Evan raised his glass. "I'll drink to that."

———

It felt like such a high school thing to do, but Caleb gave the Cat Café a wide berth as he walked by it on his way to work in the morning. He'd grabbed coffee from a little place he'd passed on the walk from his apartment. He could probably just buy a basic drip coffee maker for twenty bucks and put it in the shared office; it would make perfectly serviceable coffee. No need to frequent the Cat Café or see Lauren. Problem solved.

It wasn't even that he didn't like her. He was torn about

whether he found her stubbornness irritating or charming; a little of both, probably. Really, though, she made him think of an old scene from *The Mary Tyler Moore Show*, with Ed Asner telling Mary she had spunk and Mary taking it as a compliment.

I hate spunk!

He said hello to Rachel on his way into the office, reflecting on the fact that, well, he did hate spunk. Maybe that was post-divorce Caleb talking, but after everything that had happened with Kara and their old practice, he had very little patience for nonsense. Kara's nonsense had been covering up lies and betrayal, after all; for months, she'd pretended everything was fine when it hadn't been. And now Lauren, while beautiful and sexy, was all nonsense.

An hour later, he was in Exam 1, finishing a chart after a patient had gone home, when a big yellow Lab mix wandered in. The dog sat at Caleb's feet.

"Hi, buddy. Where are your people?"

Rachel ran in then. "Sorry, Dr. Fitch. He got away from me."

"Is this your dog?"

"No. Dr. Francis took him in last night. Someone left him tied up outside with a note saying they couldn't take care of him anymore."

Caleb knelt beside the dog and pet his ears. The dog barked happily and licked Caleb's face. Caleb laughed despite his sour mood. "Well, you seem friendly enough. Why would someone leave you?"

"It happens," said Rachel. "We get pets left here periodically, usually either by older people who don't have the energy to look after them anymore or, more often, people moving into apartments that don't allow pets. And because there aren't really any other clinics in Brooklyn that are open all night; we get a lot of the abandoned pets here."

"My old practice got a few. Mostly boxes of kittens people found on the street. Usually not big friendly dogs." The dog licked Caleb's face again and he laughed. "You house-trained, buddy? Wanna go for a walk?"

At the W-word, the dog perked up even more.

"The note said the dog's name is Hank."

"Hank?" Caleb asked the dog. He was rewarded with another face-lick. "Well, that's a good sturdy name. Do we have any leashes? I can take him for a quick trip around the block."

"Yeah, sure, there are a couple in the drawer at the reception desk. I'll get you one."

Caleb shrugged out of his white coat and returned to the reception area, where Rachel handed him a leash and a little container with biodegradable pet waste bags.

Hank was definitely house-trained. He acted like a dog who knew exactly what he was supposed to do, including barking at every other dog they passed on the street. Caleb was mystified about how anyone could abandon such a big, friendly dog. Hank was big for a Lab, sure, so he'd be a lot for a small apartment. But his tongue lolled out of his mouth, and he trotted around the block, pausing to do his business near a tree, and then resuming his happy gait.

When Caleb returned, Hank barked at the Cat Café. "Good boy," Caleb said as he reached down to rub Hank's ears.

Back inside the clinic, Caleb let Hank off the leash, and Hank flopped down in front of the reception desk.

"What's the procedure for adopting animals?" Caleb asked.

"Well, we usually keep them here for a couple of days in the kennels in back, and we'll put signs up out front saying we've got an animal for adoption, but if nobody takes the animal, we find a shelter. If it's a cat, Lauren usually takes them, but for dogs and other pets, there's a no-kill shelter in Park Slope we work with."

"Okay."

"Unless *you* want to adopt him."

Caleb couldn't help but think of his old dog Jimmy, the one Kara had gotten in the divorce. His new place in Brooklyn Heights was still a bit underfurnished and sterile, and a dog would certainly liven things up. On the other hand, he put in long hours here at the clinic. A dog like this would need a lot of attention.

"I mean," said Rachel, "this is the kind of dog you get when you're on the rebound from a bad breakup. Just saying."

Caleb looked at her.

"Sorry. Olivia told me you just got divorced."

"I did. And you're probably right. He seems like a good dog. But I don't know if I'm ready to take on a dog just yet. I *just* moved to Brooklyn. I haven't even finished furnishing my apartment yet."

"It was a bad breakup, wasn't it?"

"She left me for a younger guy and ran off to California after abruptly closing the clinic we owned together without consulting me, so yeah, it was pretty bad."

Rachel's eyes went wide. "Well, geez. That's shitty."

Caleb barked out a laugh. "To understate things."

"But, see, this dog may be just what you need." Rachel and Hank both looked at him with big puppy dog eyes.

"Okay, tell you what. Let's board him here for a few days and advertise that he's looking for a good home. If no one adopts him by, say, Friday, then I'll take him home. Okay?"

Rachel grinned. "I think you just got yourself a good doggo." She reached down and pet Hank's head. Hank licked her face. She laughed.

"We'll see."

CHAPTER 5

LAUREN TROTTED DOWN THE STAIRS from her apartment and walked out onto Whitman Street. It was a lovely spring day, the sky deep blue with wispy clouds, a gentle breeze rolling down the street. Lauren closed her eyes and savored it for a few minutes. Days like this were precious and rare—some years, New York seemed to skip right over spring entirely, going from winter jacket weather to unbearably hot in the blink of an eye—and she wanted to experience some of it before she had to spend the rest of the day inside.

Whitman Street was a wide east–west boulevard that made a straight line from the East River all the way to the Queens border, where the street changed names and became a service road off the highway leading into Long Island. Lauren had read somewhere that the family who owned the estate that had once taken up most of the land in the neighborhood had a matriarch who was a big reader, and a lot of the little side streets off Whitman bore the names of nineteenth-century American writers: Hawthorne, Cooper, Poe, Twain. Many of the businesses that lined Whitman

Street played on its namesake, from the bars and restaurants who got their names from Whitman poems to the clothing boutique up the street called Song of Myself to the bodega on the corner called Walt's Groceries.

Lauren had come to Manhattan for college and then lived there for a few years in a tiny closet-sized apartment until she'd gotten the job at the Cat Café and moved. Manhattan had its charms but didn't have the same connection to its history that Brooklyn had. Rumor had it Walt Whitman had lived in a house just a few blocks from the Cat Café for a few years. That house was long gone and had been recently replaced by a sleek, modern high-rise apartment building, but Lauren liked to think he'd walked along this street before it was named for him, that she walked in his literal footsteps.

Of course, all this Whitman memorabilia was a sign of peak gentrification in this part of Brooklyn. This had been a sketchy neighborhood in the '80s and '90s. Monique had grown up in Brooklyn and said when she'd been a kid, she wasn't supposed to walk alone around this neighborhood because there was so much gang activity. Now this pocket of Brooklyn, sandwiched between Downtown and the rest of the borough, was full of old brownstones and cute tree-lined streets with little mom-and-pop shops and cafés and restaurants. Many of the families like Monique's, who had been in Brooklyn for generations, couldn't afford it.

Lauren could only afford rent here because Diane had cut her a deal, letting her have one of the one-bedroom apartments in the building above the café, rented for a fraction of the average rent in the neighborhood. Diane often didn't seem especially interested in turning a profit so much as helping out people she liked, which seemed like a bad business strategy, even while it benefited Lauren directly.

On the other hand, the café had been turning record-breaking profits in the weeks since the coffee shop across the street had closed. Who knew there was so much money to be made by people grabbing coffee on their way to work? Or that so many Brooklyn residents preferred to buy their coffee instead of making it at home?

With a sigh, Lauren walked into the café.

Monique and Victor were behind the counter, dealing with the coffee line. Lauren waved at them and walked through to the cat area, where Paige was petting little Chloe, who purred so loud Lauren could hear her across the room. Sadie trotted into the room behind Lauren.

"Hey," said Paige. "Olivia called ten minutes ago to say they got the shipment of the food you wanted. But they're really busy and she has appointments back-to-back until this afternoon, so if you want it sooner, you have to go over there."

Sure, walk over and run right into Caleb, of course. Evan had argued that Lauren should apologize, and, okay, *maybe* she had overreacted. Caleb had been super rude, but Lauren could be the better person.

On the other hand, it was possible Caleb wasn't even working today.

Still, Lauren had *just* gotten here. "Can you go?"

"I'm interviewing help for the adoption party. My first appointment is in, like, three minutes."

Lauren glanced back at the counter, where Victor and Monique were busy helping customers. Lauren reasoned she could wait until the afternoon, although the clinic might stay busy, and the food supply was already low.

She sighed. "Fine, I'll be right back."

She walked next door, hoping Rachel or Olivia would be at the front desk, but alas, it was Caleb.

"Hello," he said when she walked in. He looked startled. "It's you."

Lauren took a deep breath, willing herself not to get angry, but man, he riled her up. "Uh, hi. Olivia said you guys got the food I ordered. I'm here to pick it up."

"Why not have it delivered straight to you?"

"It's a special order prescription thing. One of the cats at the café is allergic to poultry, so we're giving all the cats food that has no poultry products in it. That's a surprising challenge."

Caleb nodded. "You're modifying the diet of all the cats for the sake of one cat?"

"It can't hurt any of them."

"I guess not. Seems expensive, though."

"Why don't you let that be my concern and go fetch the case of food?"

It came out more patronizing than she intended, and Caleb raised an eyebrow at her before he stood. "I'll go ask Olivia where it is."

He returned a moment later and then stuck his head in the doorway. "It's in the storage room. You can come on back to fetch it."

"Can you help carry it?"

"I have an appointment any minute now."

"We'll get this over with faster if we carry it together."

"I'm a veterinarian, not a pack mule."

"You this friendly with everyone?"

"I'm very nice to my patients. And usually, they don't talk back to me."

"Please?"

He sighed and rolled his eyes. "Fine. Follow me."

Lauren huffed and followed Caleb to the storage room, where two twenty-pound bags of the cat food she ordered sat.

"All right. Come on, cat lady. We've got forty pounds of food to get next door."

She wasn't normally like this. She liked everyone, generally. She believed in being nice to people, in having empathy for everyone. But something about Caleb just rubbed her the wrong way.

"How's that little calico?" he asked as he stepped toward the bags. "What was her name?"

"Sunday. And she's fine. I guess the stone passed, because she's basically back to normal now."

"Make sure you have plenty of water out next to this expensive food. Stones happen more often when cats are dehydrated."

"Yeah, yeah."

Caleb picked up a large bag of cat food and handed it to her. "You take this one. I'll grab the other."

Olivia breezed by them. "Hey, Lauren. Coming to get the cat food?"

"Yes. Thanks for ordering it."

"No problem. There's a form at the front I need you to sign, so stop there on your way out, please."

"I will. Thank you."

"You're nice to my boss," Caleb said after Olivia was out of earshot.

"She is friendly and respects me, unlike some other people I know."

"Hmm."

Lauren carried the bag of cat food to the waiting room, dropped it on a chair, and signed the form for Olivia. They exchanged pleasantries while Caleb stood impatiently at the door with the other bag, shifting his weight back and forth between his feet.

"Is it wrong to say that I'm kind of enjoying watching him squirm?" Lauren whispered to Olivia.

Olivia laughed. "Seems a little mean, but it's only twenty pounds of cat food."

"Can we go?" Caleb called out. "This isn't exactly a bag of feathers."

"You know," said Lauren, "at my last job, whenever we needed to move something large, my boss would ask one of the male employees to do it. Ladies never did heavy lifting."

"Seems pretty sexist if you ask me."

Lauren laughed.

"Sometime this week, cat lady. I've got patients."

Lauren scooped up the bag and headed toward the door.

Caleb hadn't seen the cat room on his previous trip to the Cat Café, but he walked through it now, following Lauren to the back room where she kept supplies. It was a lot. The design was kind of retro, the colors bright and a bit garish. It read more kindergarten classroom than place for cats to live, but what did he know? And there were at least a dozen cats lounging around the room, hanging out with the six or so customers Caleb counted in a glance.

"Your vacuum must get a workout," he said, observing the cats draped on the arms of the sofa on one side of the room.

"Yeah, we have to vacuum at least twice a day, usually just before we open and right after we close. Sometimes more."

The plump cat who hung out near the counter—Sadie, if he recalled correctly—followed them into the back room and eyed Caleb as he deposited the sack of cat food into the bin on the shelf Lauren indicated. Lauren slid the top of the bin into place and secured it.

"The plastic keeps curious cats out. You'd think nothing could jump up to a shelf this high, but some of these cats have springs for legs."

"Sure."

"Come on, Sadie. You don't need to hang out in the supply room."

Sadie let out a squeaky meow of protest but followed Lauren out of the room. As did Caleb.

Lauren paused to speak with a couple of people who were sitting at a table. Caleb wondered if he should just leave. That felt rude, but it wasn't like he and Lauren were on great terms anyway.

He approached her slowly and cleared his throat, not wanting to interrupt her conversation. She turned toward him and met his gaze but didn't say anything. Her expression said, *Oh, are you still here?* Which, great. He felt so grateful to be appreciated.

He sighed and said, "You're welcome."

"Right. Thanks."

"Patients." He pointed to the wall that separated the café from the vet clinic.

"Of course. See you, Caleb."

He nodded, clearly dismissed, but paused at the doorway to try to figure out the puzzle of this particular establishment. Lauren spoke with a strawberry blond who smiled a lot and gestured toward her companion, a skinny guy with dark hair and tattoos. A diverse range of customers sat at tables or on sofas, chatting and petting the cats as if this were a totally normal thing to do. And maybe it was, but in their own houses. Why didn't these people just get cats? If the great number of patients at the vet clinic were anything to go by, this neighborhood was pretty pet friendly.

Caleb spared a thought for Hank the dog. He suspected Rachel was not really going out of her way to advertise that the dog was up for adoption, so he'd still be at the clinic at Caleb's deadline. Caleb wasn't really sure he wanted a dog in his apartment, although hadn't he just reasoned to himself that if people really wanted cats, they should just adopt cats?

Caleb shook his head and left the café.

CHAPTER 6

MONIQUE FROWNED AT SADIE, WHO was napping on the counter. The customers were gone for the day, but Monique said, "This seems unsanitary."

Lauren laughed. She walked over and picked all fifteen pounds of Sadie up. She got a squeaky little meow of protest, but Sadie turned around a few times and went back to sleep when Lauren placed her in the cat bed in the corner.

"One of these days, the health department is going to shut this whole thing down," Monique said, shaking her head.

"I mean, technically, as long as the cats are separated from where we prepare and serve food, we're okay. Or that's what the fancy lawyer Diane hired said when she opened this place. I made an exception for Sadie, but if she gets into the food, we'll force her to hang out with the other cats during business hours." Lauren knelt and pet Sadie's head. Sadie's huge purr rolled out in response. "You're a good girl, aren't you, Sadie?"

Monique laughed softly. Of all the baristas at the Cat Café, Monique was the one Lauren trusted the most. She'd been working at the café almost since the beginning, and Lauren wanted to promote her as soon as she could find enough money in the budget to pay for her raise.

Monique was a tall, gorgeous black woman, with dark skin and an amazing collection of wigs. Lauren thought of her as Brooklyn personified: She'd been born and raised in the Caribbean part of Flatbush—her parents were Haitian immigrants—and she had the hard-consonant cadence of a Brooklyn accent. She spoke five languages—English, Spanish, French, Creole, and some Arabic—which came in handy with customers. She was smart and punctual, a model employee, probably overqualified to be a barista, and Lauren valued her ease with customers.

After she finished cleaning the counter, Monique slung her bag over her shoulder and said, "I'm out. Hot date tonight."

"Have fun!"

So Lauren was alone, closing down the café for the night when she got a text from Mitch, her old friend who ran a volunteer group that trapped and spayed or neutered feral cats in Brooklyn.

I've got a box of kittens. Can I bring them to you?

The Cat Café was close to capacity. Lauren had managed to adopt out a couple of cats that week to café patrons who had fallen in love but taking on any more at this stage would make things complicated.

Sadie walked over and tapped the back of Lauren's leg with her paw. It was like she was trying to say, "Hey, dummy, take the kittens. You know you want to."

"All right, all right," Lauren said.

Sure. Bring them to the café.

Lauren sat near the counter and read a book while she waited. Mitch showed up a half hour later with a cardboard box in his hands. As Lauren let him in, she could hear little mews coming from the box.

"Oh, these guys are tiny," she said as she took the box from Mitch.

Mitch looked around, probably taking in that the lights over the counter and in the cat room had been turned off. "Did you have plans tonight? You were closing up, weren't you? I'm such an asshole. I didn't mean to just barge in. You want me to bring these to the clinic?"

"No, no, this is fine." She put the box down on the table she'd just been sitting at. "These look very young." There were five kittens in the box who looked to be two or three weeks old. Not newborns, but still tiny and a little awkward. "They still need their mom."

"Well, mom took off. These guys were abandoned. Plus, we were thinking it might be better to rescue these babies before they became feral. Find good homes for them."

"I'm not sure kittens this young can live without a mom."

Mitch frowned. He did a little shuffle with his feet, almost bashful. "I've rescued cats this young who did okay. They need a little extra care, but they should be good to be adopted in a few weeks."

Sadie was alternately smelling Mitch's shoes and looking up at the table. She hopped up on the chair and sniffed suspiciously. When one of the kittens mewed, Sadie looked startled.

"I don't know about this," Lauren said. "They'll have to be hand-fed, probably. I don't know if we have the resources for that here. I've read about kittens this young but haven't raised any on my own."

Mitch furrowed his brow. He was tall and broad, the sort of man who seemed to take up a lot of space, but he and Lauren had been friends long enough that she knew he was friendly, not at all threatening, as his size implied. Lauren didn't know exactly how old he was, but she guessed mid-forties, with light brown hair that was thinning on top. Lauren suspected he had a bit of a crush on her, but she just didn't see him that way.

But now he was frowning down at the box of kittens.

"I can ask next door for some bottles and…milk? Kitten formula? I don't even know." Lauren reached into the box and let one of the kittens nuzzle her hand. They each moved around with jerky kitten movements. "Can you tell if they are healthy?"

"I mean, I think so? I'm not a vet."

No, but Lauren had access to vets. She sighed, thinking of Caleb.

Mitch let out a breath. "Sorry, I should have thought this through more. These guys will have to be separated from your other cats until they can be checked for worms and fleas and whatever else. I should have just brought these to the clinic. I just thought they might be more comfortable with you."

"No, it's okay, really."

"All right. Are you going to be okay keeping an eye on these little guys? I should probably get back. There are a dozen new cats in the colony this week, and a couple of the volunteers are very new."

"Yeah, I should be all right. I think Dr. Francis works Thursdays, so I'll bring these guys next door and make sure they get checked out."

"Cool. Thanks, Lauren. I appreciate it."

"You're coming to the adoption event Paige is running next week, right? Well, adoption event-slash-celebration of getting our liquor license finally. So we'll have beer and wine at the event."

"Absolutely. Wouldn't miss it." He winked and left.

Lauren gathered her things from around the café and made sure the cats were all settled in for the night. She shut off the lights and walked over to the box on the table. The kittens were all still squirming and mewling...except for one. Lauren gasped and reached into the box. The little one didn't seem to be breathing.

She locked up in a rush, tucked the box under her arm, and ran to the vet clinic.

Caleb was sitting at the reception desk, doing something on the computer when she walked in. Which was just fucking perfect, but she supposed she didn't have a choice.

"I thought Doug worked on Wednesdays," she said.

"Well, hello to you, too. Doug's daughter had a ballet recital tonight, so we switched. Sorry to disappoint."

The sarcasm dripping from his voice made the hair on the back of Lauren's neck stand up, but she sighed. "Look, a friend of mine brought a box of kittens to the café a few minutes ago, and aside from the fact that I've never taken care of kittens this young and could use some help, I think one of them is in trouble."

Caleb switched to emergency vet mode immediately. "Bring them to Exam 1."

"Anyone else here?"

"No. The techs all had tonight off. Let me just lock up and put a note on the front door to ring the bell. Put the kittens on the table in the exam room and I'll be right there."

It was clear Lauren was in distress. Caleb approached the box of kittens carefully. There were five. Four of them were moving and one wasn't.

"These are too young to be away from their mother."

"I know," said Lauren. "Mitch—he runs a volunteer organization that works with feral cats—said these had been abandoned by their mother."

Caleb looked at them. "These are two weeks old, I'd say. Three at the most."

He picked up the still one and saw it was breathing but struggling. He went to work, clearing out the tiny kitten's nasal passages, which seemed to be blocked, then rubbing its belly to remind him to breathe. Lauren watched, perfectly still.

Nothing happened.

A number of thoughts ran through Caleb's head, not the least of which was that these things happened sometimes. Young kittens, especially those left on the street for a couple of weeks without a mother, often didn't make it. He knew it was how life was, yet he really wanted this kitten to live.

Lauren stared at him as if she expected him to be Jesus to this kitten's Lazarus.

"We need to get some fluids into these kittens," Caleb said, trying to act instead of face the reality that this tiny kitten probably wouldn't make it. "If you go down the hall, there's a yellow door. That's our pharmacy. There's a fridge in there that has some kitten formula in a white bottle. Can you go grab it?"

Lauren bit her lip and gave the kitten a long look before she nodded and left the room.

Caleb let out a breath. He rubbed the tiny chin of the kitten with his finger, moving down her throat to try to stimulate breathing. Caleb thought he heard a sigh or a gasp, but the kitten didn't move.

Lauren returned a moment later.

"There are some big sterile syringes in the cabinet behind my head," Caleb said, reluctant to put the kitten down. "They're in a box labeled *kitten feeding*. Pour some of the formula into one. We'll see if this little guy perks up with some food."

Lauren nodded, found a syringe, and poured formula into it.

"Like you're feeding a baby. Put the tip near the kitten's mouth."

The kitten's jaw was open slightly, and the tip of the syringe was small enough that Lauren could maneuver it into the kitten's mouth. Nothing happened for a moment, though a little formula must have dribbled into the kitten's mouth.

Then, suddenly, a definite gasp, and the kitten's mouth latched onto the tip.

"Oh my god," said Lauren.

"We're not out of the woods yet, but I think this kitten wants to fight." Caleb let out a breath as the kitten continued to eat. "Let's feed the rest of these guys, too."

Ten minutes later, all five kittens had eaten a little and the four healthy ones were letting out little squeaky mewls as Lauren pet them. But the fifth kitten had curled up in the corner of the box to sleep.

"Do you think he'll make it?" Lauren asked.

"Honestly? It's hard to say. We'll have to keep an eye on him."

"Should we make him warmer? Do you have, like, an incubator or something?"

Caleb winced.

"Sorry, not trying to tell you how to do your job."

He sighed and grabbed a towel from one of the cabinets. He wrapped it around the little kitten, who sighed in his sleep and threw out his arms in a jittery stretch.

Caleb didn't want to say they *did* have some equipment in the back room—they had the cat equivalent of an ICU bed—but this kitten was too small for most of it. There wasn't much they could do for this little guy. He glanced at Lauren, hoping she'd never read his thoughts, because she would surely call him heartless. But he'd euthanized an elderly dog earlier that day and was still reeling a little bit, which was a reminder he had to maintain a certain amount of detachment in order to do his job well.

He glanced at Lauren, who held a hand over her mouth, looking stricken as she gazed at the kitten.

"Four healthy kittens is still very good news," Caleb said. "Kittens abandoned by their mother this young often don't make it. This one kitten is struggling, but I believe the other four will be just fine. Too young to put up for adoption, but we can take care of them here until they are."

"But the fifth one."

Caleb nodded. He remembered all the times he'd saved an animal despite the odds. But he remembered every loss, too. He hated to see animals suffer, hated to see them sick or injured, and he didn't like watching this little kitten struggle to hang on. But he'd remember this night, and not just because a beautiful woman was looking over the kitten with him.

A beautiful woman who hated him, granted.

There was no animosity now, though, just concern for the kitten. Lauren reached down and ran her finger along the top of the little guy's head. He leaned into her touch, which was a good sign. The other kittens had begun to play with each other, the post-dinner burst of energy upon them, but the little one could barely lift his head to get closer to Lauren's fingers.

Still, they kept vigil for the next hour, taking turns checking on the little kitten to make sure he was warm or making sure he ate a little.

Truth be told, kittens this small needed nearly around-the-clock care, something no one in the office really had time for, but he couldn't bring himself to say no.

He'd been more of a marshmallow once. It was what had inspired him to go to veterinary school to begin with. He'd loved animals as a kid. His family had lived in a big house a fair distance from Portland, Maine—the nearest city—and they'd had room for dogs, rabbits, fish, briefly a lizard, and whatever squirrels and chipmunks and deer and moose lived in the nearby woods. For part of his childhood, they'd had a husky mix who sometimes caught squirrels and birds, and Caleb had tried to nurse a few of those back from their injuries, and sometimes was successful. As a child, he'd cried over those ASPCA commercials with the sick and injured animals. It seemed like a natural thing to make taking care of animals his job. He sometimes thought he related better to animals than to humans.

He'd felt jaded recently. He didn't used to be this hard. Having to put an animal to sleep might have ended his whole day a few years ago. He still did care about animals, but he guarded his heart a little more fiercely now. Some of that was experience, a lot of it was his divorce. He'd learned a hard lesson about trusting people.

Animals, at least, were not duplicitous.

Lauren kept shooting him skeptical looks, like she couldn't believe they were getting along. Maybe her opinion of him would have been different if they'd met a year or two ago, before everything went to hell. Maybe in another life they could be friends, at least. Or more, maybe. It was probably better for her to think him heartless. He couldn't get his heart invested—and subsequently stomped on—that way.

His stomach grumbled. He looked at his watch and realized two hours had passed since Lauren brought the kittens in. "Do you need to be somewhere else tonight? I can take care of these guys if you do."

"No. I can stay."

"Because if you need to get home, or to sleep, or whatever... I mean, I'm basically here until Olivia comes in to replace me in the morning, so it's really not a problem to watch over the kittens."

Lauren shook her head. "I won't be able to sleep without knowing if they'll be okay."

In other words, they'd both be here for the long haul. "All right. We should be prepared for the worst."

"I know. But… I just need to know how this ends. As long as he still has a shot, I'm going to worry if he's okay, and it's going to keep me awake."

Caleb looked across the table at Lauren, and their gazes met. She looked tired and worried, and yet still gorgeous. Her hair and clothes were a little mussed, wrinkles pressed deeply into the shirt she was wearing, probably because she'd had it on all day. He liked the way she dressed and styled herself, clearly putting some effort in to dress nicely and put on a little makeup, but she also had a soft beauty he appreciated.

She really was quite gorgeous, and she drew him in even when he was disagreeing with her. She made him wonder if he was capable of being with someone even after everything had happened with Kara. He wasn't ready, he knew that about himself. But Lauren made him want to try.

Still, the truth was they didn't get along outside of this current context, and as lovely and soft and sexy as she seemed now, as sweet and kind as she seemed as she pet the kittens and fretted over them, he didn't think he should give in to his attraction. Better to keep his distance. Right?

She reached across the table and patted his hand, and it was like being fourteen again, that little bit of electricity zipping through him, making him want things.

Caleb cleared his throat. "All right. Might as well eat if we're going to be here all night. Does the diner on Henry Street deliver?"

CHAPTER 7

"HEY. HEY, LAUREN. LOOK."

Lauren sat up with a start. She looked around and noticed she was in the exam room of the vet clinic. She must have fallen asleep.

They'd watched those kittens for what felt like hours, and she'd split an order of fries with Caleb after he ordered delivery from the diner. The little sick kitten had hardly moved at all, but Caleb had kept checking his breathing to make sure he was still alive. But as the night had drawn on, Lauren had become increasingly convinced the little guy wouldn't make it. The very idea devastated her, and she kept wondering if she'd done enough, if she should have insisted on more aggressive care, or if the kitten had been doomed from the outset.

Lord, she was tired. Her back hurt from the weird angle she must have twisted herself into to put her head down on the table.

She looked up and met Caleb's gaze. He had a small smile on his face. "Look." He pointed at the box.

The little sick kitten was up on his feet and cautiously checking out the other kittens in the box. They all sniffed each other.

"He's okay!" she said, jumping up. She hopped around the table. "He's okay!" Then she threw her arms around Caleb.

She hadn't meant to. The joy of watching that little kitten standing and beginning to engage with his brothers and sisters had overwhelmed her, and she'd just reacted. But now that she had her arms around Caleb and she could feel just how strong and solid he was, well... It was hard to let go.

Was she really so hard up that rubbing the surprisingly well-muscled arms of a man who clearly disliked her seemed like a good idea?

She kept a hand on Caleb's bicep but glanced back down at the kittens. The little one waved his little tail as he investigated the other kittens. Caleb's arm came around her.

"I can't believe I fell asleep."

"It *is* three in the morning."

Caleb was warm and he smelled good. Slightly medicinal, like the medical-grade antibacterial soap near the sink, but he must have used some kind of piney cologne or aftershave, too. Caleb was handsome in an effortless way, like he rolled out of bed like this every day. Pretty with smooth skin, albeit prickly. But now he wasn't being condescending or mean; he was staring at her like he might like to eat her for breakfast.

Or she was reading too much into it. But what else could that look mean?

She shifted her weight and turned to face him. He gazed down at her, a smile playing on his lips. He was tall and... Well, he had nice shoulders and a trim figure, and he was pretty foxy. Her first impression of him had been that he was the kind of guy she might like to get to know in a naked way, after all.

"I'm glad he made it," Caleb said.

"Yeah." Lauren met his gaze and stared at his eyes, which were grayish-blue and intense. His light brown hair was tousled in a very 3:00 a.m. kind of way, like he'd been up for many hours consecutively and was too tired to care what he looked like. Lauren put her hands on his shoulders to steady herself, because just looking at him made her feel warm and tingly. And being this close, touching him, smelling him, well, the tingles were in very specific places. "I'm so happy."

"Me, too. I honestly didn't think he'd make it through the night."

She leaned a little closer feeling his breath on her face. "I'm just...ah... I'm so relieved," she said softly.

"Mmm. Me, too."

"We're, ah, not fighting with each other."

"Nope."

Then Caleb swooped down and kissed her.

Warmth spread through Lauren's chest. She put her hands around Caleb's neck, trying to hold on because she knew this was fleeting, some bit of temporary insanity, but she was enjoying it a great deal.

He pulled back slightly. "We're kissing."

"I'm fine with it. Good, even."

He smiled. "Well, all right then."

He kissed her again, but this time, he hoisted her up on the counter, right next to the box of kittens. The stainless steel was cold on the back of her legs, but it didn't bother her much. She wrapped her legs around his hips and he pressed forward. She could feel him hard against her; it thrilled her that he was just as turned on as she was.

He brought his hands to her face, sliding his tongue into her mouth. She tangled her tongue with his in return. She put her arms around his strong shoulders and held him there.

The kittens were fine and Caleb was kissing her like the world was ending. What a crazy night!

But...

She pulled away. "I don't think I can do this in front of the kittens."

He chuckled and rested his forehead against hers. "Fair."

"Not that I don't want to do this, because I definitely do. Just, you know, this table is kind of cold, and the kittens are watching, and... Gosh, you're sexy."

He laughed. "So are you. But I take your point." He stepped back.

She slid off the table with some reluctance. "But we could, like, take this to my place after your shift is over. I live right upstairs."

He raised an eyebrow. "Convenient."

"Yeah. Uh, when does Olivia come in again?"

"Not for another four hours."

"Is there a sofa we can make out on or something?"

He laughed and looked in on the kittens. "Maybe. This seems very out of character for you."

"Hey, I can be sexy and spontaneous. And these are unusual

circumstances. It's like, thank-god-we're-alive sex. Except in this case, thank god the kittens are alive."

"So, just to be clear on your intentions, if I come with you back to your apartment, you intend to jump me."

She grinned. "Yes, that's accurate."

His grin mirrored hers. "I will take your offer under advisement. In the meantime, it's probably about time for these little fur balls to eat again. Want to help me?"

"Absolutely. I'm on it."

_____

Rather than making out on the sofa in Olivia's office, Lauren fell asleep there. Caleb bustled around the office, trying to keep himself busy, periodically looking in on the kittens. The longer Lauren slept, the less hope Caleb had that they'd end up in her bed. Probably she'd remember that they didn't much like each other. That he thought she was flighty and she thought he was cold.

Although there'd been nothing cold about the kisses they'd exchanged at three in the morning. Caleb had been about to rip their clothes off to show how hot they could be when she'd put the brakes on. Which was probably for the best. What had he even been thinking? Lauren was hot, yes, but she was bossy and ridiculous. Still, she'd been so worried about those kittens, and then relieved when the little one was okay, and then she'd had her hands on him, and, well, there was only so much resistance he could put up.

Olivia arrived precisely on time at six, and Caleb explained the situation with the kittens. They looked in on the kittens together. All five seemed to be doing just fine, mewling and playing with each other. Caleb carried the box to the back room, where Olivia got them set up in a kennel.

"I can take it from here," she said. "Not the first litter Lauren has brought us from the feral rescue organization, but I haven't seen kittens this young in a while. But we can put them on a regular feeding schedule and get the techs to help out. I'll ask Rachel to put up flyers saying we've got kittens up for adoption in a few weeks."

"Thank you. I'm sure Lauren will appreciate it."

"She spend the night here fretting about these guys? Is that why she's asleep in my office?"

Caleb's pulse sped up a little. Obviously, he couldn't say that she was here, biding her time until they could go up to her apartment. "Yeah, she wouldn't leave."

Olivia nodded. "That seems right."

"Yeah, she's kind of a pest that way."

Olivia laughed. "Like I said, not the first time. About six months ago, she brought in a feral that had been badly injured in a fight, and she wouldn't leave until after the poor cat got out of surgery."

"Was the cat okay?"

"Yeah, he lived. We patched him up and found him a nice home in a controlled feral colony upstate."

Caleb nodded. Some feral cats would never make good pets because they were too wild and likely to claw or bite people. Caleb assumed Olivia was referring to the old, abandoned army fort upstate that had been converted into an isolated location for feral cats to live. Scientists studied the colony there to learn more about feline behavior.

"I'll just go wake her up then," Caleb said.

"All right. I'll give these little guys some food."

Caleb gave each of the kittens a little scratch behind the ears. Then he walked back down the hall to Olivia's office. Lauren was curled up on the couch there, snoring softly. Caleb hated to wake her, but he couldn't just leave her here all day. He knelt beside the sofa and gently nudged her shoulder.

As had happened in the exam room earlier, she awoke with a start, shooting upright. She stared at Caleb for a long moment, then looked around the room. She must have remembered where she was and why she was there, because her features relaxed.

"It's after six," Caleb whispered. "Olivia's here, so I'm punching out for the day."

"The kittens?"

"They look good. Olivia's feeding them now."

"Good." Lauren smoothed down her hair and shifted her weight on the sofa. "So, ah, your shift is done?"

"It is."

"The invitation still stands, you know. My staff can take care of the café this morning. They have the morning rush down to a science."

Caleb felt a bit of relief. Maybe she didn't hate him so much after all, or they'd reached some kind of a truce. Likely nothing romantic would come of this, but a bit of fun in bed with a woman as sexy as Lauren was never an unwelcome occurrence. Wanting to seal the deal, he leaned over and kissed her. She put her hands on his shoulders and kissed him back, snaking her tongue into his mouth. It would be so easy to hook his leg over her on the sofa and...

"Upstairs," she whispered against his mouth.

"Yeah, getting caught making out in my boss's office is not a good look."

"Not so much, no."

Caleb stood and set himself to rights, and then helped Lauren off the sofa. She was still warm with sleep, and she gazed at him affectionately as he grabbed his bag from the drawer in Olivia's desk where he'd stashed it. There were still a lot of ways that this could go wrong in the short distance from this office to Lauren's apartment, and Caleb probably should make up some excuse. He definitely didn't want to have an excuse, though.

And then he remembered...

"Hank."

"Huh?"

"My dog, Hank."

"You have a dog?"

"Yes. He was... He was abandoned here at the clinic and he kind of grew on me. He's at my apartment now. Way overdue for a walk."

"Oh. That's disappointing. But you should know that your compassion for your pet is kind of turning me on."

Caleb laughed. "Well, hold that thought long enough for me to call my dog walker."

CHAPTER 8

THEY BURST THROUGH THE DOOR of Lauren's apartment after breaking a land-speed record to get from the vet clinic into the residential part of the building. Lauren had barely gotten her key out of the lock before Caleb shoved her against the door from the inside, slamming it closed. There was no prologue or pretense here; instead, they kissed and groped each other against that door. Caleb reached down to grab Lauren's thigh and pulled her leg up to wrap around his hip. They writhed against each other, tasting each other, groaning when things felt good. Lauren pulled Caleb's shirt out of his trousers and slid her hands up the inside to feel his warm skin. God, he was hot. She could feel the traces of his abdominal muscles, the soft fuzz of his chest hair. She pinched one of his nipples and he hissed into her mouth.

"Where's the bed?" Caleb asked.

Lauren couldn't make words. Instead, she shoved him toward the bedroom door, which was about six feet from the front entrance. He didn't even look around, just went where she pushed him. She sent a little prayer to the gods of preparation that she'd actually made the bed the morning before and her room wasn't too messy, then she steered Caleb toward the bed. His foot must have hit the leg of the bed frame, because he tripped, landing on his back on the mattress.

He didn't protest, though. In fact, when Lauren crawled onto the bed on top of him, he whispered, "Yeah, that's what I'm talking about." Lauren laughed and kissed him. Caleb put his arms around her and leaned up into the kiss, then bucked his hips against her.

"Oh, yeah," Lauren said. "Let's do more of that."

Caleb grabbed the hem of the shirt Lauren wore and pulled the whole thing off over her head. She sat straddling his hips, and he reached up and touched her breasts over her bra. It wasn't the sexiest bra she owned, just a practical plain beige situation with a little strip of lace at the edge of each cup, but Caleb stared at her as though she were the sexiest thing he'd ever seen. She could give him more. She reached behind her and unhooked the bra, then pulled it off. Caleb's eyes went wide, then something in his gaze darkened, turning primal.

He leaned up and pulled off his own shirt without bothering to unbutton it. The white undershirt he'd had on under his standard-issue blue oxford shirt landed on the floor next to Lauren's discarded bra. Caleb leaned up, grasped Lauren's waist, and took one of her nipples into his mouth. His hot tongue was magic, shooting electric currents through her body, and she sighed and put her hands around his head to keep him there. She could feel him hard between his legs.

"Too much clothing," she murmured.

He tapped her thigh and she took that as a sign to get off him. As soon as he had space, he undid his belt and pulled his pants off. In a further sign that none of this was planned, he had on a pair of threadbare boxers that didn't leave much to the imagination.

He had light hair everywhere, though, from his disheveled coif to the hair dusted along his chest, to the slightly darker hair that formed a line pointing into his boxers. And he was cut, like he spent a lot of time in a gym: rounded arm muscles, defined pecs, strong abs. His blue eyes seemed to glow a bit as he stared at her.

She took the hint and slid off her jeans, pulling off her socks in the process. The pink cotton panties were again not exactly her sexiest lingerie either, but Caleb still placed a hand on her hip and hooked his thumb into the waistband.

It had been awhile since she'd gotten naked with a man. She hadn't gotten much action at all since Derek aside from a thirty-second affair right after the breakup—she'd been too busy with the café and hadn't gone out of her way to date. She felt self-conscious suddenly. Here was the hottest guy she'd ever been with—unassuming veterinarian in the streets, underwear model in the sheets—about to take off her panties, and a million thoughts spun through her head. She hadn't shaved in a while, he might not like what he saw, she hadn't planned to get naked with anyone this week—or month, to be honest—and this kind of spontaneity was so unlike her...

But then she decided to just roll with it. Caleb slid her panties off and said, "Oh, yeah," which was reassuring.

He positioned her on her back on the bed and slid between her legs, his boxers still on. He kissed her and cupped her breast in one hand, then slid that hand down her stomach and between her legs. She was wet and ready when he slid a finger inside her. Her body practically screamed, *Yes, let's do this.*

She slid a hand down his back, cupped his very smooth ass in her hand, then reached into his boxers to wrap a hand around his cock. He sucked in a breath when she touched him.

"Condoms?" he asked.

"Bedside drawer. But, uh, check the expiration dates." She rolled her eyes and dropped her head back on a pillow. "That might be the least sexy thing I've ever said."

He chuckled and opened the drawer. He tossed a couple of condoms over his shoulder, probably old expired ones, and then held one up and said, "Eureka."

"I don't...do this a lot."

"Hey, that's okay. No judgment. This one doesn't expire until next year, so we're good."

"Phew." Lauren laughed nervously.

"Unless you don't want to."

"Oh, I want to. Couldn't you feel how ready for you I was? Let's do this."

Caleb grinned. He really was unbearably cute when he smiled. Handsome, yes, but he had a dimple in his right cheek.

She kissed him. She felt him maneuvering beside her, probably getting his boxers off so he could put on the condom. He pulled away slightly and looked down. His bare cock was something to behold, hard and large and smooth. Lauren ran her hand over his chest as he rolled on the condom. Then he took her hand, rolled her onto her back, and positioned himself between her legs.

"You're the sexiest thing I've ever seen," he said.

"God, back at you. I didn't know you were hiding all this under your white coat, Dr. Fitch. It's like a fun, sexy secret."

He laughed softly. "I thought you were hot the first time I laid eyes on you. I've been wanting you ever since."

She kissed him and nipped at his lower lip. "Then without further ado..."

Caleb ran his fingers along the entrance to her body, then slipped two fingers inside her. She moaned, loving the pressure of his fingers but wanting much more. She grabbed his cock and steered him toward herself. When she felt the blunt head of his cock at her entrance, she shifted her hips to welcome him and murmured, "Yes, that's what I want." When he slid inside, it hurt a little, but it was exactly what she needed. She felt full, stretched, aroused like crazy.

"Move," she said, and she kissed him.

He thrust in and out and got a rhythm going, touching her everywhere his hands reached. He cupped her breast, twisted his body so he could suck on a nipple, ran his hands over her hip, her belly, her neck, her hair. The warmth of arousal spread through her body and tingles and electricity pulsed from between her legs to her fingers and toes.

Why had she put off doing this for so long again? Being with Caleb made Lauren feel like the world could end in three minutes and it would be fine. She kissed him, nibbled at his earlobe, his jaw, his collarbone. She ran her hands over his pecs and abs, pinched his nipples, experimented with touching him in different places to see how he would react. She gently bit the spot where his neck met his shoulder because that made him groan and whisper something unintelligible. And through all that, he made her feel like nothing else existed in the world except the two of them making this powerful friction that would soon propel them both off a cliff.

What a way to go.

She shoved her fingers into his hair, felt the silky strands of it, then dug her fingers into his shoulders as she groaned. She was half delirious with lust and cried out when he reached between them and pressed a thumb against her clit. Yes, right there, that was it, just a little more pressure...

The orgasm hit her all at once, ripping through her body and making her arch her back and throw her head back. Everything went blissfully white and quiet for a second, and then she came back to herself in time to feel Caleb shudder in her arms and come inside her. She held him through the aftershocks as he murmured nonsense in her ear.

After a moment, he slid off of her and lay beside her. "That was *something*," he said.

"Something good, I hope."

"Something *great*." He panted and turned his head to look at her. He smiled.

"Your smile could knock someone out. I'm glad you don't whip it out much."

He laughed. "I know I'm not the most cheerful person."

She wanted to laugh and say something sarcastic, but she didn't want to break the moment, so instead she patted him on the chest. "You sure smiled a lot this morning. But I'll keep your secret."

Caleb returned to the bed and slid under the covers with Lauren. She curled around him.

He didn't know what to say. He was here with a woman he thought was incredibly sexy, and nothing about seeing her naked was disappointing, but he was aware their personalities were not the most compatible. Maybe that would change now.

He felt a little snoozy and closed his eyes, deciding to revel in the feel of her body curled against his.

What felt like a moment later, she said, "Are you sleeping?"

Without meaning to, he snorted. "Am I?"

She leaned over him and looked down at his face. "Not anymore, apparently. Sorry for waking you up."

"Probably for the best. I should go see poor Hank before he thinks I've abandoned him."

"Mmm." She kissed him. "So you *are* a dog person."

"Guess so. This dog had my number from the first moment he showed up at the clinic."

Lauren sighed happily. "You're cute, you know that?"

"I like to think I'm just an animal person. In vet school, I had to take care of horses and cows and lizards and all kinds of things. The veterinary medical center at Tufts took everything."

She grinned at him. "So you went to school in Boston. Is that where you're from?"

"Well, I'm from Maine originally, a little ways outside Portland. But I lived in Boston for a long time. That's where I was before I moved to Manhattan."

"Ah, okay. I grew up in Ohio but moved to New York for college and never left."

"Yeah, that's something I've noticed since moving here. New York kind of fall into three categories. People who were born and raised here and will never move, transplants who think this is the greatest place in the world and will never move, and people who talk about moving reluctantly because they have to for whatever reason."

"And you?"

"Well, you know, I thought about moving after my last practice closed, but here I am, so maybe this city is stuck with me."

He had thought long and hard about going somewhere, anywhere else after Kara had run off. He'd felt humiliated and furious and just wanted to put everything behind him. But Kara had done him the favor of running off to another city, so Caleb had decided to give New York one last shot.

He was reluctant to mention all that to Lauren, though. The divorce had made him feel like a failure, like he hadn't been good enough for Kara. Still, Lauren should probably know the reason he wasn't super eager to commit to a relationship.

Her phone rang somewhere in the room. With a sigh, Lauren rolled away and dug through the clothing on the floor. "Shit, I forgot to call in. They're probably wondering if I've died."

She found her phone in her jeans pocket. And apparently their moment was over, because she pulled a sheet over her naked breasts as she answered the phone.

"I'm so sorry, Monique. I was feeling under the weather this morning and forgot to call. Are you guys able to hold down the fort without me? Oh, shit, Victor called out? Is Paige there? Okay, ask Paige to help you at the counter. She knows how to use the register but not the espresso machine. I'll get there as soon as I can." Lauren glanced down at herself. "Er, can you give me forty-five or so? Okay. Soon as I can, I promise." She hung up and sighed.

"So I guess this is over now," Caleb said.

"Yeah, sorry. One of my baristas called out and there's been some pandemonium at the café during the morning rush." She got out of bed and pulled on a pink robe. "I'm not going to work smelling like sex, though, so they'll have to make do while I shower."

Caleb lay back on the bed for a moment. He looked around the room. The walls were painted a soft gray, and Lauren's furniture was mostly dark wood. It was a nice, feminine room; the bedspread was pink, there were little stuffed animal cats on most available surfaces, and there was a vase full of dry pink roses on her dresser. Also cat toys on the floor. "Do you have a cat here?"

"Yeah. Her name is Molly. She's a grouchy old lady. She's here somewhere. She doesn't really like people, or other cats, or really anything besides me, so we couldn't keep her at the Cat Café. She'll probably hide until you leave."

"So your cat lady bona fides are solid."

Lauren laughed. "You could say that." She started picking the clothes up off the floor.

"Well, this was...nice. Guess we have to go back to real life now."

She stopped and looked at him. "Guess so."

"Is this a thing now?"

Caleb felt like a dick for even saying that, but he didn't see much disappointment on Lauren's face, either. He kind of wanted it to be a thing, but maybe that wasn't a good idea.

"A thing?"

"I just mean," Caleb said, sitting up. "The ink on my divorce papers is still drying. And the whole process was...not pretty. I'm not really ready to date right now."

"You're divorced."

"Yeah. This was great and, honestly, I want to do it again, but I don't really have it in me to do anything romantic."

"Well, I guess you're in luck."

He watched her futz around the room, unable to read her tone. Was she bitter? Honest?

She dropped her clothes in a hamper and said, "My ex-boyfriend just got married. It was... I don't know. I'm still processing how I feel about it. I thought I'd marry that guy once, but it wasn't meant to be, and now he's married to somebody else. So I decided I'm going to focus on myself for a bit. Relationships...end. They don't go how you plan. And rather than deal with the frustrations of that, or with dating, which I don't really have time for, I'm prioritizing myself. Doing what makes me happy, what fulfills me. If the right guy comes along, awesome, but if not, I'll be okay."

Caleb appreciated that. He was still adjusting to being on his own—he and Kara had lived together since vet school, and before that he'd had roommates, so he'd never had his own place before. He hadn't gone as far as prioritizing himself so much as just trying to find some kind of normalcy. It seemed remarkable for someone to choose themselves; Caleb had always figured that once he'd recovered, he'd date again, even if he planned to never get married again.

He must have been staring, because Lauren stared back.

"Like, I get it," she said. "Breakups are the worst. Can I ask what happened?"

"She cheated on me, then closed the clinic we ran together without consulting me, and then the cherry on top was her running off with the guy to another state."

Lauren winced. "Oof. I'm so sorry."

"I'm…making my peace with it. But, like I said, things got messy, especially when we were dividing up our business assets, and I just… I can't put myself through all that again. I know 'it's not you, it's me' is a cliché, but it really is me."

"But it's me, too, is what I'm saying." Lauren sat at the foot of the bed. "Derek getting married really threw me for a loop. He and his wife knew each other for, like, five minutes before he proposed. My friend, Lindsay, says a lot of guys just hit a certain age and suddenly ready to settle down. So it's not *me* per se. But I felt like it was me. I dunno. Sorry, you don't need to hear all this."

"It's all right. I'm familiar with that feeling."

"Bottom line is we don't have a romantic future. And I'm okay with that."

Caleb knew he had no business in a relationship while he still harbored so much bitterness toward Kara, but hearing Lauren state the situation so bluntly was oddly upsetting. Disappointing, even. Why would that be? Lauren was sexy and great in bed, but she was also kind of a presumptuous know-it-all cat lady who ran a business in which people sipped coffee and pet cats. They'd spent most of the time they'd known each other bickering. Even if he wasn't still a mess over his divorce, getting involved with this woman seemed like a silly idea.

And yet.

Her robe was starting to slip off her shoulder to reveal the edge of her breast, and it was basically the sexiest thing he had ever seen. He wanted to reach into that robe and cup her just-more-than-a-handful breasts.

"Your eyes are all red," Lauren said as she got off the bed.

"Yeah, my contacts have been in for a few hours longer than they should have been."

"Aha. I thought I saw you wearing glasses."

"I do a lot of the time, but dogs licking my face are occupational hazards, and it's hard to get the smudges off sometimes." He cleared his throat. "Even if we have no romantic future, this was nice. Just putting it out there that I'm incredibly attracted to you and would not say no if you wanted to take me back to your place and jump me again."

"You kind of jumped me."

He felt himself smile. He liked this woman a lot when they weren't arguing. "It was a mutual jumping."

"Well, I need to hop in the shower. But it's a pretty big shower. Room for two if you want to conserve water."

So, no romantic future, but perhaps some sexy fun in the short term. Hard to say no to that. He tossed the covers aside. "Well, if it's to conserve water..."

CHAPTER 9

LAUREN SAT ACROSS FROM EVAN, Paige, and Lindsay at Pop. She was bursting to talk to them about what had happened with Caleb but was worried about how all of it would look. She couldn't just say, *I slept with a guy I have no future with and who I don't really like that much. High five!*

Lindsay was an old friend from college who hopped around careers like they were hobbies; she'd recently bailed on a dead-end job as a line cook at a restaurant in Park Slope to begin a career as a restaurant reviewer for a popular urban food website. These days, she ate everything as if she were thinking of the most pretentious way to describe it. She sipped a martini now as if she were a sommelier at a wine tasting, which was especially silly given that the glass was garnished with a tuft of cotton candy on the rim.

Lauren loved her friends, but they could be a lot sometimes.

Evan narrowed his eyes at Lauren. "Something happened."

"Well, that's vague," said Paige. "Of course something happened. Something happens every day. I mean, Mitch came by today to talk about the adoption event, and I think he hit on me? But it's hard to tell because he was subtle about it."

Lindsay frowned. "Mitch is the feral cat guy, right? The big guy?"

"Yeah," said Paige. "You make him sound like a mountain man when you describe him that way. I assume he lives in some apartment in Brooklyn with eight adopted cats, but it's not like he lives in a hut in Prospect Park. He's a perfectly nice guy. Not my type, but..."

"You want me to talk to him?" Lauren asked.

"No. Especially not with your boss voice. It's fine. It was a little awkward is all."

"No boss voice," said Evan. "We're at a bar. Paige is your friend and not your employee when we're sipping cocktails."

If only it worked that way. Lauren had known Paige for years, too. Paige had been an event planner for a massive international bank. Her main task had been planning quarterly meetings for the executives at luxury hotels around the world. She'd made enough money to live well but had found corporate life soulsucking. After her boss had made one too many comments about how her ass looked in a skirt suit, she'd quit and come to work for Lauren.

"What I *meant*," said Evan, "is that Lauren has a look on her face like she has news. I'm guessing it's related to a dude."

"How do you do that?" asked Lauren.

Evan shrugged. "It's a gift."

"So, uh, well. I slept with Caleb."

Evan gasped.

Paige said, "And Caleb is... Oh, wait. Caleb Fitch. Dr. Fitch. The veterinarian. I thought you hated that guy."

"Me, too," said Lauren.

"You're gonna have to explain," said Lindsay.

"I got this," said Evan, holding his arm out in front of Lauren as if he didn't want her to step forward. "Dr. Caleb Fitch is the new veterinarian at the clinic next to the Cat Café. He's quite foxy, although unfortunately heterosexual."

"I'll say," said Paige. She fanned herself with her hand.

"He's also a bit prickly, and he and Lauren got off on the wrong foot. They've had a couple of big arguments. But they only hate each other in the sense that they want to jump each other's bones." Evan turned back to Lauren. "Glad you finally got that taken care of. When is the wedding?"

Lauren looked around and flagged down a waitress. After she ordered, she said, "Look, he's... Yes, he's foxy as hell. But he's also kind of a dick. He thinks he knows everything, he's stubborn, he doesn't seem to have normal human emotions, and he's a *dog person*. A dog person, guys. I can't date a dog person."

"Heaven forfend," said Evan.

"No, she's right," said Paige. "That's like a Yankees fan dating a Red Sox fan."

"A Montague dating a Capulet," said Lindsay.

"A pork roll person dating a Taylor ham person," said Paige.

"That's the most New Jersey thing you've ever said," said Lindsay. "The Empire dating the Rebel Alliance."

"A Coke person dating a Pepsi person," said Paige. "Definitely doomed from the start."

"And besides," said Lauren, "he just got divorced and doesn't want to be in a relationship. So it's not going to be a thing. Just... We had sex. That happened."

"Girl, this calls for more cocktails," said Evan. "We should get Claire to send over a whole pitcher of that blue martini thing you like."

"Ugh," said Lauren. She didn't want her friends making a big deal of this. She'd just needed to tell someone.

"He was good, though, right?" asked Evan.

"Yes, very." And he really had been. They'd gotten each other off in the shower afterward, and that had been amazing, too. Lauren had gone to work feeling sleepy and sated, which had probably helped keep her mellow during the morning rush chaos. Monique had told her afterward that she admired Lauren's calm.

"The problematic ones always are," said Paige, shaking her head.

The waitress placed a martini in front of Lauren, so she took a sip.

"This calls for a toast," said Evan.

"To what? My non-relationship?" asked Lauren.

"Hey, you banged a hot guy," said Lindsay. "That's enough sometimes."

Lauren laughed and lifted her glass. "All right. To banging hot guys."

"You're gonna marry him so hard," Evan said, clinking his glass against Lauren's.

"You could not be more wrong, Ev," said Lauren. "Recently

divorced, dog person, doesn't like me much. What part of that spells future wedded bliss?"

"When he proposes, you owe me ten dollars," said Evan.

"Or not! Who says she has to marry the first guy to come along since Derek? Not all men are relationship material," said Paige a little defensively. Then she grinned and held up her glass. "To hot guys!"

"I'll drink to that!" said Lindsay.

They all clinked glasses. Inside, Lauren sighed. It would be nice to have someone in her life, sure, but she was focusing on herself, and that meant repeat performances with guys who, no matter how sexy and charming, were not potential future mates was probably not a solid strategy. Or maybe it was, because she'd gotten hers in the end. Maybe some kind of *with benefits* arrangement could be made.

Or she could stop trying to overthink it and just enjoy a night out with her friends. The subject changed anyway when Paige said, "So I went into the bookstore the other day and saw Pablo is working there now."

"I know," said Evan with a groan. "My coffee habit was bad enough, but now I feel obligated to buy a book anytime I casually drop in. There's only so much space in my apartment."

"You could just ask him out," Lindsay said. "Otherwise, you're going to be that man who dies because his great piles of books fell on him."

"This has occurred to me, but I don't think it's our time yet."

"This means Evan hasn't worked out if Pablo is gay or not," said Paige.

"His biceps are pretty beefy. I bet he's got a good right hook. I'd like to not be on the other end of it if I hit on him and it's unwelcome. Or I could just forget about him, because Robert called the other night."

All three women groaned. Robert was Evan's ex-boyfriend, a sweet guy who was...fine. Lauren thought he was okay. Which meant he wasn't good enough for Evan. Apparently this was a point they all agreed on.

"What?" said Evan. "Look, I'm not getting back together with him. He was nice but dull. I get that. So, he called, just to be nice. He's dating a young man named Elvis now, if you can believe that."

"Elvis? Really?" asked Paige.

"Yes. And apparently he's a hunka hunka burning love. But my point is Robert invited me to this housewarming, which, if what I recall of Robert's social circle remains the same, promises to be a smorgasbord of single gay men."

"What about Pablo?" asked Lauren.

"I'm keeping my options open."

Paige lifted her glass. "To keeping options open!"

They all clinked glasses again. Lauren laughed. Thank god for her friends.

———

Caleb checked on the kittens just after he got to work the next morning. All five were still thriving. Rachel had set up a little pen for them to play in and given them some little balls and things, and the kittens were having a great time pouncing on each other.

Although Caleb did not want any kittens in his home, it was hard to deny that these little guys were pretty cute.

Rachel wandered into the back room. "They have names yet?"

"No. I figured whoever adopted them could name them."

"I've been calling them each by their coloring. Gray, Mittens, Stripy, White Nose, and Giant."

"Giant?"

"It's like the reverse of calling a big guy Tiny. I'm calling the little one Giant. I think he's got some spunk. Don't you, Giant?" She reached down and scratched the little kitten's chin.

"What's on the agenda for today?"

"You've got a goldendoodle who needs booster shots at ten and a Great Dane with a cough at eleven. Mrs. Liao is bringing in one of her cats this afternoon, although I don't recall which one."

"How many cats does Mrs. Liao have?"

"Eight."

"Eight? In a Brooklyn apartment?"

Rachel grinned. "I'm betting that place is...pungent."

"And I thought Lauren was a crazy cat lady."

Rachel gave the cats one last head rub each and then turned to walk back toward the waiting room. Caleb followed. Rachel said, "Lauren *is* a crazy cat lady, but she keeps it to the café."

"She has a cat at home, too."

Rachel raised an eyebrow. "And how do you know that?"

"It came up in conversation when she brought the kittens here." That was plausible enough. He'd enjoyed his morning with Lauren immensely, but he didn't want to discuss it. It was his business.

And it didn't really mean anything; it had been just some fun after a tough night. She didn't want a relationship, and neither did he.

He'd been in love once and it had been terrible. After vet school, after they finished internships in different cities and somehow made a relationship work, he and Kara had set up a practice together in Boston, looking after the cats and dogs and hamsters of the wealthy brownstone class who lived in Back Bay. They'd put their pooled money into a storefront on Newbury Street sandwiched between an ice cream parlor and a novelty gift shop. They'd operated in the red for the first few months, which had been tremendously stressful, but they got enough business to start turning a profit just before Caleb had maxed out their credit. And Caleb had always figured if he and Kara could get through all *that* together, their relationship was indestructible.

Caleb would have been happy to stay in Boston. Sure, he preferred big dogs to the little ones a lot of his clients carried around in fancy bags, but most of the patients were good dogs (and cats and bunnies and gerbils and hamsters and guinea pigs), and he and Kara had been happy working together.

He'd been a different person back then. Hardworking and content. He didn't constantly feel the edginess that had been trailing him since the divorce. Perhaps that was why the move to New York had made sense when Kara had suggested it. A vet school buddy of Kara's had gotten a lead on an established veterinary clinic in Morningside Heights that the owners wanted to sell. "We've gotten everything we can out of this place" had been Kara's argument when Caleb had asked why she wanted to move. So they'd picked up their lives and gone to another city, left their friends and their community behind, and bought the clinic on 110th Street, just a few blocks down Broadway from the Columbia campus.

Caleb had thought they'd been happy there, too, but something had felt off. He hadn't been able to put a finger on what the issue was. Whenever he brought it up to Kara, she suggested it was because they were still adjusting to life in a new city.

And then one day Kara had said she'd met someone else and they were moving to LA. She had wanderlust, Kara had explained, and didn't want to be tethered to any one location, and besides, they'd been together since the first year of vet school. Hadn't their relationship run its course?

No, Caleb had argued. Their wedding had been the two of them making a lifelong commitment because they loved each other and would work together to keep their relationship sacred through good times and bad. They didn't make a commitment just to end things when they got bored.

Dividing up the business had been the worst part. He'd been furious about Kara making these unilateral decisions without consulting him, about putting the clinic up for sale without telling him, about fighting him over every dollar, every piece of equipment, every filing cabinet. He hadn't wanted to sell the clinic, but he hadn't want to run it without Kara, either, and he'd learned the hard way that owning a business with one's spouse and a joint bank account and a Gordian knot of tangled finances got to be quite messy. She'd used her half of the assets to hire one of the best divorce attorneys in the city, and he'd spent hours and hours in various law firm conference rooms haggling over which things they would keep, which they would sell, and who got which cut of the profits.

He understood intellectually that Kara had probably been restless all along and just hadn't said anything, that this situation was unique and not every woman would bail on Caleb rather than try to work things out, but he still didn't feel like he could trust anyone. He'd known everything was not hunky-dory between him and Kara, but most of his attempts to get her to talk about it had been rebuffed, and he hadn't been given much chance to try to fix things. He suspected Kara didn't want them to be fixed. That was on her, not Caleb, but still, he couldn't help but think he wasn't good enough for her.

But they'd been in New York less than a year when Kara had handed him divorce papers, and he'd lived in Brooklyn all of a month now, and this place was nice but still didn't feel like home. He didn't have much of a community here. But he couldn't really go back to Boston and try to rebuild some happy past. Too much baggage, too many memories.

He let his first patient of the day into the exam room and reflected on the fact that he was lonely. Maybe that was what had led him to Lauren's bed. He'd needed some kind of human connection.

Ugh, what a dreadful thought for the day. He focused on the dog in front of him, a blond fluff ball only identifiable as a dog because his tongue lolled out of his mouth.

"Hi, buddy," he said, patting the dog's head.

He needed to do something besides just go to work and go home, maybe. Find a hobby. Meet new people.

The owner of the goldendoodle was a middle-aged woman who grinned at him like he was the hot guy in an old Diet Coke commercial. All right. He smiled at her then looked at the chart. "Charlie here needs a couple of boosters. I'll go get his shots ready."

He ducked out of the room and took a deep breath. Yeah, he needed to do…something. Make some sort of change. The current limbo he found himself in was okay for now, but it was no way to live long-term.

CHAPTER 10

CALEB WAS MANNING THE FRONT desk when Olivia came in one evening a week later. She was taking the night shift that day, but had been running late, and now she was out of breath.

"Ugh, sorry," she said. "I had an appointment in Manhattan and the subways are just...well. I got stuck at Broadway–Lafayette for, like, twenty minutes trying to transfer, and I swear, if I read one more story about some city program the mayor wants to spend money on that is not the subway, I am going to march down to City Hall myself and tell him my thoughts on *that*."

Caleb laughed. "I'm sorry it took you so long to get here, but it's fine. I didn't have anything else going on tonight."

But Olivia was already pulling her cell phone out of her bag. She murmured, "Great, voicemail," and then listened to the message. "Oh, Lauren wanted to know if we have any more cardboard cat carriers we can spare. We've got a whole case of them in the back. Could you drop a few off to her on your way out? I'll take over now."

"Yeah, no problem."

"You're not still avoiding her, are you? I know you guys have argued in the past. I don't want to put you in an uncomfortable position."

"It's fine, really. We're not going to be best friends or anything, but I think we reached some kind of truce when she brought over that box of kittens."

"Oh. Good. I mean, since we do so much work with the Cat Café." Olivia shrugged out of her jacket and hung it on the hook behind the desk. "How's that dog of yours, by the way?"

"He's great. Friendly and well-behaved. I didn't think I wanted a dog in my new apartment, but he's the best roommate I've ever had."

Olivia chuckled. "He's a good dog, in other words."

"Probably exactly what I needed right now."

"Pets have a way of doing that. I've got a cat at home that just showed up on my fire escape one night. I live in a huge building with sixteen other units, but this little cat chose *my* fire escape, like he knew I'd be a good cat mama, and then one time I opened the window and he moved right in."

Caleb nodded. In his experience, pets often chose their owners rather than the other way around.

"Anyway, what I wanted to say," said Olivia, "is that if you wanted to bring that dog here during the day instead of leaving him at home alone, that's fine. He was very good with the other animals those few days he was here, so I feel pretty confident we can leave him up here by the desk most of the time, unless you think he'll bolt."

"Nah, I doubt it. He hasn't tried to bolt from me yet. He's very sweet. Just a big, friendly dog."

"Excellent. Totally your call, but I've always run a bring-your-pet-to-work style office. It just so happens that most of the other vets have pets that don't leave their homes right now, although Doug has a German shepherd he brings by sometimes."

"Thanks. I hired a dogwalker to take care of Hank a few times a day but having him with me here on overnights would be a help. I appreciate it."

Olivia smiled as Caleb got up and gathered up his things. "No problem. I endeavor to make this a pleasant place to work."

Caleb smiled as he grabbed his jacket. He really did appreciate Olivia. "Well, I'll just grab those carriers from the back."

Olivia had a recurring order of collapsible cardboard cat carriers for when they adopted out cats and small dogs, so there were plenty in the back room. Groups of five were held together with plastic ties. Caleb grabbed a bundle, swung by the office to grab his bag, and then said good night to Olivia.

He felt pretty good about popping in next door. Maybe this could be part of his new lease on life. He could make friends with the café staff and the other vets. He'd accepted an invitation to a cookout at Dr. Gardner's place that weekend, where there'd be spouses and friends of the other vets at the clinic, so that would be good. He didn't generally love parties, but this was a low-key thing with some people he already knew, and he did like the other vets at the clinic. It was kind of nice to work with people he wasn't romantically attached to.

The Cat Café was closed, so he hit the buzzer. Lauren's voice rang through the intercom, "Who is it?"

"It's Caleb. I've got some cat carriers from the clinic."

The door buzzed and Caleb pushed inside. The café area was empty, so he walked back through the second door.

When Caleb walked into the cat area, Lauren's back was to him. It sounded like she was singing the Sia song, "Chandelier," but there was something in there about cats and she name checked several of the café's feline residents. "I want to meow with Sadie the cat…"

"I don't think those are the lyrics," he said.

She started and turned around. "Uh… I sometimes change the lyrics to pop songs to be about the cats."

Caleb couldn't decide if that was cute or crazy. Some of both, he decided.

Lauren took the cat carriers from him. "Thanks for these. We wanted to have some on-hand for the adoption event we're hosting next week and realized we were a few short."

"You're welcome. Is it just you here right now?"

"Yeah, Monique and Paige just left about ten minutes ago. We closed at six."

Caleb looked at his watch. It was almost seven, much later than he thought it was. Olivia had been quite late. "Do you just let the cats hang out here all night?"

"For the most part. There are a couple that need to be separated, so we put them in kennels in the back overnight. I've got a scrappy little street tabby we named Tyler Durden who likes to pick fights with the other cats when no one is around. It took me a whole month to figure out why there were little tufts of fur all over when I came in some mornings. But he's good with people. I think he'll be fine in a home with no other cats."

"Okay." Caleb was still a bit baffled by all this, but he liked that at least the secret mission of the café was to find more permanent homes for these cats. It was like a shelter with a coffee shop. Still a little strange, but at least the cats were well taken care of, from what he could tell. And now he felt awkward, so he said, "Well, I'm just gonna…"

"No, stay a minute. Can I get you a cup of coffee?"

"Okay, but nothing fancy. Plain old regular coffee is fine."

"And your usual is coffee with cream, no sugar."

"How did you remember that?"

Lauren grinned and tapped her temple. "I'm very good at my job."

That grin was incredibly sexy, like Lauren knew all the secrets in the world and was willing to share, for a price. A sexy price, hopefully. Caleb couldn't help but smile back.

"Have a seat near the counter and I'll be right with you. I'm just gonna make sure these guys are all tucked in."

Caleb walked back to the café area toward the counter and sat at a table nearby. He reasoned he could probably figure out how to work the giant coffee maker—add water and coffee grounds, how hard could it be?—but he didn't want to muck up any existing system. He pulled out his phone to check his email, and Sadie walked up. She chirped and rubbed against his leg. He relented and pet her.

"Do I meet with your approval?" he asked the cat.

She started to purr loudly, so Caleb took that as a yes.

Lauren appeared at the door. "Hey, Sadie, get in here. You don't belong out here at night."

Sadie sat defiantly at Caleb's feet.

Lauren rolled her eyes and slapped her thigh. "Come on, cat. You can't stay out here all night. Go hang out with the other cats."

Sadie stared at her for a long moment but stood and sauntered over to the door. Lauren grabbed her and carried her the rest of the way, then locked the door.

"Sorry," Lauren said. "Sadie's special. She's a permanent cat here because I haven't been willing to part with her. We call her the office manager because she bosses everyone around. She gets free rein during the day, but she would for sure get into stuff around the counter without supervision, and the last thing I need are complaints about cat hair in people's morning coffee."

"Doesn't that happen anyway?"

"Sure, in the back room." Lauren hooked her thumb back toward the cat room, then walked over to the counter. She got the coffee maker going. "When people are here, she mostly stays away from the counter, but I don't need dusty footprints on the counter or anything like that. Plus she has lots of places to play and nap in the other room. I think she just generally prefers people to cats."

"How very like a cat."

Lauren laughed. She reached into a little refrigerator behind the counter, and Caleb took a moment to appreciate her ass. When she stood back up, she had a couple of croissants in her hand. "Aha. Monique sometimes leaves the day-old stuff in the fridge for me. These croissants are really good. I get them from this little hole-in-the-wall French bakery in Prospect Heights. They are..." She made a chef kiss.

"Lovely."

"I mean, they were delivered fourteen hours ago and have been in the fridge for a bit, so they aren't at peak freshness, but they can't be sold now and are still pretty dang good." She sighed. "When we first opened, we were giving the leftover pastries to a homeless shelter close to the river, but ever since the Star Café closed and everyone is coming here instead, the morning commuters have been cleaning us out. These two croissants represent all that is left after the plunder this morning."

"I'm honored you're willing to share with me then."

Lauren poured two cups of coffee and put the croissants on a plate, and somehow managed to get all of that to the table without spilling anything. She probably had some table-waiting experience in her past. She sat across from him and dug into one of the croissants.

"How are the kittens?" she asked.

"Really great. I checked on them when I grabbed the carriers. They're all pretty lively now. Rachel gave them names based on their physical traits."

"I know. I dropped in to check on them yesterday."

Of course she had. Lauren was just the sort of busybody who wouldn't take anyone's word that the kittens were okay.

Caleb sighed. His whole resolution to make friends and try to find a community here wasn't going to get anywhere if he let everyone annoy him.

"Anyway," said Lauren, "those kittens will be too young for the adoption event we're hosting here next week, but I can definitely let people know there will be kittens up for grabs in a few weeks. We can make flyers or something. People love kittens."

"I usually try to talk people out of adopting kittens."

"Really? Do you prefer puppies?"

He sighed. "It's not that. Kittens and puppies are just a lot of work. They're energetic, they eat a lot, they get into places you don't want them to go. Not to mention, as you must know very well, it's harder for adult animals to get adopted because people love kittens and puppies, but grown cats and dogs make perfectly good pets if you're into that sort of thing."

"Said like a man who likes a big, slobbery dog."

"Well."

"What kind of dog is Hank?"

"Yellow Lab and...something else. Definitely not a purebred. I can't tell what the something else is, though. He's on the big side for a Lab and has a shaggier face than any Lab I've ever seen, and he has some random patches of darker fur, but is otherwise basically a yellow Lab. He's a good dog, though. He came house-broken and mostly trained."

"But someone left him at the clinic?"

"Yeah. Could be anything. The previous owners moved or died or who knows? My gain, I guess. It's nice to have a dog at home again. My ex took ours in the divorce."

"That bitch," Lauren said with a bit of a smile.

"Yeah. That was probably our most vicious fight."

"Over the dog?"

"I really liked that dog."

Lauren nodded. "Sure. I'd be pretty upset if an ex wound up

with one of my cats. Mostly, though, I just end up with other people's cats. And you're right, it's harder to adopt out older cats, but we try here. The point is to lure people into adopting by letting them spend time with the cats first."

"Does that work? Do people fall in love with the cats and want to take them home?"

"Yep. A few times a month. We let it be known that all the cats here, except for Sadie, are looking for forever homes. I figure if this place ever closes, I'd just take her home. Molly can cope with a new roommate."

Caleb sipped his coffee. "This is some place you've got."

He looked her over. She looked good today. Her long brown hair was up in a messy bun, her long bangs loose over her forehead. She had on a soft-looking pink sweater and dark jeans tucked into stylish brown boots. Her clothes hugged her body in an appealing way, and Caleb enjoyed a moment of remembering what she looked like under her clothes.

"Maybe we should talk about what happened," Lauren said.

Caleb's knee-jerk response was, *Do we have to?* But he said, "That is the elephant in the room, I guess."

She sat across from him. "I'm not trying to make it a thing, but it just feels weird not to acknowledge it."

"No, I get it. I'm acknowledging it. We slept together. It was good. I'm not opposed to doing it again."

Lauren rolled her eyes. "Well, there's a ringing endorsement."

"What?"

"'It was good. I'm not opposed to doing it again.'" She

dropped her voice in imitation of him, and the way she said it did make it sound quite lackluster.

Of course, it was anything but. Caleb was still thinking about Lauren in bed all these days later.

"Well," he said. "We know where things stand. We had an amazing...morning together, but neither of us can do a relationship right now. So where does that leave us?"

Lauren stared at Caleb. His facial expression made him look like he was fighting with himself about something. This guy clearly had some baggage Lauren would do well not to look into. That was fine, she could work with that. Because she wanted him again. In, like, a primal, monkey sex way, not as a potential romantic partner.

"Crazy idea," she said. "We could be friends."

"Friends."

"Friends who have sex sometimes?"

He laughed. He really was so very cute when he smiled. He should do more of that and less scowling.

"Seems reasonable," he said. He sipped his coffee. "This is good. Very strong."

"A little too strong if you ask me." She sipped her own coffee, and it was bold and bitter. Lauren liked a strong cup of coffee, but not this much so late in the day.

"Hmm," Caleb said, clearly enjoying the punch in his cup. "I'd try to talk my way back into your apartment, but I really do need to get home before the dog tears apart my living room. He's been gnawing on the rug when he gets anxious. I'm going to start bringing him to work with me, because I think he gets lonely."

"Where's home?"

"Brooklyn Heights. I'm renting a one-bedroom not far from Borough Hall. I usually walk here in the morning, and it's a nice walk. I'll probably walk home now, in fact."

Lauren nodded. That was a swanky zip code. Recently divorced veterinarians apparently did all right for themselves. Lauren silently thanked the charity of eccentric older ladies with money to burn for her apartment.

Lauren recognized belatedly that there was an invitation in Caleb's voice; he was asking her to walk home with him. Did she want to do that? Something about having to actually go somewhere gave the moment more importance.

"Well," said Caleb. "Maybe I should go."

"Finish your coffee, at least."

He smiled.

They sat in companionable silence for a minute. Searching for something to talk about, Lauren said, "So, Boston, right? That's where you lived before you moved here?"

"Yeah, my ex and I had a clinic in Back Bay. Do you know Boston at all?"

"I went there once to visit a friend from college. Her husband has a very park-the-car-in-Harvard-Yard accent." She affected the best Boston accent she could.

Caleb chuckled. "As a New Englander, I should be offended by that, but we had some clients who spoke like they just walked off the set of *The Departed*."

"You don't have an accent."

"Believe me, I put some work into that. It comes back when I'm home. But if you're ever in Portland, I can tell you all the best places to get a lobster roll."

He'd turned his accent on—"*lobstah* roll"—which made Lauren laugh. "Do you go up there much?"

"Not as much as I'd like. My ex got the car in the divorce, too, in that she literally drove off in it when she left town."

"So she got the car and the dog. What did you get in the divorce?"

He sighed and looked away, probably not super willing to talk about it. "I got a slightly larger percent of the clinic sale, basically. Her lawyer was a real shark, though."

"Sorry. I didn't mean to bring it up."

"It's all right." Caleb rubbed his forehead.

Lauren knew better than to push him into talking about it, so she said, "What other Boston movies are there? *Good Will Hunting?*"

Caleb offered her an indulgent smile, like he knew what she was doing. "I remember really liking that movie, but I haven't seen it in years. I had a buddy in college who went to the same high school as Ben Affleck and Matt Damon, although a few years later obviously, and he was really proud of that fact."

"Well, I went to the same high school as Guy Fieri, so take that."

"Who's Guy Fieri?"

"He's that Food Network guy with the bleached hair and the goatee who wants to take you to Flavortown."

Caleb laughed. "Oh, sure, that guy. Where are you from again?"

"Columbus."

"Right, okay. Well, my high school produced no one very famous. A second-tier NFL linebacker, a soap actress, the drummer for a punk band that had one hit in 1982, but otherwise no one of note."

"Except you!"

"I'm hardly famous."

"No, but you are successful." Lauren grinned. "I went to my ten-year reunion last year, and my main goal was to show how cool and successful I am out here in New York City. I had just gotten hired at the Cat Café, so I was all, 'I manage a business and I live in Brooklyn, how cool am I?'"

"How did that go over?"

"My former classmates were way impressed with the fact that I lived in New York City and kept telling me that my life must have been very glamorous or very dangerous. Although I think most people were like, 'Wait, who are you again?'"

Caleb nodded. "I didn't go to my ten-year reunion. And my graduating class only had sixty students, so I definitely knew everyone."

"Small high school."

"Small town." Caleb looked around the room. "So your classmates were not impressed by your glamorous life as a cat café manager?"

"Well. Some were." Lauren watched Caleb look around, trying to interpret the look on his face. "You don't take this very seriously, do you?" she asked.

"What, the Cat Café? Whatever you're doing seems to be working. This place is always busy when I walk by."

"You're a vet. You know people find petting animals soothing. The cats here are all pretty docile and friendly. After all, we send the hard-luck cases to you."

"Yeah, I guess that's true. Olivia and I had to neuter a couple of feral cats yesterday. One of them was real nasty when he came out of anesthesia. I was worried he'd scratch my eyes out."

"Yeah, the ferals can be mean. I assume Mitch will bring those back to the colony behind the Brooklyn Museum."

"So that's an official colony, huh?"

"Yeah. They mostly stay away during the day, but they hang out in the parking lot at night. The museum thinks they are kind of a menace, but it's really the safest way to control the feral population in Brooklyn. They can't be in homes, and we can't just euthanize them, at least I wouldn't be able to. So Mitch—he's the guy who brought me the kittens—he runs an organization that traps and tags the cats. They spay or neuter any they find that are untagged then release them back to the colony. And still, new cats sneak in all the time."

"Are feral cats a problem in Brooklyn?"

"They are. Monique lives in Prospect Lefferts Gardens, and she says there are feral cats all over, and they are real bold. They go through her trash at night, like raccoons." Lauren sighed. She assumed Brooklyn's feral cat population included strays, cats that escaped, or cats that were abandoned by their owners. There were several no-kill shelters in Brooklyn, and there were veterinary clinics and places like the Cat Café that would take in house cats if people couldn't care for them anymore. Those cats could have better lives in new homes rather than being turned out on the street. It broke Lauren's heart to think about.

"Were you this passionate about cats before you worked here?" Caleb asked.

Lauren tried not to hear the mild disdain in his tone. "Sure, I've always been a cat person. I've gotten more involved in the pet communities here since coming to manage this place, though. I know people at all the shelters, I try to attend meetings of this pet owners group in Park Slope, and I've met my share of cat people. And I've learned a ton about feline behavior since I've worked here." She smiled. It was a lot of work and it could be stressful, but this was a dream job in a way. Not the sort of thing she ever saw herself doing, but running a business that made people happy was something she enjoyed daily.

"You think it's silly," she said.

"Did I say that? If it makes people happy, who cares what I think?"

Lauren tried and failed to read his tone. "You're not...the warmest person."

He rolled his eyes, which got Lauren's hackles up. He said, "You're hardly the first to say so."

"I don't mean to offend you. I'm just making an observation."

"I've gotten used to putting some professional distance between me and my patients."

"Am I one of your patients?"

He frowned. "No."

"I'm not asking you to be anyone but yourself, but this

professional distance thing you have can be... I don't know how to describe it. I just wish you could figure out how to turn it off. See the world a little differently."

"Oh, here we go."

"Don't roll your eyes at me. I don't know if this is, like, a divorce thing or if you've always been like this, but if you're really this jaded, why even bother? Do you not care about your patients?"

"Of course I care about my patients!" Caleb's tone was sharp. "I love animals. That's why I got into veterinary medicine to begin with." He rubbed his forehead. "I even like cats sometimes. Do I want one as a pet? No, not especially. But that doesn't mean I'm not a good doctor."

"I didn't say you weren't!"

"You kind of implied it."

Lauren groaned. "Look, cards on the table? I find it frustrating that you maintain this distance, or whatever it is. I get that you don't want any romance, I probably wouldn't either if I'd just gotten divorced, but you could try to not be a jackass all the time."

"Who's being a jackass? I was trying to make conversation. Then you started down this road, talking about what a cold bastard I am. That's not a news flash, by the way. And cards on the table? Yeah, I think this place is a little silly. I appreciate the work you do for pet adoptions, but if I wanted cat hair in my coffee, I'd drink the stuff Rachel makes at the clinic every morning."

Lauren let out a frustrated grunt. "I keep forgetting we can't stand each other. Us getting along for a few minutes there distracted me."

"Here's your reminder, I guess."

"Why did I ever sleep with you?"

"Interesting question. Neither of us was in our right minds, I guess."

"Shit." Lauren rubbed her forehead. She still didn't regret sleeping with him as such, because it had been good, but this conversation was a good reminder of how incompatible they were. "If that's how you feel..."

He grunted. "I'm not *trying* to be a dick. I guess we just rub each other the wrong way...when we're not rubbing each other the right way."

Lauren laughed despite herself. "That was bad."

"I know. It just sort of popped into my head. But otherwise, I don't know what to tell you. You don't care for my personality. It's not like I can easily change it. You knew what you were getting into when you slept with me."

"Yeah, I did. Maybe you should just go home, Caleb."

"Fine."

Without any further word, he grabbed his bag and left the café.

CHAPTER 11

"WELL, I HATE HIM AGAIN."

Evan and Paige glanced at each other. They were the only ones at a table in the back of the cat area of the café, during the slow period just after lunch.

"Dr. Fitch?" Paige asked.

Lauren dropped into a chair. "He came by the café last night and we had a fight. I don't know why I thought we could even be friends. Clearly the other morning was just a weird fluke because we were tired and stressed and relieved the cats were okay. So that's over."

Evan shook his head. "Nope."

"No?"

"I don't think it's over. I think it's just the beginning. I think you guys are so bent out of shape over each other that all that passion bubbles up as arguments. If you just fucked instead, you wouldn't fight."

"That's garbage, Ev."

"Is it? That morning you banged each other, did you fight?"

Lauren thought back on it. She guessed they hadn't argued at all. "No."

Evan crossed his arms. "I rest my case."

"One cannot build a relationship on just fucking," Lauren pointed out.

"I dunno. I spent several very promising months with that guy Brent." Evan turned toward Paige and said in a loud whisper, "Dick like a porn star. We spent basically the entire first month of our relationship exploring what he could do with it."

Paige giggled.

Lauren rolled her eyes. "Did you marry that guy? No."

"Anyway, despite the fact that you are definitely going to fall in love and marry that guy and pay me ten bucks, you said you didn't want a relationship anyway, so what's the problem? Screw his brains out, then go back to hating each other if you like."

"You don't make any sense," said Lauren.

"Well, you can be angry but getting laid or angry but not getting laid, and I know which of those *I'd* choose."

"He kind of has a point," said Paige.

"Ugh, don't encourage him."

"Is he coming to the adoption night?" asked Evan. "I can talk to him if you want. Get the real scoop. Ask if he likes you."

"I am an adult woman, thank you very much, not a seventh grader. And I already know he's attracted to me. He just doesn't like me very much. And speaking of the adoption event, that's what we're here to discuss, not my love life."

"You brought it up," Evan pointed out.

Lauren opened her notebook to a clean page and clicked her

pen a couple of times. "Look, is there anything remaining on the to-do list?"

Paige looked at her own notes. "We're basically covered. There's a case of plastic cups in back for drinks. The bartender is all set to arrive a half hour before doors open. We should probably buy a few more bottles of wine just in case, but we can also just run down to the corner liquor store if we're getting low."

"Food?"

"Ah, you're going to love me." Paige grinned. "I called all of our regular food vendors and asked if they could donate anything. So we'll have some pastries, and Pierre's Bakeshop is bringing some savory things. So there will be mini-quiches and something else. All free of cost to the event."

"You are a rock star."

"Evan designed signs for each of the cats up for adoption, so I got those printed today," said Paige. "I figured we could post them around the room. And I talked to Olivia when I went out for lunch. She's got flyers made up about the kittens you brought in, and she said you could stop by this evening to grab those."

"Cool, thanks."

"We should be nice to them because they gave us a pretty fat check in exchange for having their name all over everything. So maybe don't murder their new vet."

"I won't. This week. After the adoption night, all bets are off." Lauren sighed. "Sounds like we're in good shape, though."

"We are," said Paige. "I know this is the first time we're serving liquor, and that adds some variables, but this should really go well. I'm looking forward to it."

"Me too. Thank you, guys, really. I know this is your job, Paige, but you've really kicked ass planning this one."

"Thanks, boss."

"Pierre is really giving us food for free? That's wild."

Paige laughed. "I think I said, 'It's for a good cause' about eight hundred times before he relented, but yes."

"I should give you a raise."

Paige grinned. "I don't want to tell you what to do, but..."

Paige did deserve a higher salary. Lauren knew she could be assertive when needed; she'd likely charmed fancy hotels into discounts when she'd done event planning for a bank. It bothered Lauren that the café couldn't afford to pay her more because she was worth three times her salary. But if Paige was happy working for peanuts so she didn't have to go back to her corporate job, Lauren was grateful.

The bell over the front door rang and Diane's voice drifted toward the back. It sounded like she was with at least one man, and they seemed to be arguing.

"I wonder what that's about?" Lauren said.

She got up and walked to the café area. Diane was there with two men in suits, which seemed very strange. Monique was behind the counter and wore an alarmed expression. Lauren pulled the door to the cat room closed and walked over to the men. "Can I help you?"

"Ah, Lauren," said Diane. "Lauren is my manager here. Lauren, this is Mr. Randolph and his assistant, Mr. Newton. They work in real estate."

Lauren shook each man's hand while thinking that "they work

in real estate" sounded a lot like a euphemism. She took it to mean Mr. Randolph was an investor and not an agent. And then her stomach flopped. Was this the developer buying up property on Whitman Street? Was he here to buy Diane's building?

Would she sell after all?

Lauren tried to smile and not let the horror she felt show on her face. The assistant, Mr. Newton, was not doing as good a job at that and looked thoroughly disgusted.

"You know it's illegal for animals to be anywhere food is served," he said, eyeing Sadie's cat bed in the corner. Sadie was currently asleep on a sofa in the cat room, which Lauren was grateful for, because this looked like the sort of man who might report them.

"Our lawyer says the current set up is compliant with the law," Lauren said.

"It's dangerous having animals and food so close to each other."

Mr. Newton was a skinny man with a nasal voice, and he was clearly grossed out by the idea of an animal getting anywhere near his food.

"I take it you don't have pets," Lauren said.

"God, no. Cats carry disease, you know. Having food near a cat is a good way to get toxoplasmosis."

"There are no litter boxes anywhere near the food. And you can get toxoplasmosis from uncooked meat, too."

"Okay!" said Diane. "This business is thriving and I'm committed to it continuing to thrive, so we have a lawyer on retainer to make sure we're following the letter of the law, and I can assure you the cats and the food do not interact. Customers who don't want to eat near the cats can eat out here. They are free to choose to eat with the cats, too. It's really no different than if you had dinner at your own house with your dog in the room, now is it?"

Mr. Randolph had been silent during this whole exchange, but now he said, "Thriving? There are no customers."

"It's the slow time of day. And we do have a customer in the back," said Lauren. After all, Evan paid for his coffee. Most of the time. "It'll pick back up later this afternoon. And we've been doing great business in the morning, especially since the café across the street closed."

"Yes," said Mr. Randolph. "I own that building now. I'm here meeting my neighbors, you see."

Sizing them up, more likely. Why else would he get in touch with Diane first? Lauren would have bet Randolph had designs on this building and was here to look at the retail space. Sure enough, he said, "Mind if I peek in there?" He gestured toward the cat room.

"All right."

Not surprisingly, Newton stayed put, standing near the counter with his hands shoved in his pockets. Diane shot Lauren a look that briefly expressed her displeasure at the situation.

Randolph came back a moment later and said, "Cute." To Diane, he said, "And next door is a veterinary clinic?"

"Yes. One of the biggest in the neighborhood. They're actually the only clinic in this part of Brooklyn that does emergency medicine and stays open all night."

Randolph nodded thoughtfully. "Interesting. Good to know.

Well, it was nice meeting you ladies. Maybe I'll see you around the neighborhood."

Randolph left with Newton in tow. Diane stayed quiet until they'd vanished from view. Then she said, "He's trying to buy the building."

"I figured. I heard a developer bought the Star Café."

Diane turned to Monique. "Can I have an herbal tea, dear? Do you have that rooibos today?"

"I do," Monique said, fetching a cup.

Once Diane had her tea, she headed toward the cat room, so Lauren followed her there. Diane greeted Paige and Evan before settling on a sofa.

"That Randolph fellow wants to buy this building, too," said Diane. "Which is comical. I have no intention of selling. Honestly, I think he wants to buy up buildings on this block to level them and put in a mall. No appreciation of history, these developers. This building has been here since 1923! It's got character! There's a rumor that Truman Capote slept with a man who lived in this building! How can you tear it down to put in a mall that no one is even going to shop at?"

"Or they'll put up a flimsy new apartment building that looks all sleek and modern on the outside but falls apart once tenants move in," said Paige. "A friend of mine lives in one of those new buildings in Crown Heights and all her appliances broke down the first month she lived there *and* the building has mice."

"Gross," said Evan.

"It doesn't matter," said Diane. "I'm not selling. I figured I'd meet with the guy when he contacted me to see what he's about, but he practically got out the tape measure when he was in here, and I did not approve of that." She shook her head and groaned. "What's up with you girls? And Evan? How are you all?"

"Lauren hated the new vet, then she loved the new vet, then she hated him again," said Evan.

"Traitor," Lauren muttered.

Diane laughed. "That sounds fun. Winnie and I got our start that way, actually." Winnie was Diane's late wife.

"Oh?" said Evan, leaning forward.

Diane sipped her tea and gave Evan an appraising look. "Our first meeting was very awkward and we got off on the wrong foot. That was, gosh, 1975, maybe? I had just finished law school, and I went to this reception for female law professionals. Safety in numbers, you know. It was very hard to get a job if you were a woman in those days, unless you wanted to take dictation for one of the partners, which I did *not*. Winnie was a paralegal for a huge, evil corporate firm in Midtown, and I got a little idealistic with her the first time we met."

Lauren chuckled, picturing it. Diane had a bit of a retired hippie vibe. Winnie had died before Lauren had met Diane, but she'd seen pictures, and she could just picture someone as crunchy granola as Diane meeting a buttoned-up paralegal.

"Anyway," Diane said, "I ended up getting a job at her firm, because I have principles but I also had rent to pay. So of course I ran into her in the company cafeteria one day, and she let me have it for being a hypocrite, which I deserved. Things were pretty prickly between us for a while. But gosh, she was just so beautiful. My Winnie had a lovely face and these pretty blue eyes, and she wore her hair long in those days, and I had such a crush on her even though we generally argued whenever we ran into each other. And then one day I ran into her and we didn't argue. I didn't know if she was gay, and I didn't know how to ask her, but we got to be friends, and then one day we got to kissing, and the rest is history."

"That's so sweet," said Paige.

"So what I hear you saying," said Evan, "is that you met this woman and then you argued whenever you met and then one day, instead of fighting, you made out, and then you fell in love."

"That's about it, yeah," said Diane.

"Don't even, Evan," said Lauren.

Evan crossed his arms and looked smug. "Because Lauren and Caleb fight, except one time, instead of fighting, they made out."

"Evan!" said Lauren. Although she probably should have felt relieved Evan didn't say she and Caleb had slept together.

"I can't believe you told her that," said Paige, giggling.

Diane laughed. "Oh, honey, I know exactly how that goes."

"We're not compatible," Lauren said. "We're not! He's an arrogant know-it-all whose heart has been replaced with robotic parts or something, because he doesn't seem to feel human emotions. He's rude. He thinks the Cat Café is ridiculous. And he just got divorced and doesn't want a relationship. What on earth could we be to each other?"

Evan mimed making dollar bills rain.

"What does that mean?" Diane asked.

"Evan bet Lauren ten bucks she'd marry Caleb," said Paige.

"He's going to lose that bet," said Lauren.

"I'm not. You just heard how hard she protested. She *loves* him. She's going to *marry* him."

"Nope," said Lauren.

Diane clapped. "Oh, I do love you guys. But Dr. Fitch seems like such a nice young man. I'm surprised you don't get along."

Lauren sighed.

"I'm not even saying you and Dr. Fitch will be like me and Winnie. Because Winnie was one in a million. God, I miss her sometimes."

Lauren reached out and touched Diane's arm comfortingly.

Evan, who had always been uncomfortable with deeply emotional moments, said, "But you can see certain parallels."

"Maybe," said Diane. Her smile was enigmatic.

Lauren shook her head. "You're wrong."

"I take cash or check," said Evan.

Lauren rolled her eyes and left to check on Monique. She heard Evan and Diane laughing together behind her.

———————

Caleb was manning the front desk when Lauren walked into the clinic. When she spotted Caleb, she frowned.

"It is I, chopped liver," he said.

Lauren sighed. "Is Olivia here?"

"No, she left about twenty minutes ago. Her daughter had a sporting event of some sort. That kid does, like, eight sports, so I don't remember which one it is tonight. Soccer? Who knows?"

"Yeah, thanks. Damn."

"What do you need?"

The grimace Lauren made told Caleb all he needed to know about how much esteem she held for him. But she said, "She said she had flyers for the kittens that I could distribute during the adoption event. She said to come pick them up tonight."

"Yes, I have those." Caleb pulled a manila envelope from a drawer in the desk. "Olivia doesn't know you and I are sworn enemies, so she left them for me to give you."

"You're not my..." Lauren pressed a hand to her forehead, took a deep breath, and held her hand out for the envelope.

Caleb held the envelope for a moment. "You're going to take this the wrong way, but I find you incredibly hot when you're mad at me."

It was a dumb thing to say. He knew it would offend her. But once the thought popped into his head, he couldn't stop himself from saying it. Because the truth was, though he didn't relish arguments, part of him enjoyed riling her up.

"That... That was a terrible thing to say."

"It's true." Might as well lean in, he reasoned. He grinned at her. "You're standing there glowering at me, and you've never looked sexier."

She frowned. "Isn't that, like, sexual harassment?"

He felt guilty for a brief moment, thinking maybe he'd crossed a line, but the way her face went crimson indicated maybe she was into it, too. Was he an asshole? Probably. "You don't work for me. I'm not even propositioning you. I'm just stating a fact."

She looked flustered, which was gratifying. "You're an arrogant prick, you know that? You think just because you lay on some bullshit backhanded compliment, I'll sleep with you again."

He shrugged. "Will it work?"

"No. Remember how we don't even like each other? Not two days ago, you came into my place of business and told me how silly it was."

"Actually, you told me I thought it was silly."

"You didn't disagree."

"It's not for me to say!" He shot out of his chair. "You know what I think? I think you provoke me on purpose. I think you think I'm pretty sexy when we're fighting, too. In fact, I think that we're making a mistake yelling at each other now when we could just be ripping each other's clothes off."

Her jaw was loose, her gaze intense. "Give me the flyers."

He held the envelope behind his back. "Tell me I'm wrong."

She blew out a breath that made her bangs jump. "Okay. Fine. Maybe I enjoy our sparring matches a little. Gets the adrenaline up. But are you seriously suggesting we fight and then have sex, as if that's a normal way to conduct a relationship?"

"What relationship? We don't have to be friends, even. But I think you're hot, you think I'm hot, as I recall, we were pretty hot together, and so we could do something about that."

"So what are you proposing? An enemies-with-benefits relationship?"

Caleb laughed. The absurdity of the situation hit him all at once. But then he realized it wasn't actually a terrible idea. "I mean…yeah."

Lauren nodded slowly. "Is anyone else here?"

"There are no other humans in the clinic right now, if that's what you're asking, but I should warn you Doug is due back any minute. We ran out of coffee this morning and he can't get through the overnight without it, so he ran to the bodega on the corner. But then I'm off work and, as I recall, you live right upstairs."

"You make an interesting point."

Caleb wasn't sure if he was a jerk for feeling a little smug that he'd persuaded her. He wasn't even sure she'd been persuaded. And this was nuts. Was he really propositioning a woman he couldn't seem to get along with?

Yes. Because she got his blood pumping the way no one had in a very long time.

He handed over the envelope. Lauren took it and lifted the flap to look inside, then slid the envelope into her bag. This was where she should have probably thanked him and left, but instead she stood there, staring at him.

"So," Caleb said.

"Just sex. That's what we're doing. No romance, no flowers, no chocolates, none of that."

"Basically. Only if you're into it, though. If you're not, I was joking."

"But you weren't joking. You want to have sex with me."

Caleb walked around the desk and stood in front of Lauren with no furniture between them. "I do. But only if you also want to. I know what I said was inappropriate. I don't want you to feel like I'm pressuring you or anything. But if you think about it, this could be ideal. Neither of us wants a relationship, but we could probably stand to have some fun."

"Sexy fun."

"Of course."

He couldn't read her facial expression. She did look great today, though. Her long hair fell around her shoulders, her purple button-down strained a little at her breasts, and her short corduroy skirt showed off her gorgeous legs.

"I'll pick another fight with you if it makes a difference," Caleb said. "Cat lady."

She shot him a wry smile. "Actually, you want to grab some dinner before we do anything else? I skipped lunch today and I'm starving."

"Sure. That Italian place across the street any good?"

"Yeah. A little pricey, but they make their own pasta and mozzarella in-house."

Of course they did. Brooklyn was full of places like that. The owners were probably some Italian family from South Brooklyn with a marinara recipe they'd passed down for generations. Caleb salivated thinking about it.

Doug came back in then, carrying a whole sack of groceries.

"You moving in?" Caleb asked him as he unpacked the bag near the coffee maker in the waiting room.

"It's the overnight shift. I need snacks. This is the city that never sleeps, but the only thing you can get delivered here at two in the morning is pizza."

Caleb laughed. Around his old place in Boston, everything was closed by midnight, even some of the bars, and no food could be delivered after nine. New Yorkers didn't know how to cope with the fact that things closed and not everyone wanted to work all night.

He caught sight of Lauren in his peripheral vision, her face inscrutable. Actually, it looked like she was trying really hard to look friendly and placid and utterly failing. She was still hot and bothered. Caleb wondered if he could keep that going through dinner.

"Well," Caleb said. "If you don't need anything else, I'm gonna head out."

"Yeah, I'm good. Hello and goodbye, Lauren," said Doug.

"I came by to get the kitten flyers," Lauren said, patting her bag. "Are you coming by the big party next week?"

"If I'm not working, then yes."

"We're going to be fighting to the death to decide who has to work the overnight the night of your adoption party," Caleb explained. "Or, you know, we'll draw straws or something."

"We heard there'd be free liquor," said Doug. "It's gotten contentious."

"You're liquoring people up to talk them into adopting cats, aren't you?" said Caleb.

"I would never," said Lauren with mock outrage. "I'm merely throwing a party. The aim is for people to adopt cats, yes, but we also want them to have a good time. Well, and Paige figured free booze would attract some of the local hipsters." She rocked on her heels. "Can I see the kittens?"

"Oh. Yeah, I'll take you back there."

Lauren looked in on the kittens while Caleb went to the office to grab his stuff. When he popped back into the back room to fetch her, she was cooing and making baby noises to the kittens.

"They're so cute with their little scrunchy faces." Lauren's voice got higher and squeakier as she spoke.

"They seem to be doing pretty well. I've been keeping an eye on Giant because he's slow to eat sometimes, but he's playing with the other cats and he seems very friendly."

Lauren looked up. "Could he still be sick?"

"I think he may have a weak stomach, but he can live a full life if his eventual owners are careful with what they feed him. Or he'll grow out of it. It's hard to say with kittens this little."

Lauren stroked Giant's head, and he purred gently and pressed up against her hand. She cooed at him.

"We usually wait until they are about twelve weeks old to adopt them. They can eat regular kitten food by then. So they're with us a few more weeks." Caleb let out a breath. Her compassion was charming, but he didn't want to spend all night squatting next to a kitten pen. "You read to go?"

"Yes. Bye, little kittens. See you soon!"

They left together a few minutes later after a lot of baby talk to the kittens. As they waited to cross the street, Caleb noted this felt suspiciously like a date.

But, no, they were just fueling up for the hot night they were about to have. They didn't like each other much. This was not a relationship.

If he kept telling himself that, he might start to believe it.

CHAPTER 12

DINNER WAS...CIVIL. THERE WAS a brief argument about whether to order red or white wine; Lauren won and they ordered a bottle of white. It was a draw about whether cat pheromone diffusers actually worked to help keep cats calm—she'd seen them in action, Caleb remained skeptical—and they'd agreed to disagree about something regarding raw food diets for cats. The final argument was over dessert—they agreed to split something until it became clear Lauren wanted tiramisu and Caleb wanted cheesecake and there would be no compromising. There were instead two half-eaten desserts.

Lauren let Caleb into her apartment and closed the door, feeling a little awkward now. They really didn't see eye to eye on anything, did they?

Except the crazy thing was Caleb was right; the more they argued, the more worked up Lauren got, the more sexually aroused she was. Caleb was very handsome, his light brown hair getting a little long on top and sometimes falling into his eyes, a couple of days' worth of beard growth on his jaw giving him a slightly scruffy look, and his crazy athletic body all adding up to a quite appealing package.

So basically, whenever they fought, she also wanted to rip his clothes off.

But she wasn't sure how to get the ball rolling now.

"I'm feeling the need to call you fat and stupid," she said.

He laughed. "To quell your desire or to ramp it up?"

"The latter. Why is it that fighting with you gets me so revved up?"

"There's probably some brain science behind that."

"I've got some beer in the fridge if you want a drink while I catalog your faults."

Caleb followed Lauren into her kitchen. She was a little more self-conscious about her living space now that she knew he lived in Brooklyn Heights. Her place was clean but sparsely decorated, a large open space with a bedroom off to the side. The sofa was secondhand, the TV had been a gift from her parents, and the dishes had once belonged to Evan, who had spotted some colorful china on sale one day and decided to replace half his kitchen. Most of the cups in the cabinet had logos printed on them, one of the bookcases tilted slightly, and the computer desk in the corner had come with her after an old roommate had left it behind. Her mattress, at least, was fairly new, but it wasn't until recently that she started making enough money to even just live without roommates, let alone replace all her old furniture.

Caleb didn't say anything. He just smiled when she reached into the fridge and then handed him a beer.

"My ex-wife hated beer," he said. "We hardly ever had it at home."

"I like beer. But not IPAs. I don't know why every craft brewery tries to cram as much hops in their beer as they can now, because bleh. But give me something lighter like a *Kölsch* or a pilsner, and I'm happy. This is a pretty good amber. It's got kind of a caramel-y quality."

Caleb looked at her with awe. "You know the kinds of beer."

"I know a lot of things." She smiled. She'd arrived at the ripe old age of twenty-nine without getting married, and though she'd never been the sort of woman to modify her behavior to impress a guy, she'd been growing more set in her ways of late. And since all that mattered as far as Caleb was concerned was her physical attractiveness, she'd order dessert if she wanted to and drink beer if she wanted to, and basically just be herself because she could be.

She'd left an old afghan on the sofa the previous night, which she shoved off to the side now so they could sit.

"If I weren't here," Caleb said, "what would you be doing right now?"

"What a weird question."

"I'm curious about women, I don't know."

"Nothing that interesting. I usually just watch TV in my jammies most evenings."

"Yeah?"

"Although, honestly? Usually when I get home, the first thing I do is take off my bra."

Caleb sat back on the sofa and sipped his beer. "Don't let me stop you."

"All right."

It wasn't a lie. Lauren often did come home, dump her stuff, wriggle out of her bra, and then go about the rest of her evening.

The bra she had on now had a wire that poked her on the left side, one of those bras she kept putting back in the drawer long enough to forget it was uncomfortable. She met Caleb's gaze, then reached under her shirt, undid her bra, wriggled around, and pulled it off under the bottom of her shirt.

"Not through a sleeve?" Caleb asked.

"This shirt doesn't really allow for that. Also, we're not in *Flashdance*."

Caleb grinned. "I saw that movie when I was ten. It had a profound influence on my adolescence. So you'll forgive me the fantasy."

Lauren smiled back. "You have such a funny, formal way of talking sometimes."

"Too much time in school, I guess."

"How much college for you?"

"Well, five years of undergrad. Then four years of vet school, then another year of an internship, and then a residency. I finally graduated when I was twenty-eight."

"And now you are..."

"Thirty-two. Turning thirty-three in September."

"And already divorced."

"Yeah. That wasn't part of the plan."

"Did you see it coming?"

Caleb frowned. "I think part of me did. It's not that we were having problems, we just kind of shifted into coexisting rather than talking and having a real relationship. I wasn't... I mean, we weren't honeymoon happy, but I wasn't unhappy, either. We just...were. Then she told me she was seeing someone else. That I didn't see coming."

"Did you know the guy? Not to be nosy."

"It's okay." He laughed softly and shook his head. "No, I didn't know him. She met him at the gym. And we went to different gyms. I forget why. I think she thought mine was too much of a meat market. And then, lo, she found some meat." He sighed. "Sorry. I hate talking about this because I inevitably kind of fall into this bitterness that I'm tired of and don't want to feel anymore."

"I'm sorry I asked, then. And not even in a snotty way."

He nodded. "No, I get it. Hard not to be curious. What about you and that ex who got married?"

She didn't want to talk about Derek, but she supposed turnabout was fair play. "We dated for almost six years, and then one day we realized we were headed in different directions. He wanted the wife and kids with the picket fence in the suburbs. That kind of life horrifies me. I'm never leaving the city. So we hit an impasse. Then he married the next woman he dated." Lauren took a deep breath. "It's not even that I want him back, because I don't. It just…hit me wrong, I guess, when he announced he was getting married. Like, I'm mad he won the breakup."

"He won the breakup?"

"Yeah. I've hardly dated since we broke up, but he's married now."

"I don't think you can assign a real value to that."

Lauren rolled her eyes. That was such a Caleb response. "I'm not saying it's rational. I'm just saying that I felt… I dunno. Like I failed because he's happy now but I'm just… I mean, I'm not *un*happy, but I'm not in a relationship. Not that I even feel the need to define myself by being in a relationship, because that's some sexist, heteronormative bullshit, I'm just *saying...*" She stopped talking and looked at Caleb, who was smirking. "I'm rambling. Sorry."

"It's okay. You're what, late-twenties? Hard to get to thirty without any baggage. I'd think you were weird if you didn't have any."

"You already think I'm weird."

He laughed. "True."

Lauren was a bit relieved when Caleb made the first move, because she couldn't figure out how to get them from this conversation about their failures into the sexy times. Because she did not want to talk anymore. She wanted Caleb naked, in her bed, and she wanted him to do unholy things to her, but she couldn't quite figure out how to make that happen. Should she just say it, should she touch him, should she—

He kissed her.

He put his hand on her cheek, a gesture so sweet she almost forgot they weren't supposed to like each other, and then he leaned in and pressed his lips against hers. The kiss alone was enough to kick her motor into gear, and arousal spread through her body like a comforting warmth. She pulled his shirt out from his pants and slid her hands up his chest. He sighed into her mouth.

"Let's take this to the bedroom," she said.

"Perfect."

They stood and she led him toward her room. Then a thought popped into her head as they crossed the threshold. "What about your dog?"

"He'll be okay for another hour or two. It's not like I'm spending the night. That's not what this is. Right?"

Right. Lauren had quite forgotten this was just sex. It wasn't romantic. There would be no cuddling, no spending the night, no kisses over waffles in the morning.

She shook it off and led him to her bed.

It didn't take them long to get naked, their clothes tossed all over the room. It didn't escape Caleb's notice that there was a fresh box of condoms on the bedside table, and when he looked in the drawer, the old ones had been removed. That she had anticipated this was encouraging.

When he turned back to her, she lay staring at him. She was on her back, her head pillowed by her arms, her perfect breasts raised up a little. Her body was lovely, curvy in the right places, soft in a way he found appealing. He touched her belly, ran a hand up her side and cupped her breast. He couldn't not touch her. He loved how soft and smooth her skin was, how beautifully shaped her breasts were, how hard and pink her nipples were. He bowed his head and took one of those nipples in his mouth. She moaned when he did.

He wanted to taste all of her. He set the condom aside and then trailed kisses from between her breasts to her navel and finally between her legs. She was already wet, and he relished her taste, sweet on his tongue. When her fingers wove through his hair, he applied more pressure, making her hiss and sigh and groan. He licked her clit and slid a finger inside her, and the way she smelled, tasted, and writhed around on the bed aroused him like nothing else had in a while.

She came on his tongue.

She'd whispered it was coming, but he felt it when her back arched off the bed and her body vibrated around him. He kept licking and stroking her through the orgasm, then slid up her body and kissed her lips.

His cock, hard as it had ever been, pressed against her, and he was about to reach for the condom when she tilted her hips up and the tip slid inside.

"You're gonna kill me," he said breathlessly. "Hold that thought, please."

"I need you inside me right now."

"And I need to be inside you, but I need to do one thing first."

He managed to roll the condom on before his brain leaked out of his ears, and he finally slid home in one smooth movement, her body warm and tight, he pressed inside her. It felt amazing to move in her, tight and tingly and hot, and he knew he was about to go off like a teenage boy.

"I'm not gonna last long," he said.

"If you do it right, I'll come again." She was equally breathless, her face and upper chest flush, beads of sweat on her forehead.

God, she practically glowed.

"Do it right?" he asked.

She grabbed his hand and positioned his thumb on her clit. He understood exactly what she needed and he moved his thumb in a circular motion. She hissed and arched off the bed again.

It became a challenge to keep up anything like a rhythm,

and he felt like he'd gone primal, that he was just rutting around looking for release. He tried to give her what she needed, putting pressure where she needed it.

But it was too good. Lauren dug her fingers into his back, he surged forward, and then everything went white as he came. He clutched her body to his and pumped his hips and groaned.

When he came back to himself, he rolled off her, but reached for her body. "I want to make you—"

"No, you're good. I'm good. I came twice, Caleb. That hasn't happened in years."

"You came twice."

"Don't look so smug."

He laughed and rolled out of bed to run to the bathroom. When he came back to the bed, she was still laying there pretty much as he'd left her.

"Having a problem there?" he asked.

"All my limbs are Jell-O now. I just want to lie here forever."

"Well, move over. I want to lie down for a bit."

"Right."

She shifted slightly toward the side of the bed. He lay down beside her. Then she snuggled up to him and laid her head on his chest.

It was...nice.

They lay together in comfortable silence for a long time, and Caleb put his arm around her and pressed his hand near her shoulder. He regretted that he'd have to get up to leave in a few minutes. Not only did he have to get home to Hank, but he couldn't stay here. If he did, his walls might come down.

"I wasn't always this way," he said softly.

"Mmm?"

"You asked me that recently. If I was this much of a bastard before the divorce. That's not how you phrased it, but that's what you meant."

"And you're saying you weren't."

Caleb let out a breath. "A divorce will take all the idealism right out of you." If his heart wasn't open—to a potential romantic partner, to the animals he treated—then it couldn't be broken the way it had been that day Kara had handed him divorce papers and told him she was seeing someone else.

"It's hard to picture you as idealistic."

Caleb laughed.

He ran his hands through her hair. He would have loved to spend the night, just talking about whatever, maybe showing her the kind of man he used to be, but he knew better. "I should get going."

She made a protesting noise.

"I'm sorry, Lauren. I gotta get home to my dog."

She rolled away. "I know. Of course. He's probably eaten your rug by now."

She sounded angry, and he couldn't really blame her. But he couldn't tell her why he wasn't staying, either. That had the potential to pull down his walls, too.

It was too soon. He was still too raw. And this...thing...he had going with Lauren was never supposed to be anything but sex.

He got up and started putting his clothes back on.

She sat up and pulled her sheet over her breasts. "You are coming to the adoption event, right?"

"Do you want me to?"

"We were hoping a few of the vets would be on-hand to answer questions for anyone interested in adopting a cat."

Ah, so it was a business situation, not that she wanted him there for support. That was probably just as well. He shouldn't feel so disappointed, especially since he was the one getting ready to leave.

"Yeah, I'll try to be there," he said. "Depending on how the Jell-O wrestling goes with the other vets and all that."

She laughed softly. "Right. Well. Say hi to Hank for me."

"Yeah, I..." She was clearly miffed now, and he didn't want to leave her like that. "Lauren, I'm sorry. It's too late to make other arrangements, and I..."

"It's fine. I know what this is between us." She smiled, but it seemed hollow. "Good night, Caleb. I'm sure I'll see you around this week. We seem to be forever randomly running into each other."

"Right. Good night."

Then he made himself leave.

CHAPTER 13

SINCE LAUREN HAD BEEN MANAGING the Cat Café, they'd held adoption events once a quarter or so to make room for new cats. They were usually pretty well attended, but this party was something else. Apparently "free booze" was the only thing one needed to say to attract New Yorkers to an event.

The café's full staff was there. Victor was posted at the cat room door to make sure none of the cats got out. Monique was overseeing the adoption paperwork and fees. Paige had gone into corporate event planner mode, walking around the room to make sure everyone was fine, helping people pick out cats, shaking hands with the shelter volunteers and veterinarians and other invited guests. The hired bartender was slinging drinks. And a handful of Lauren's other friends were pitching in to make sure everything went well. Lauren didn't have much to do as a result, so mostly she just mingled with the crowd.

She spotted Evan standing near one of the sofas. The little tortie named Chloe stood on the arm of the sofa and kept leaning up into Evan's hand to be pet. Evan was humoring her.

"Thank you for coming," Lauren said to him.

"Of course. You can't talk me into adopting another cat, but I can be supportive."

"Are you sure?"

"Sam is a lot of cat."

Lauren smiled. Evan had been among the first to adopt a café cat, a chubby gray street cat named Sam who was too sweet and lazy to survive among the feral cat population from which he'd been rescued, but who had enough feral in him that he was savage toward the occasional bug that got into Evan's apartment. Evan was convinced his apartment remained roach-free because word had gotten out among the roach community that any bug that got near Sam would be disemboweled.

"How are things otherwise?" Lauren asked.

"Fine. Is Caleb still your nemesis?"

"Yep."

"You're so gonna marry him."

Lauren rolled her eyes. "How's that whole 'sleep with a guy who's not Pablo' thing going?"

"Ugh. Not well. That housewarming party I went to? Everyone was in a couple. Everyone! How can that be? Is this just how my thirties are going to be? I thought I had more time."

Lauren tried not to smile at Evan's histrionics, so she said, "More time for what?"

"Before my classy yet understated destination wedding at a B and B in the Finger Lakes."

"Right, of course."

"I mean, come on, no one in New York settles down until

they're *at least* thirty-five. I've still got a few more years until I get there." He sighed. "I don't want to get married tomorrow. I just want to have some fun. Find a nice fellow to fool around with."

Lauren tried to school her face so she wouldn't let on that she had one of those in Caleb. She still wasn't entirely sure what to make of the fact that she was sleeping with a guy she didn't get along with otherwise. In bed, everything was peaceful and harmonious. Out of bed, things were still pretty messy.

This was normally the sort of thing she'd share with Evan, but she didn't want his judgment—or his gloating—and there was no reason any of her friends needed to know about all this. At least not until Lauren had a better handle on what *this* was.

And speaking of the devil, Caleb himself strolled into the Cat Café then.

"Your future husband is here."

"Bite your tongue. He isn't my future anything."

As if making that point, Caleb greeted nearly everyone else in the room before making his way over to Lauren.

"Hello," Caleb said placidly when he was close enough.

Evan sipped his cocktail and made a "See?" face.

"Hi," said Lauren. "You know my friend Evan?"

Caleb frowned, which meant he didn't. He shook Evan's hand. "I'm Caleb Fitch. I'm one of the vets from the clinic next door."

"Yes," said Evan. "Lauren has mentioned you. I'm Lauren's best friend. I'm very protective."

"Right." Caleb's frowned deepened, which was gratifying.

Monique walked by, her clipboard in hand. "Lauren, can you give me a hand?"

"Oh, hey, gotta go," said Lauren. She followed Monique to the back room to carry more cardboard carriers and other supplies back out front.

"Callie and Steve have been adopted," Monique said. "They went home with a really sweet newlywed couple who live in Carroll Gardens."

"Together? That's great!"

"Yeah. I'm happy they found a good forever home, but I always feel a little sad when our cats leave."

"I know exactly what you mean." Lauren felt a pang of sadness, too. Callie was a brown-and-black striped tabby and Steve was a black tuxedo cat, and the two of them had been nearly inseparable since they'd moved in, so it was good they were adopted together. But Lauren would miss them both, just as she missed all the cats who came through the café. She felt a pang at knowing she probably would never see those cats again.

As if sensing she needed a cat, Sadie wandered over and headbutted Lauren's shin. Lauren bent down to pet her. "You're stuck with me forever, kitty," Lauren told Sadie.

Sadie chirped happily in response.

Once Monique was set, Lauren walked over to the bar. Lindsay stood there flirting with the bartender. Lauren managed to say hello to Lindsay and order a gin and tonic in the same breath.

Lindsay sipped a cocktail and grinned at Lauren.

"I thought you couldn't make it," said Lauren.

"I tried to make an excuse to be here in my professional capacity. These are great cocktails. See?"

"Great cocktails? From our rented bartender, with the middle-shelf liquor from the store up the block."

Lindsay brought the cup to her lips and gave Lauren a thumbs-up. Then she said, "I'm not missing a lot tonight. Did you see that new streaming show, *Baking Bread*?"

"No. When do I have time to watch television?"

"Fair. But it's really soothing. It's basically just this silver fox baker who shows you how to make a different kind of bread each episode. I could watch him knead bread all day. He has amazing hands."

Lauren laughed. "Sure."

"Anyway, the guy from that show, Jack Brentwood, is from Brooklyn and just opened a new bakery on Court Street, so I was supposed to go check it out tonight, but I postponed."

"Really? Why? That seems more interesting than a party for cats. Not that I don't think a party for cats is the best thing ever, just, you know."

"I do know, but Jack Brentwood reminds me too much of a certain pastry chef ex. I was all set to go over there and tell him what other things he could knead, but then I wondered if Brad might show up, which is silly because why would he even? Brad's probably got his own bakery in some posh Manhattan neighbor-hood now. Still, I called Jack Brentwood to reschedule so I could come here tonight and get drunk with my friends." Lindsay lifted her glass to toast Lauren.

Lauren signaled to the bartender that she could use a refill. She forgot how over-the-top Lindsay could be about her ex-boyfriend. She basically walked around with an annotated map of New

York City that told her which blocks to avoid to ensure she never randomly ran into Brad. Lauren had tried to tell her a few times that, in a city of eight and a half million people, the odds of running into anyone were pretty slim.

Except on the F train. Lauren always ran into people she didn't want to see on the F train. It was clearly cursed. She'd seen Brad on the F a couple of months before, in fact, but had hidden her face behind a book and neglected to mention it to Lindsay.

Lindsay said, "Enough about *Brad*. I take it from the cutesy matching T-shirts that a number of vets from the Whitman Street clinic are here. Is one of them *your* vet?"

"He's not my anything, but Caleb is the tall guy awkwardly talking to Evan."

Lindsay looked and whistled. "Well, he looks like a tasty dish. And you decided not to sleep with him again because..."

"We hate each other's guts."

"I'd be willing to overlook that to get him between the sheets. I won't, of course, because of the sisterhood." She patted Lauren's shoulder. "But I'm just saying."

Lauren was tempted to say something glib like, "You can have him," but the truth was she didn't want anyone else to have him. Maybe they weren't destined for a great romance, but as long as they had...whatever they had, she wanted Caleb to herself.

"This is quite a crush," said Lindsay, surveying the room.

"I hope people actually adopt cats or donate to a shelter and aren't just here for the free booze."

"They will. Who could resist these little guys?" Lindsay bent down to pet Patches, a marmalade-colored cat.

"You want one?"

"I already have two, thanks to you."

Lauren sighed. "Well, anyway. I better mingle more. Thank you for coming, though."

"Sure. Let me know if you need anything."

"Say nice things to the guests about how great it is to have cats."

Just then, Lauren spotted the comedy duo of Randolph and Newton in the crowd. Both had on business suits. What the hell were they doing here?

Lauren approached them. Newton held up his hands as if he were afraid to touch anything.

"Alcohol *and* cats," said Newton.

"It's a private event," Lauren said. "The rules are different. Nice to see you gentlemen. What brings you here? Interested in adopting a cat?" There. Kill 'em with kindness, she figured.

"Ah, no," said Randolph. "Just being friendly neighbors."

"This is a private event, but it's open to the public," said Newton.

"It's all on the up-and-up. We consulted our lawyer before putting this on, and he says it's fine. Also, you may recall, the state of New York changed the law last year. This is all kosher as long as the animals are not allowed in the space where food is prepared. Given that everything was donated from elsewhere, there's no issue. If you're not comfortable eating with the cats, there are a couple of tables near the counter, away from the cat area." Lauren kept her tone light and friendly.

"I'd really prefer that," said Newton. He snagged a mini-quiche from a nearby tray and then left the cat area.

"He's a bit of a germophobe," said Randolph. "So you're in charge of all this?"

"I'm the manager of the café, yes. But my event planner Paige did most of the work for this particular event. We have these adoption parties quarterly to make room for new cats."

"Interesting. Very interesting business you have here. Seems a little flash in the pan, though, no?"

"We've been open for more than a year. Business is up lately. That seems like more than a flash. There's a cat café in Chinatown in Manhattan, in fact, that has been around for six years."

Lauren was curious about why this guy was here, and it made her nervous. She couldn't help but think they were here to calculate how long it would be until they went out of business. If the Cat Café went under on its own, it saved Randolph the hassle of evicting them if he bought the building...hypothetically. Or replacing the café with something more lucrative, like a bank or a cell phone store. Since technically Diane owned the Cat Café, the café closing would put her at the sort of financial disadvantage that might make her more inclined to sell as well. Lauren reasoned there were a lot of possibilities here, and many of them involved shutting down the Cat Café if Randolph had his way.

She looked around. Diane chatted with what looked like a middle-aged gay male couple—they were similarly groomed and also holding hands—and she wore a purple dress that was a little too formal for the occasion. She held a travel coffee cup with kittens on it in her hand, rather than drinking out of a glass from the bar. It was all very Diane.

Lauren wanted to get out of this conversation but didn't want to ruin Diane's evening by inflicting these guys on her. So Lauren said, "If you're not interested in adopting a cat, we are also taking donations for no-kill shelters in Brooklyn to help them cover their expenses. You can see Monique at the door if you're interested in donating."

"I'll take that under advisement."

Randolph continued to stand there, looking at her in a way that made her uncomfortable, like he was trying to wear her down. To what end, she didn't know; it wasn't like she owned this property.

Then Randolph said, "Do you get much business from the tenants in the apartments upstairs?"

Oh, this was bad. If he was inquiring about the tenants upstairs, he was likely wondering if he could evict them, too. Not wanting to admit *she* was one of those tenants, Lauren said, "Some. A lot of people who live between Henry Street and the subway station at the end of the block stop in here for coffee on their way to work. Some of them stop and pet the cats, but a lot of them just get their morning cup o' joe and a pastry." Lauren was thinking about starting a loyalty program with little cards, a "buy ten, get one free" sort of thing for the morning crowd, hoping to keep her customers loyal when a new coffee shop inevitably opened nearby. "Any ideas with what you will do with the old Star Café space now that you own it?"

"Not yet," said Randolph.

When no more information seemed to be forthcoming, Lauren said, "Well, it was nice chatting with you. I better mingle and make sure my staff is doing okay. Please help yourself to anything on offer and remember to talk to Monique about donations on your way out!"

Lauren slid away before Randolph could rope her into further conversation. He seemed to take the hint and went to the bar. His presence here was deeply unsettling, but Lauren didn't want to let that hamper her enjoyment of the evening. Instead, she sought out Paige, who stood on the corner surveying her kingdom.

"Successful evening," Lauren said.

"Much bigger crowd than I was expecting!"

"It's good, though. Maybe people will be charmed and continue coming back to the café."

"Was that the real estate developer you were just talking to?"

"Yeah. I don't know why he's here. I wouldn't worry too much. Diane said she wasn't selling. End of story, as far as I'm concerned. He can keep trying, but as long as Diane digs in her heels regarding selling, we're fine."

Paige smiled. "Good, good. In the meantime, let's get some more cats into good homes!"

———

The odd thing about talking to Evan was that Caleb got the impression Evan was rooting for him.

Well, that, and when they first shook hands, Caleb felt a spike of jealousy. It was unfounded—a few minutes of speaking with Evan revealed he was gay—but that it had happened at all was an unpleasant surprise. Caleb had no claim on Lauren. They weren't seeing each other exclusively. They weren't even in a relationship. Hell, they weren't even friends. They were two people who verbally sparred sometimes and then had sex.

He moved about the party. All of the vets had to wear official blue Whitman Street Veterinary Clinic T-shirts so they would be easily identifiable to the party guests, which meant he fielded some questions from potential cat parents. He knew most of the cats at the café were rescues who came from shelters, so he also assumed the cats had been screened for devastating diseases like feline leukemia and the feline version of HIV. Maybe the years of treating sick cats had made him too pessimistic, but all these people drinking and thinking taking home a cat was a good idea made him a little wary.

Which was why he inserted himself into a conversation with a woman who was telling a prospective cat adopter that she didn't take her cat to the vet regularly because the cat stayed inside all the time and didn't need shots.

"You really should, just in case," Caleb said to the woman.

"Well, sure," she said, glancing at his shirt. "You want us to pay you hundreds of dollars every year."

"No, I want to prevent the spread of feline diseases should your cat escape your apartment or otherwise be exposed to other cats."

"He would *never* escape."

"I passed four different missing cat posters on the way to work just this morning. You never know."

The woman just scoffed at him.

So he wasn't feeling very sociable when he finally ran into Lauren again. She looked to be a couple of cocktails into her evening, but she greeted him pleasantly enough.

"All right, cat lady. Do you screen or do a background check on any of the people who adopt cats?" he asked.

"We make them answer a series of questions to make sure

they're ready to take in a cat. The cats who live in the café have already been spayed or neutered and their shots are up to date, so that's already taken care of. We get everyone's contact information, and Paige calls them to follow-up in a few weeks. That's really all we can do."

Lauren's tone struck Caleb as blasé. "That's all you can do."

"It's not like we're giving out state secrets here. And you guys at the clinic don't do any more than that when you allow pets to be adopted."

"No, but most of the adoptions are to people who are already clients."

"Sometimes, my cold-blooded friend, you have to trust your fellow human beings to be good people. What's the alternative? A lot of these cats would die on the streets or in kill shelters otherwise. At least this way, we give them a chance at a good home."

"It's not that I don't trust people…"

Lauren leveled her gaze at him, as if to say, "Oh, please."

"I'm only worried about the welfare of the animals."

"Sure, you are."

The mocking note in her tone felt like she was goading him. On purpose? He couldn't tell.

He rolled with it. "I'm just saying, letting any rando off the street adopt a cat could lead to these cats being mistreated, and that's not what you want."

"Of course not. We do screen people. Are you accusing me of something?"

"No. I would never accuse you of anything."

She scoffed. "Oh, really?"

"Have I ever?"

"You've called me flighty on a few occasions. And you, buddy, are stubborn and untrusting."

Their raised voices were starting to attract attention around them.

"You're *too* trusting. You live in some strange fantasy land of cats and unicorns where everything is perfect, and it's ridiculous. People aren't nice. That's not how the world works."

"That's not fair. I'm doing good work here. If you can't see that—"

"Oh, I can see it. But be realistic. And lower your voice—people are staring at us."

"Fine," she whisper-shouted. "Are you really mad at me or are you making an argument to make an argument?"

"Some of both."

"You asshole. I can't believe you would pick a fight with me at an event I put on, in my place of business."

"You pick fights with me at *my* place of business all the time. You did just a few days ago, in fact."

"You are such a jerk. Why do I keep thinking we can even be civil?"

"Because you are foolish and idealistic?"

Lauren let out a frustrated grunt. "And you're an arrogant prick. God, you piss me off." Then she turned on her heel and marched into the back room.

Caleb looked around. Some of Lauren's friends—people he recognized but couldn't name, not really disproving her point—looked at him expectantly.

"Fine, I went too far," he told his audience. "I'll go apologize."

He made a big show of looking put out about it, and then jogged after Lauren. He walked through a series of open doors and found her in a big walk-in closet that seemed to be used mostly to store extra cat food and litter.

"Shut the door," Lauren said breathlessly.

Caleb did as he was told.

"Are you as turned on as I am?" Lauren asked.

"It was about to get embarrassing for me out there."

Lauren reached forward and grabbed his crotch, the palm of her hand against his very hard cock. "I think we have, like, ten minutes before people start to notice I'm missing."

"I'm supposed to be apologizing. I'm sorry if I went too far there."

She worked at the fly of his pants. "Shut up and fuck me. We can talk about it later."

He grabbed the hem of Lauren's skirt and shoved it up. He looked around. There was a narrow table that looked like it was about the right height. Would it support Lauren's weight? Only one way to find out. Caleb lifted Lauren onto the table and slid off her panties. She opened her legs. He was already half-hanging out of his pants, so he fished out his cock and kissed her.

"Do you have any—?" he asked.

"No, but I am on the pill."

"I don't have anything."

"I don't either."

With that, he pushed inside her.

It was fast and intense. Lauren threw one arm around Caleb's shoulders and used the other to brace herself against the table or the wall or whatever would keep her from falling. Caleb drove forward, shocked by how good it felt to be inside her bare, amazed that she trusted him this much, lost in the feel of her body around him.

It was over almost as fast as it started, with Lauren biting into his clothed shoulder to keep from crying out, and then Caleb shuddering and coming inside her.

They stayed panting on the table for a moment, Lauren still clutching at him to keep from falling. With some reluctance, Caleb withdrew. As they each put themselves back to rights, Caleb said, "That just happened."

"I do trust you, you know. You're always unfailingly honest."

"I trust you, too. At least as far as *this* goes." He gestured between them.

But the truth was, he *did* trust her. Maybe not with his heart, but he'd never known her to lie or be deceitful. Although now that he heard what he'd said in his own head, he worried he'd sounded condescending.

Lauren said, "I've never done it in a closet before."

"Me neither, actually. And Lauren, I didn't mean—"

"It's fine, don't apologize. Do I look okay?"

She looked gorgeous. A little disheveled. He reached over and smoothed down her hair. He tugged her shirt back into place. "Your lipstick is smudgy."

She hopped off the table. "My bag is in the office. Come with me."

He followed her down a short hallway to an office. She pulled a purse from a drawer, produced a compact mirror and a couple of what looked like wet wipes. She tossed one at him. He saw it was an individually wrapped make-up wipe.

"You've got my lipstick smudged on your face," she said, gesturing around her own lips.

He sighed and ran the wipe over his face as she fixed her lipstick. When she was done, she took the wipe from him, dabbed at a spot on his cheek, gave him a quick peck on the lips, and then ran her hands over his hair.

"Do I look passable?" he asked.

"You'll do." Lauren patted his shoulder. "All right. Let's get back out there and pretend we still hate each other."

Caleb laughed. "Don't we?"

He couldn't read her facial expression, but she managed to twist it into a smile. "Let's go."

He trailed her back into the main room, where the party was still in full swing without them. The blond woman who worked as the event organizer glared at Caleb, which seemed about right. Evan bent his head to talk to Lauren out of Caleb's earshot.

He should probably just leave the party. Bow out before he gave anything away about what had just happened between him and Lauren in a closet. He did want to get to the bottom of whether or not Lauren was offended and dodging him or if she really didn't care what he said. Maybe she actually liked it when he criticized her, which was kind of fucked up. Then again, he'd kind of started it with the whole fighting-with-you-turns-me-on thing.

He could wait for Lauren and try to talk her upstairs or back to his place, but that felt an awful lot like something a boyfriend would do.

He sought her out in the crowd. Now she was talking to someone Caleb didn't know, laughing as if she'd just heard the funniest joke, and he knew she would be just fine here.

He turned to leave. On the way out, he paused near the woman handling adoption paperwork, who he thought might be named Yvette or Monique or something French. He said, "I'm Caleb Fitch. I'm one of the vets from next door."

The woman smiled. "I know." She pointed her pen at his T-shirt.

"Right. I just wanted…to let Lauren know I had to leave, but I think this is a great event. I hope it ends up being as successful as it looks."

"We've found forever homes for four cats so far."

"That's great! Just, um, tell Lauren I had to go. I'll see her soon. Okay?"

The woman gave him an odd look, but she said, "Okay. Have a good night. Dr. Fitch."

CHAPTER 14

"I'M HAPPY TO REPORT," PAIGE said the next afternoon, "since it may have gotten lost in the alcoholic haze at the end of the party, that six cats were adopted. Trey from Pet Kind is bringing over five new cats this afternoon."

The Cat Café staff was sitting in the cat room for a staff meeting-slash-postmortem on the event. They'd raised nearly $1,000 for shelters as well. Brian Randolph had made quite a significant contribution, which Lauren found curious.

Lauren nodded. "We did a great job, team. That was our best adoption event yet."

"It was the alcohol," said Monique.

"That's cynical," said Paige. "I mean, free drinks obviously got some people in the door, but it didn't open their wallets or convince them to take a furry friend home."

"Do we know anything about the new cats?" Lauren asked.

"Trey emailed me some stuff," said Paige. "If I remember correctly, three are girls, two are boys. All are adults, but I don't think any of them are older than four."

"Sounds good. All rescues?" asked Lauren.

"Yeah. Trey always picks good cats for us."

Lauren tried to picture this Trey. Paige was much better at maintaining relationships with Brooklyn shelters and rescue organizations. Trey was a familiar name, but Lauren couldn't remember what he looked like. Tall, skinny, bearded maybe. Probably. That described half the men in Brooklyn.

"Does anyone else get sad when the cats leave?" asked Victor. "I miss Callie. It won't be the same around here."

"I do miss the cats," said Lauren. "But they've all gone to good forever homes. That's the goal here. We can be sad that six cats have left, but also happy they will be well cared for."

"Anyway," Paige said. "Huge success. People are already asking about the next one. I've got it penciled in for August. Maybe we can do some kind of summer theme."

"Great. If that's all, I'm calling the staff meeting. Get back to work, everyone." Lauren stood. She was pleased with the adoption event results, but she was feeling a little off her game.

She should really stop telling herself that Caleb wasn't the issue. Because he was on her mind and had been all day. Because they had once again argued, this time with plenty of witnesses, and then they'd had mind-blowing sex in a closet. Lauren wasn't even mad about the fight—she suspected he'd picked it precisely so they would have sex somewhere nearby. That didn't bother her. What bothered her was that Caleb could make her feel that amazing and then just…bail. Because not ten minutes after they'd reemerged from the back, he was gone. All he'd left was an incoherent message from Monique that became "he said to say hi" in the game of telephone her staff played.

Why would he just leave?

Well, probably because they weren't actually dating and he didn't actually owe her anything.

"Boss? Hello? Earth to Lauren."

Lauren looked up. Paige was looking at her expectantly.

"Sorry, I spaced out. Guess I didn't sleep enough last night."

"Oh, really? Did someone at the party catch your interest?"

"Not because of sexy reasons. Did you ask me a question?"

"Yeah, I just… Well, I was talking to Lindsay last night, and she brought up again that if we have that kitchen on premises that is just a big empty space right now, we really should use it. I was wondering if we could revisit the plan to hire a pastry chef."

"Yes, I want to. Let me put some numbers together and have a talk with Diane. Who…wow. How is it that lately, I just have to say a person's name aloud, and they appear?"

"Unknown superpower?"

Diane breezed over. "Hello, my girls. I heard the adoption event last night was a smashing success. Sorry I didn't get to talk to you much. I fell into conversation with a fellow who wants to run for city council. I figured I'd offer him some encouraging words."

Lauren laughed. "Well, we found six cats new homes."

"That's great news. The party was a delight. You girls do good work. And Victor does, too." Diane fluttered into a chair. She had on a purple chiffon caftan over a white shirt and pants, her short hair perfectly coiffed. The fuchsia lipstick was a bold choice. "I had a wild idea. Tell me what you think."

Paige glance at Lauren, looking mildly alarmed. Every so often,

Diane came to them with a crazy idea that often ran contrary to how Lauren would prefer to run the café. Since Diane owned the café, they had to either try to implement her odd ideas or tell her why they weren't possible.

Diane launched into her spiel. "I went to a fundraiser for a young lawmaker in Manhattan last week, where I met a woman who runs a writing program for kids, which got me to thinking about writers. Writers and cats specifically. I wonder if there are writers' groups in the area who would like to use our space, maybe after regular hours, for meetings or to write together or that kind of thing."

"We can look into that," said Lauren. It wasn't a terrible idea. One of Diane's previous wild hairs had been to make the café a space for students to study during certain hours, but the kids had been so loud it had bothered some of the cats. But older writers might be fine. The only trick would be to talk staff into staying after hours. Or hiring new people. "We should schedule a meeting to talk personnel soon."

"Are you having an issue with someone?"

"No, I need more someones, now that the morning rush has gotten so nutty."

Diane smiled. "Sure, we can discuss that. I have an appointment in a few, but I'll let you know when I have time. How are things otherwise? How is Dr. Fitch?"

"Lauren and Dr. Fitch still hate each other," said Paige.

"Aw, come on," said Lauren. "Way to blow my cover."

"They had a huge fight in the middle of the party last night. Did you not see them argue? He was kind of a jerk. I think he stepped over the line."

Diane smiled. "I did catch part of that. He apologized, didn't he?"

Given that his apology had involved sex in the closet, Lauren pressed her lips together so as not to give anything away. She felt her face heating anyway. "He did," she said, hoping she sounded noncommittal.

"He's really sweet with animals," said Diane. "I guess that's his type. Good with animals, terrible with humans."

"It's not that, exactly," said Lauren.

Diane and Page both turned to look right at her.

Lauren sighed. "He just rubs me the wrong way, is all." Or he rubbed her in all the right ways, which was becoming more of an issue as time went on. Surely this enemies-with-benefits situation had an expiration date. In no way was it sustainable. And the minute Caleb met some woman he did actually like and want to spend time with, this whole thing was over.

"You may yet make it work," said Diane.

"You and Evan are both crazy," said Lauren.

Diane smiled. "Love and hate are just different sides of the same coin. And it's not hard at all to flip a coin over."

Lauren sighed. "Trust me, there's no future for me and Caleb."

"They're on a first-name basis," Paige whisper-shouted to Diane.

"I noticed." But perhaps Diane recognized further pushing was futile, because her next question was, "And how are things with you, Paige?"

Paige laughed. "Well, if it's true a girl has to kiss a lot of frogs before finding her prince, I'm in luck, because all the dating apps are sending my way are frogs lately." She held up her phone. "Maybe I'm too old for dating apps. I mean, fond as I am of these hipster boys who know a lot about craft beer and kinds of avocados but can't balance a checkbook."

"There's more than one kind of avocado?" asked Diane.

Paige looked forlornly at her phone. "Aside from the internet, how do people even meet anymore?"

"Well, in my day, people met in person and looked at their phones much less. Were there no eligible bachelors at the adoption party last night?"

Paige frowned. "Not really, no."

"What about that Mitch fellow who runs the rescue organization?"

"He's nice, but not at all my type. Also, like, fifteen years older than I am."

"So dating is going well," Lauren said.

Paige laughed. "I'm not trying to be picky, I just haven't met anyone worthy of a second date in a while. But my prince is out there somewhere."

"It's good that you haven't given up hope, dear." Diane patted her knee.

The *unlike Lauren* was implied.

———————

Olivia walked in with a cup of coffee and a grimace. Caleb sat at the front desk, updating charts while Rachel was at lunch, and he found Olivia's expression alarming.

"What's going on?" he asked.

"I saw Diane at the Cat Café."

"Diane...?"

"She owns the building. So she's our landlord, but she basically lets us operate without interference."

"Okay."

"She's a nice woman, but she's a bit of a busybody. She's currently dishing with Lauren and Paige like she's their mom. Well, more like a kooky aunt than a mom, I guess. She'll probably come here next to tell you you're too thin and she's got just the woman to set you up with."

"That does sound like my mother." Although, his mother hadn't been pushing him to see other women yet. She understood he was still smarting from the divorce. She had, however, never been Kara's biggest fan and didn't seem particularly brokenhearted when the marriage had ended.

"So brace yourself. Diane tries to mother everyone who works and lives in the building. It's just her way."

"Seems unusual. I haven't lived in New York that long, but it seems like more of a 'keep your head down and get where you're going' kind of place. I don't think I could even come up with the first name of the guy in the apartment next to mine if I tried really hard."

"And that is how it should be. I say hello to my neighbor when we pass in the hall, but otherwise, if I'm home, I just want people to be quiet and leave me alone. And at work, I only want to talk to people who work here and the patients." Olivia sighed. "What's up next today?"

"You have a Pekingese with the sniffles coming in at two. Then I have a follow-up appointment with that dachshund from last week with the lump we removed. Let's hope the blood tests continue to look good."

"Yeah, I hope so. The tumor was benign, right?"

"It was, yes. I think the blood tests should be fine, but I want to do a full panel."

Olivia nodded. "Seems smart. Better to rule out something more sinister." They'd discussed before that cancer in pets was particularly heinous. They had the capabilities to administer chemotherapy to small animals at the clinic, but it was such a tough call choosing whether to treat cancer aggressively in a way that might make the animal sick or to let the animal live out the rest of its life as comfortably as possible. And that was without accounting for costs. Those decisions often devastated the pet owners and were upsetting to watch as the doctor.

An older woman with white hair breezed in then. Caleb remembered her vaguely; they'd met right after he'd started working here. "Hello, doctors. How are things today?"

"Good," said Olivia. "How are you, Diane?"

"I'm fine, dear. Please don't tell me you need to hire more help, though. Lauren wants to hire more people. Possibly also a pastry chef."

"A pastry chef?" asked Caleb. "To make pastries for cats?"

Diane let out a belly laugh, as if that were the funniest thing she'd ever heard. "Maybe!" She gave Caleb a light punch on the shoulder. "Rumor has it you and Lauren haven't been getting along."

Good to know that was common knowledge. "It's not that we don't get along…"

"It's that they don't agree on anything," said Olivia.

Caleb tried to remember when Olivia had even been around for one of his arguments with Lauren, and he remembered suddenly that she'd been around a few days ago when they'd had quite a loud fight about proper kitten care in the back room, and then had quickly made up by making out on top of a stack of bags of cat food. Hopefully Olivia had only heard the first part.

"Did you see them sparring last night?" Olivia said, reminding him she'd been at the adoption party, too. "I couldn't tell if they wanted to tear each other up or tear each other's clothes off."

"Hey, now," said Caleb, embarrassed his boss had witnessed him arguing with Lauren more than once. "I try to get along with her. She just gets under my skin."

"Uh-huh," said Diane.

"She's too much sunshine for Caleb the Grouch," said Olivia.

"Am I really that grouchy?"

Olivia gave him a "please" look.

And maybe he had been a little. He supposed this tendency to keep everything at arm's length had infiltrated every part of his life, spreading like a disease. At first, he was just trying to keep his heart safe from emotional entanglements, and he wanted to keep professional distance from his clients so when a dachshund with a tumor showed up, it didn't break his heart. But maybe he'd been rude to everyone.

When had he become this person? He didn't like this person much.

He sighed. "Well, anyway, I did apologize to Lauren after we argued last night and she…took it well. I don't see us becoming friends or anything, but I will try not to argue with her in public anymore."

Diane laughed. "That's delightful. I mean, don't stop having public arguments on my account. It's fun to have some gossip to speculate about. I'm an old retired lady, I need some fun sometimes."

Caleb wasn't thrilled she was having fun at his expense, but if he remembered correctly, she was a widow who lived alone, and her only real job seemed to be running this building. So, fine. He could be the butt of the joke for a little bit.

Although, as Diane and Olivia talked about the kittens and when they would be adopted, Caleb sat at the desk and thought about whether any of what was happening with Lauren was sustainable. How long until someone caught them or discovered what they were really up to? How long until Lauren got sick of him? How long until she met a guy she actually got along with?

He didn't want whatever was between them to end, but he recognized it had a short shelf life.

"Maybe I should take those kittens off your hands."

Olivia plastered a smile on her face and said, "Five kittens is a lot of work. And we've already got some interest from the adoption event."

Diane nodded. "Oh, well. It just seems a shame to break up siblings. But consider this me expressing interest in at least one of the kittens. I'm all set up for cats upstairs. Thompson would like a younger sibling."

"Of course," said Olivia. "I'll make sure we set at least one aside for you."

"Lovely. A couple more weeks, you said?"

"Yeah, we like to make sure they are big enough to eat on their own before we let anyone adopt them. We're still bottle-feeding them some, but they should be weaned pretty soon. They're eating some regular cat food, too. They're a pretty scrappy bunch."

"I think Thompson would enjoy that."

Caleb was saved from having to engage further when his afternoon dachshund patient showed up. He was pretty grateful for that dog, even though he'd have to now draw enough blood to do a full panel of tests. Drawing blood from a dog was among his least favorite things to do as a vet, and he still preferred it to continuing to let Diane subtly mock him.

"I'll, uh, just go check on those kittens while I'm back there," he said as a way to bow out of the conversation.

"Be nice to Lauren next time you see her. She works hard."

Right. "I'll try."

CHAPTER 15

LAUREN REALIZED, AS SHE LAY with her limbs tangled with Caleb's in her own bed, that though she was in one of those relationships—or not—in which she never went to her lover's place, it was more because of expedience and convenience than anything nefarious on his part.

When she'd first moved to the city, she'd had a roommate who dated a guy who never allowed her at his place. Turned out it was because he had a live-in girlfriend, and Lauren's roommate was his side piece. Thus Lauren had long been skeptical of guys who didn't want to take their potential sex partners home. She didn't even know what block Caleb lived on, but given that they both worked in the same building as Lauren's apartment, that was likely due to laziness more than malevolence.

He was apparently equally contemplative, because he said, "Have you told your friends about me?"

"I may have said something the first time we slept together, but as far as they know, I hate you again now."

Caleb murmured something Lauren couldn't hear, then said, "Do you hate me?"

"Not right now."

"Is it because of all the orgasms?"

She sighed dramatically. "They certainly help. Anytime you want to win me over, just go down on me like that again."

"So if I said, 'Dogs are better than cats' and 'One should have red wine with red meat' and then went down on you, you'd be on board with my platform?"

"I'll consider the wine thing, but you're wrong, cats are clearly the superior animal."

He put his hand on her hip. "Shall I try to persuade you?"

"I won't stop you from *trying*."

He laughed. Then he rested his head on her chest. "I'm not quite recovered from the last bout, but I'll put it on my to-do list."

Lauren ran her hand through Caleb's hair. It was hard to deny this was…nice. More than nice. Being with Caleb made her feel powerful in a way, like she was the sexiest thing he'd ever seen, maybe the sexiest woman in Brooklyn. And now, tangled up with him in bed, she felt content. One could get used to such things.

And under normal circumstances, maybe she'd tell her friends about this, but her friends had few boundaries, and she wasn't ready to let them in on this yet. Plus, she'd never be able to explain it. How she was sleeping with a man whom, in public, she despised. But the truth was she didn't despise him so much anymore. Whether that was the endorphins from all the good sex talking or how she genuinely felt, she couldn't say right then.

And then Molly hopped up on the bed. She gave Caleb a wide

berth as she walked around the edge of the mattress and then curled up in a ball near Lauren's shoulder.

"So you *do* have a cat. She's not imaginary."

"Nope. She doesn't really like people, especially men, but I guess she's either decided you are okay or her need to sleep near me has overwhelmed her desire to avoid you. Hard to say."

Caleb chuckled, then reached across Lauren to hold his hand near Molly. Molly gave him a cursory sniff, then lifted her head to rub against his hand a little, then went back to her ball of sleep. Caleb retracted to his side of the bed.

"I see what you did there," said Lauren.

"What did I do?"

"You tried to get her to like you. Tested the waters a little."

"Sure."

"You *do* like cats."

"It's not that I dislike cats, it's that I prefer dogs."

Lauren rolled onto her side, careful not to disturb Molly, and faced Caleb. "I wonder what Molly would do if you brought Hank here."

Caleb recoiled. "I don't see that ending well. Molly doesn't look very big, but I've seen tiny cats do a lot of damage."

"Or they will be fast friends. Molly's never met a dog, so I don't know what she would do." Molly didn't get along well with other cats, but she might like different animals. "Do you remember, when we were kids, there was a movie with a kitten and a pug who were friends who went on adventures together?"

Caleb narrowed his eyes. "I have no recollection of that."

"I can't remember what it was called, but it was really cute.

And the whole point of the movie was to show that even a cat and a dog can be friends. Like you and I having a civil conversation right now."

"When I was a kid, we had a golden retriever named Floyd, who was about the sweetest dog I've ever known. We also had a couple of cats who moved into an old barn on my parents' property. Both cats clearly had it out for poor Floyd. I wanted to bring the cats into the house, but in my one attempt, they tried to claw Floyd's eyes out. So dogs and cats can be friends, sure, and I've seen that in my practice. But not always."

"Your childhood trauma explains a lot."

Caleb laughed. "I did build a nice home for the cats in the barn. My family wasn't really using it for anything except storage, so I cleaned it up and put some pet beds in there and I brought food to them every day. So, see? I'm not evil."

Lauren shot him a sultry grin and reached over to twirl a lock of his hair. "No, not evil. I think you're a big softy on the inside. You love all animals, even cats. You'd have to, in order to be a good vet, and the rumor around the café is your patients like you. But don't worry. Your secret is safe with me."

"I appreciate that. Although..." Caleb shifted his weight and propped himself up on his elbows. "I'm coming to realize the divorce left me more jaded than I thought. I didn't used to be as much of a dick as I've been lately."

"Are you...apologizing?" Lauren put some mocking in her voice.

"Shut up. No, not really. Just... If you'd met me a year ago, you might have actually liked me. You're right, I do love animals. I like taking care of them. I like the puzzle of diagnosing problems. A vet's knowledge of medicine has to be even broader than a human doctor's because anatomy varies so much between animals. I also have to have knowledge of what each species or breed's common issues are. Like, rabbits have sensitive stomachs, bulldogs tend to have respiratory issues, beagles get epilepsy, cats get UTIs. That kind of thing. And I love all that stuff, love studying the whys and hows of it." Caleb sighed. "I have to remind myself of that sometimes."

"Why is that?"

"I think I've just been going through the motions since the divorce. I have always put distance between myself and my patients to an extent because getting attached just leads to heartbreak. But it's like there's a wall between me and the rest of the world. It's one of my own making, no doubt, but... I guess I didn't realize how much I was cutting myself off."

Lauren didn't want to cheapen the moment by making a joke, because she appreciated that Caleb was sharing this much of himself. She could hear the frustration in his voice. She slid a hand across his chest and gave him a little hug. When he sighed, she kissed him softly.

"What was that for?" he asked.

"Be careful. You start talking about yourself in that way and I may start to like you."

He lay back down on the back. "You're a weirdo. I tell you I've become a jerk, and you're like, 'Mmm, give me more.'"

"No, what I heard you say is you've been a jerk, but you don't want to be. You're being smart and introspective. You went through something really difficult and you're still dealing with the aftermath, but it sounds to me like you're coming out the other side. I appreciate your honesty. It's almost admirable."

He cracked a smile. "Almost?"

"If I compliment you too much, it will just go to your head."

He rolled his eyes. "Here I am, sharing with you, pouring my heart out, and you mock me?"

Lauren ran her hand across his strong chest. She kissed his chin. "I'm not mocking you. I'm...providing comic relief after a serious moment."

"Right, of course," he said, but he smiled.

Lauren couldn't help but wonder what he must have been like before the divorce. Had he been happier? Less grouchy? Had he been idealistic, hopeful, nice?

Would she have liked him then?

Probably. A man as sexy as Caleb with a pleasant disposition to match? That sounded like Lauren's dream man. Of course, he'd been married back then.

And, well, despite his grouchiness, Lauren kinda liked the man he was now. She smiled at him, probably looking silly, but Caleb reached up a hand and ran it through her hair, meeting her gaze and continuing to smile.

If her friends could see the way she and Caleb were grinning at each other now, they wouldn't believe it. And that was fine; she didn't need to tell them yet.

Hank nearly pulled Caleb's arm out of the socket as he pulled him down the street. Caleb had decided to go for a long walk to clear his head. In the short time he'd lived in this neighborhood, he hadn't explored it much, and having Hank lead him around was a decent excuse.

Hank was a huge dog. He was dumb and friendly but still kind of a beast. Labs were sometimes susceptible to obesity, but that wasn't really the case here. Hank wasn't fat, just large for a dog, close to a hundred pounds. So he could put some good force on the leash. Caleb worried he'd have little choice in where they went today.

But when they got up to Montague Street in the heart of Brooklyn Heights, Hank seemed more interested in sniffing everything. Montague was bustling at this time of day, people popping in and out of the various businesses and restaurants. It was charming, in a way, the nineteenth-century brownstones juxtaposed with the brightly lit signs of the modern stores that lined the street. The short, narrow streets of Brooklyn Heights almost reminded Caleb of a much smaller town, like a little village tucked into the wider city.

Caleb's attitude toward New York City since he'd moved here had been "Why not?" It hadn't been his first choice; he'd mostly just tagged along with Kara. He was still getting his bearings, not used to the tempo or size of the city. Boston had been just as expensive but felt more compact. Here, it could take an hour or more to get to some parts of the city, the subway ran all night, and he could get nearly anything his heart desired delivered almost instantly. He'd picked Brooklyn Heights on the recommendation of a vet school buddy, and it was a very nice neighborhood, but he didn't know much about it besides that it was expensive and looked to be full of Old Money.

He let Hank lead him toward the end of Montague Street, which Caleb knew must have terminated near the river. He'd been in the neighborhood for such a short amount of time, though, that the sign pointing toward the promenade surprised him. He had a vague understanding of the neighborhood's geography from looking at maps, but he hadn't ever walked to this section of it.

This end of Montague was gorgeous. Old brownstones were largely left unchanged by a century of progress. Caleb could easily picture what this neighborhood must have looked like at the end of the nineteenth century, with women bustling about on their errands wearing voluminous skirts instead of jeans, with men in hats and suits instead of T-shirts. This pocket of Brooklyn was out of time, perhaps. And just ahead, Caleb could see a slice of the East River.

"Want to check it out, Hank?"

Hank barked and happily let his tongue loll out of his mouth.

Caleb laughed and said, "All right. Come on, buddy."

There was a short walkway, and then, suddenly, the scenery stole Caleb's breath.

The promenade was a long esplanade that overlooked the East River and lower Manhattan. Caleb brought Hank up to the railing and found himself gazing at the skyscrapers of the financial district, One World Trade Center surrounded by dozens of tall buildings Caleb didn't know the names of. The Brooklyn Bridge spanned the river just ahead, and it was a remarkable sight, that old bridge connecting Brooklyn and Manhattan just as it had for nearly 140 years. To the left, a fair distance away, was the Statue of Liberty, holding her torch up in welcome.

This was the city in all its glory. Caleb had never seen it from an angle like this before. He'd flown into New York a couple of times since moving here, and he always spent the descent gazing out the window and trying to identify the landmarks. There was a lot about this city he still didn't know yet or hadn't explored. He'd done a lot of the obvious tourist stuff with Kara when they'd first moved here, but since she'd left, he'd mostly kept to himself, just traveling between his home and his work.

Caleb walked with Hank up the promenade a little. Attached to the railing was a framed photograph of this same view, but before 2001, the Twin Towers still standing. The picture was jarring, upsetting in its way. Caleb didn't have roots here, had never even been to New York until a few years ago, but he'd met enough New Yorkers through his job to know people did have deep histories and memories. Brooklyn in particular was an odd mix of people who had lived here for years, whose families had been here for generations, and people who had moved here five minutes ago because it was trendy or it was what they could afford. Lauren had told him that she'd originally moved to Brooklyn because she couldn't afford Manhattan, but parts of Brooklyn were even more expensive than Manhattan now.

Caleb brought Hank over to a bench and they sat so Caleb could people watch for a few minutes. There were joggers, probably passing by for the view. There were people out casually walking. A few office workers eating lunch. A woman he recognized as a barista from the coffee shop near his apartment leaned on the railing and looked at Manhattan.

Caleb couldn't complain much about gentrification since it got him a nice apartment in an affluent neighborhood, but he'd been reading a lot about how Brooklyn was changing. Whitman Street ran through a part of Brooklyn that was quite gentrified, cute little mom-and-pop shops lining the long boulevard that ran from the East River all the way to Queens. The street changed after it intersected with Flatbush Avenue; the eastern part of it was old warehouses and self-storage places and train yards and housing projects. Of course, in order for this whole swath of Brooklyn to be cute and charming, a lot of people had either been priced out or pushed out of their homes.

He sighed. The promenade overlooked the highway, which added some noise to this otherwise peaceful place, and what Caleb thought must have been Brooklyn Bridge Park nearby. He didn't much mind the noise; he was willing to overlook that for this view.

So maybe this neighborhood did have some magic to it.

Caleb had thought he'd take a job at a clinic and work there until he figured out what to do next, and part of his plan had been to probably start his own practice, likely in a less expensive city. But working for someone else had its perks. Being able to focus on his patients without fretting about finances was the major advantage. Being part of an established practice and not having to worry about finding new patients was another. He still felt a bit like an outsider in this community, but the longer he worked at the clinic, the more they tried to include him. There was a routine, a rhythm, and he enjoyed having that in his life.

And then there was Lauren. It... It wasn't a real thing and probably never would be, but having her in his life challenged him in a way, and being with her at night reminded him that he was still capable of feeling. What would he do when they inevitably ended whatever was happening between them? How would he feel when she began dating someone else?

Best not to think of that right now.

Caleb leaned back on the bench and let the sun bathe him. He felt more like his old self than he had in a while, content instead of tense and angry. Was that this place? Was it because Kara was gone, because he was here, because the pieces of his life were falling into place? He didn't know and he didn't want to question it too much.

He looked down at Hank, who was lying on the paving stones, his tongue out, his eyes taking it all in. He looked happy, too. "What do you think, Hank? Should we stay awhile?"

Hank barked, probably at a bird that had landed on the railing, but Caleb took that as a yes.

CHAPTER 16

SPRING FELT LIKE IT LASTED about a day and a half. When Caleb had lived in Boston, the joke was if you didn't like the weather in Massachusetts, wait five minutes. And that applied here, because after several disgustingly warm days, New York was finally blessed with gorgeous weather.

Caleb left work in the early evening, looking forward to walking home in this weather, maybe grabbing takeout from the Tex-Mex place near his apartment, and just watching TV with Hank.

As he walked outside, so did Lauren.

"You guys closed for the day?" Caleb asked.

"No. Paige is closing today. Diane actually told me I work too much, so she's forbidden me from staying until close on days when I come in to open."

Caleb smiled. "Forbidden you, eh? Don't you close at six? Which is in about ten minutes?"

"Yes, but we're staying open tonight to host a writers' group after hours. Paige can handle it. If this goes well, we may start a book club or something next. Diane's letting me hire a couple of extra people, so if we start staying open later, it's not an undue burden on the current staff."

"Sounds like you're expanding."

"Yeah. It's weird. I'll admit, when I took this job, I loved it, but I thought it was kind of a novelty. I used to manage a coffee shop, and a cat café opened up nearby, tucked into this storefront around the corner, but it lasted maybe four months."

"And you took the job anyway?"

"Diane is persuasive."

Caleb wanted to ask more about that, but he felt like an idiot just standing on the sidewalk. "Uh, you have plans tonight?"

She smiled. "Not really, no."

"I'm headed home myself."

"Oh." She seemed disappointed by that.

"I was going to walk. Would you like to walk with me? Maybe get some dinner close to my place? Meet Hank?"

"Really?"

"Yeah."

She smiled, which made warmth spread in his chest, a feeling he didn't want to analyze too closely. "Sure, that sounds nice."

It wasn't until they turned the corner to walk north toward Caleb's apartment that it registered: He'd asked her to do something and she'd said yes and they'd exchanged nary an angry word. Caleb didn't want to think too hard about what that meant. Had something in their relationship changed? Should it have? Did he want it to?

Best not to think about it. Asking her to come home with him had been an entirely spontaneous decision. He had no motive beyond wanting to spend time with her. And why did he want to spend time with her?

Nope. Not going there.

They walked and made small talk about how nice the weather was for the next block. Then he said, "So how did you end up going from a coffee shop to managing a cat café?"

She laughed. "I don't know. Life is strange sometimes. My college degree is in art history."

Well, that figured. Caleb didn't want to be judgmental, but Lauren did strike him as the sort of person who would spend a lot of money on a degree in something useless.

"I see your face," she said. "You're not wrong. My original plan had been to go to grad school and get a job as a museum curator, but one internship at the Met taught me those jobs are pretty hard to come by. But I had a job as a sales associate at Bloomingdale's, mostly fetching shoes from the back for customers. After I graduated, I got a promotion, and then I saw the opening at the coffee shop and got a job as a manager. Diane used to get tea there regularly, so we'd get to talking. I mean, you've met her. She treats everyone like they're her old friends. When she offered me the job, I thought she was kidding."

"So, wait, she just randomly offered you the job?"

"Pretty much, yeah. That's kind of how Diane is. She operates by instinct, not logic, but her instincts rarely fail her. So I came to check out the space, and she showed me the business plan for it. I already knew how to run a café, but adding the cat component was an interesting challenge. I had cats as a kid, but nothing like this. But I was over working at the coffee shop and having to put out fires with wealthy patrons who yelled at me for everything, from not carrying coconut milk to the depth of the roast on the coffee beans to the speed with which my employees made lattes. So when Diane offered me the job, it seemed like a fun opportunity, and at the time, I figured if it was a flop, it might be the kick I needed to try to find a job that was more fulfilling. Luckily it worked out."

Caleb shook his head. He couldn't imagine taking such a leap of faith. "So you just…took a job managing a business you didn't think would last, working for a woman you didn't know very well?"

"Well, it sounds silly when you say it like *that*. It was a good opportunity. Was I supposed to sell bossy rich people overpriced hot beverages for the rest of my life?"

"No." That seemed like a waste of Lauren's talents in fact. "I'm just…" But he was trying not to start a fight with her. His instinct was to argue, to point out how foolish such a choice had been, to demonstrate she was flighty and impulsive. But that was this jerk version of himself, the one who kept everyone at a distance. The one who was lonely now. "It's not something *I* would do."

She nudged him with her shoulder. "Nice save."

"I'm trying to turn over a new leaf. Not be such a jerk."

"It's fine, you know. Don't try to fight your own nature."

He laughed. "No, it's just… I've always had a plan. In high school, I knew I wanted to be a veterinarian. I studied biology and animal science in college, I went to vet school, I opened a practice. I did all the things I was supposed to do. I'm not… I don't like spontaneity. This evening notwithstanding."

They walked silently for a few minutes. Then Lauren said, "Ah, I see."

Something in her tone rubbed him the wrong way. "What do you see?"

"That was why your divorce threw you for such a loop. You didn't see it coming and it wasn't part of the plan. You met your ex-wife in vet school, right? You got married after you graduated? That was all part of your plan. Your wife left you, and it threw a wrench in your plan."

That was...quite astute, actually. But it also showed why he and Lauren would never work as a couple. He needed more stability in his life. She would uproot him on a regular basis.

"Well, now that you've assessed me psychologically, how was your day?" he asked.

"Fine. Busy. We had enough customers today to more than justify my desire to hire more people."

"That's good."

"You? How was work, honey?"

Her tone was a little facetious, the *honey* a joke, so he ignored it. "It was fine. A little stressful. This morning, I treated a lizard with a cold. Then I had some dog owners in this afternoon who were *a lot*."

Lauren smiled. "You know, I don't really like the term *owner* for people who have pets. It implies the animals are objects instead of friends and companions."

Oh, boy. Caleb didn't *want* to argue, but that was pretty silly. "Are you one of these pet parent types who goes on about your fur babies? Because the couple who brought their dog in today kept saying that. I mean, no offense, I guess, but that always sounds weird to my ears."

Lauren frowned, which indicated she'd probably called a cat a fur baby a time or two in her life. "I mean, I'm not so naive as to think taking care of a dog or a cat is the same as taking care of a human baby. Actually, I think cats are more like teenagers. You have to put out food and clean up after them, you try to keep them out of trouble, but otherwise, they basically get along on their own."

"Sure."

"But anyway, maybe *parent* is not the right word, either. I don't know. *Pet caretaker?*"

"Makes the pet sound like an old house."

Lauren sighed. "But *owner* doesn't work. First of all, I'd argue cats really own us. They often just show up and move themselves in. *Pet friend?*"

Caleb laughed. "I don't know." He thought this whole argument was silly, but he was enjoying talking to Lauren.

They were nearing Borough Hall, which meant they'd have to make some choices about which direction to walk in if they were going to get dinner. "How do you feel about Vietnamese food?"

"I like it. Are you changing the subject to avoid picking a fight with me about how ridiculous I'm being?"

"A little. But basically, soon we'll have to decide if we want Asian or Mexican food to the left or burgers or sandwiches to the right."

"Vietnamese is fine. Have we...turned a new leaf?"

"You sound condescending, but I really am trying to not be a jerk. I'll pick a fight with you if you really want, cat lady."

"Well, let's wait until we get to your place. No need to make a scene."

Caleb's place turned out to be a garden apartment with its own entrance in a brownstone a few blocks from Borough Hall. Lauren had long thought "garden apartment" was just a euphemism for "ground floor," but in this case, French doors at the back of the apartment really did lead out to a garden that the house's owner maintained.

The apartment was nice, although sparsely furnished. There was a butter-yellow sofa in the narrow living room that faced a nice TV and several bookcases stuffed with veterinary textbooks, doorstopper history books, and some battered fantasy novels. A galley kitchen in the middle was small but had clearly been renovated recently, and it led to the bedroom in the back.

And, of course, there was the huge dog who hopped happily in greeting when Lauren and Caleb had walked through the door.

In other words, it was downright swanky for a bachelor apartment, and it demonstrated how fussy and clean Caleb was, and also how few things he owned, although Lauren guessed he'd lost some things in the divorce.

The poor dog was nearly apoplectic with excitement to be meeting a new person. Lauren knelt on the floor and scratched his ears. "Hi, buddy. I'm very happy to meet you, too." He licked her face in response, which tickled enough to make her laugh.

Caleb dropped the takeout bag on a little table just outside the kitchen and said, "Dig in. I'm going to take Hank out back and then feed him."

While Caleb took care of Hank, Lauren unpacked the bag of food from the Vietnamese restaurant. It seemed like they'd ordered half the menu, probably because Lauren had been indecisive. There were bun noodles and spring rolls and meat on skewers and a plastic tub of pho. She thought about raiding Caleb's cabinets for plates and silverware, but he came back inside with Hank before she got there.

"Plates?" she said.

"Yeah, hang on. Be right with you."

Lauren leaned in the archway that led to the kitchen and watched as Caleb went through what was probably his evening routine. He told Hank to sit, then crossed the kitchen and scooped some dog food from a huge plastic container into Hank's bowl. Then he stood up and said, "Go get it." Hank bounded across the kitchen and started gobbling up his food.

"He came trained," Caleb said. "He was well cared for before he was left at the vet clinic. I can't figure out why someone would just abandon a dog like that, but their loss is my gain, I guess. He's a good dog." He pulled a couple of plates from a cabinet and forks from a drawer and joined Lauren at the table.

They had a pleasant meal, carrying on conversation as easily as they had on their walk here while Hank nosed around at their feet waiting for food to drop. Caleb explained that he and his ex-wife had honeymooned in Asia, touring Japan, South Korea, China, Vietnam, and Thailand. They'd essentially eaten their way across all five countries. Even after all that had happened, he seemed nostalgic about the trip. He still loved Asian food.

"You know, it's funny," Lauren said. "I worked with a woman at Bloomingdale's who once dated an Indian man, and after that relationship imploded, you couldn't even say '*tikka masala*' around her without her losing her mind. She's missing out. I'd never let a man force me to give up Indian food. I love curry too much."

"I tried that Indian place near the vet clinic. Their lunch special is more food than any human should eat in one sitting, but it's so good I want to."

Lauren laughed. "Yeah, that place is good. The Thai place on Bond Street is just okay. A little bland, but I like their pineapple fried rice. There was this great Thai place near my old apartment in Manhattan. The decor is kooky, but they make the best pad thai in Manhattan."

"Where did you live before?"

"Upper East Side, but before you judge, I was on Second Avenue during peak subway construction when it was so loud all the old ladies who lunch moved out and rents went down, so I could afford it. It was a strange apartment. The toilet was in one little room on one end, and the rest of the bathroom was on the other. It made mornings with my roommate require some choreography."

"Olivia told me when she first moved to the city after college, she lived in an Upper West Side studio that didn't have a bathroom. She had to share with everyone else on the floor. I thought that kind of stuff was a myth."

"Hey listen, moneybags, we all have to make sacrifices to afford to live here. If Diane didn't give me such a steep discount, I couldn't afford to live anywhere within three subway stops of the Cat Café."

"Did the apartment come with the job offer?"

"No, actually. I was commuting from the Upper East Side, which was awful. I had to walk all the way to Lexington Ave to get the subway, then ride the train for an hour very early in the morning to make it to the café by opening, then walk another six blocks when I got here. So when my lease was up, I mentioned to Diane that I was thinking of moving closer, just in a, 'Hey, if you know of anyone looking for a roommate in Brooklyn, let me know' kind of way. I'd been working at the Cat Café for maybe six or seven months at that point. And Diane goes, 'I just lost the tenants in a one-bedroom upstairs,' and she offered it to me for a rent she knew I could afford, since she pays my salary. It's basically half what anyone else in the neighborhood would pay for a one-bedroom."

"Wow."

"On the flip side, I'm kind of at her beck and call. I help her out with errands and stuff when she needs a hand. That's the trade off, I guess. I don't mind at all, though. She's really very nice."

Caleb frowned. "She's nosy."

Lauren smirked. "So you've met her."

"I have, yeah. Always asks me a lot of questions about my personal life."

"Yeah. She does that. Worse than my mom."

They chatted about their families. Lauren's parents lived near Columbus, Ohio, and she had a brother who was currently finishing his law degree at Georgetown. Caleb was an only child, and his parents lived in Maine. He did have a hint of a New England accent—there was something very Boston about the way he pronounced certain vowel sounds—but it had faded to the point that it wasn't always detectable.

Talking and sharing personal trivia with Caleb was…nice. And it felt like a date. But she and Caleb weren't even in a real relationship, were they?

"So you like food," Caleb said.

"I *love* food. Who doesn't?"

"I dated this girl in undergrad who wouldn't eat in front of other people."

"Like, at all?"

"Yeah. We only dated long enough for me to figure that out. We'd go out to a restaurant, and she'd order a meal, eat none of it, and ask for a doggy bag."

"I will admit to ordering a salad on dates sometimes so the handsome stranger I'm dining with won't judge my choices, but I can't imagine just not eating."

"You haven't ordered a salad any of the times we've had dinner together."

"We're not dating, are we?"

"Fair."

Lauren didn't want to dwell on that point, so she said, "My friend Lindsay is a food writer, so she's gotten me into some pretty swanky restaurants."

Caleb smiled. "I've gleaned from talking to the other vets at the clinic that an important component of being a New Yorker is talking about the best meals you've eaten."

"Lindsay got me into Gramercy Tavern to try their tasting menu because she went to culinary school with one of the sous-chefs. So good. I didn't know food could taste like that." She mimed drooling. "What was your best meal in New York?"

Caleb laughed. "My ex and I ate at Morimoto for our last anniversary. The sushi was actually a little plain, but the rest of the seafood was some of the best I've ever had. Clean and fresh. And remember that I'm from Maine. I grew up eating seafood right off the boat."

"Yeah?"

"One of my cousins is a lobsterman and has a little mussel farm off the coast."

"You can farm mussels?"

"Yeah. You drop these ropes into the water that are covered with what is basically mussel seed, or baby mussels. Then they grow right there on the ropes."

"And they're safe to eat?"

"Yeah, totally. They grow bigger and taste better than mussels found in the wild."

"I had no idea. You know about all kinds of animals, don't you?"

"It's true, I do."

"What's the weirdest pet anyone brought you?"

Caleb chuckled. He appeared to think about it for a moment. "One of my patients in Boston was a fennec fox. Those are the ones with the huge ears."

"You can have those as pets?"

"Not legally, and I wouldn't recommend it. This guy was tame, but they're little predators."

"I mean, so are cats."

"True, but fennec foxes belong in a desert climate, not a house. House cats have adapted to indoor living over many generations. The fox was a cute little guy, though. About the size of a Chihuahua. On the other hand, he had this squeal that would blow out your eardrums."

Caleb cleaned up after they ate and then invited Lauren to his bedroom. As he closed the curtains, she said, "*This* wasn't a date, was it?"

"No," he said. "This was two…people…eating dinner."

"Is that what we are to each other? People?"

"People who sleep together."

Well, all right. Not a lie. "You know, we haven't really argued today."

"I can change that if you want me to, cat lady."

Lauren sighed and sat at the foot of the bed. Hank wandered over, sniffed her leg, then retreated to a dog bed in the corner, flopping down with a *whump*.

"I don't *want* to fight. But what are we doing here if it's not that?"

Caleb turned toward her and frowned. "Do you want me to draw a diagram?"

"So this is just sex, and the fact that somehow, in the last few weeks, we actually started getting along doesn't matter?"

"We were clear from the word *jump* that we weren't going to have a romantic relationship. Neither of us wanted that. Right?"

"You're right." But Lauren didn't know what to make of the changing nature of their relationship. Given that they'd just walked and talked and eaten food together for nearly two hours, it sure felt like they were dating. Maybe Lauren hadn't really been with anyone since Derek, but she knew what dates felt like. Was Caleb really in this much denial?

Was Lauren?

What did she really want here? Did she really think she had a future with Caleb? No, not really. But she was growing to like him. And that was a problem.

"Did I ruin it?" Caleb asked.

"Ruin what?"

"The mood. I don't know. Sex shouldn't feel perfunctory."

Lauren stood. "Maybe I should go."

"No, sorry, that was a stupid thing to say. Sorry, it just was starting to feel like the standard date narrative. We chatted, we had dinner, and now we're going to have sex. But even though I like plans, scheduling sex is the one thing that takes the fun out of it. So I'm awkwardly trying to put the moves on you and failing completely."

"Do we have no passion if we're not fighting?" Lauren was legitimately concerned about that. He was still smoking hot, his hair and clothes a bit disheveled at the end of a long workday, his body still cut, his broad shoulders and slim hips still appealing, his handsome face still drawing her attention. But suddenly, things seemed awkward between them. Maybe they just didn't know how to initiate sex when they were both getting along. But that was insane. Normal couples got along well and then had good sex and didn't need petty arguments to get the ball rolling. What the hell was wrong with them?

"No. Of course we don't need to fight. Ignore anything I say. I'm being an asshole."

Lauren decided to turn the tables on him. They would either make this work or they wouldn't. "Do you want me?"

Caleb's expression softened. "Yes. All the time." He stepped closer.

The truth was, she wanted him too, at a bone-deep level. He was sexy, of course, but the more she got to know him, the more she was drawn to him. It wasn't just that he was hot, though he was; under all his grumpiness, he was compassionate and thoughtful. The kind of guy she could fall in love with, if they could go for more than a half hour without disagreeing, and if he hadn't sworn off relationships.

Her own baggage was starting to feel like it didn't matter much. Derek, *schmerek*. He was married in New Hampshire. He didn't matter anymore.

"I want you," Caleb said, sitting beside her on the bed and putting a hand on her cheek. "The first time I saw you, I wanted you. Every time you come into the clinic, I feel an inappropriate jolt. Whenever you pick a fight with me about something silly, I want you. Just talking over dinner, and I want you."

"I want you, too," Lauren said. "That's all that we need to get started, no?"

"I suppose so."

Caleb bent his head and kissed Lauren. He moved his hand along her jaw and his fingers played with the hair at the base of her skull. She nearly lost the ability to breathe, it was so tender and sweet. She put her hands on his shoulders and pulled him closer, opening her mouth to let him in more.

He was sexy, but he was familiar, too. Not in a bad way, more like she'd unlocked a secret. She knew some of the nuances of his body, knew what things made him hiss or moan, knew where he liked to be touched. They'd slept together enough now that she was beginning to understand what he really liked in bed, what revved him up, what made him come.

So she knew if she pressed against him, he'd grasp her and hold her closer. She knew he liked her breasts, liked to rest his hand on the curve of her hip, liked the way she tasted.

Knowing these things about him made her feel powerful, made her feel sexy.

She pulled away from him slightly and took off her shirt. She met his gaze and raised an eyebrow. He practically swooned, looking delighted as he ran a hand down her chest and cupped one of her breasts.

The fact that they were doing this in secret heightened how powerful she felt. The only people who mattered here were the two of them. There was no pressure, no obligation to anyone else. Just two people who were into each other doing what they wanted. Maybe she didn't need any more explanation than that.

She gave Caleb a gentle push back toward the bed. He took the hint and scooted back and lay down. She climbed on top and straddled his hips. He immediately put his hands on her, covering her breasts, her waist, her belly. He slid his fingers under the underwire of her bra, so she reached back and unhooked it, then pulled it off. He groaned in response.

"Do you feel less awkward now?" she asked.

"Not awkward at all." He bucked his hips against her, and she could feel he was hard. "I want you to ride me just like this."

"That can be arranged."

She pushed his shirt up his chest, and he leaned up to pull it off. She had to stand back up to take off her jeans, unfortunately, but Caleb made the most of losing contact and took off his own pants and underwear. When Lauren straddled him again, they were both naked.

"Feels like we need more foreplay," Caleb said, sitting up slightly and taking one of her nipples into his mouth.

"Nope. I've been thinking about this since dinner. I want you inside me now."

"Yeah?"

"Yeah. I'll ride you like a motorcycle."

He laughed softly and shifted their position slightly on the bed. "Have you ever ridden a motorcycle?"

"Well, no. It was an expression."

"Lauren?"

"What?"

"Kiss me."

Lauren leaned down to kiss him, and as she slid her tongue into his mouth, she felt his erection poking at the entrance to her body. She shifted her hips slightly, and one of his hands went between them, and then he entered her slightly.

She stood up, taking him inside her in one fluid motion.

"Oh, god," he said.

That's what she wanted. She wanted him messy and panting and out of his mind with lust. She moved against him, bracing her hands on his chest and lifting her hips on and off him. He bucked his hips a few times, as though frustrated he couldn't set the pace, but this was hers. She was in charge here.

He thrust his hands into her hair, brought their lips together to kiss her, cupped her breasts in his hands. When she sat back up, he put one hand on her hip to try to control the pace and the other danced over one of her nipples.

This. This right here. This was what she wanted. He filled her up, touched all the best places, made her feel like the only thing in the whole world that mattered was the connection made by their bodies. She could likely come just from the way he touched her chest, but the fact that he was also bucking against her as she rode him was creating exactly the kind of friction that would get her there even faster.

And suddenly, all that mattered was getting to that orgasm, was tumbling over the cliff with him. She rode him hard, fast, loving the way his body rubbed against hers. And just when she was about to fly apart, he said, "Holy shit, I'm gonna come."

She got there first, the orgasm bursting within her. She threw her head back and settled her knees into the mattress as she rode it out. A moment later, he grasped her hips and seemed to stop breathing as he shook a little. She felt him come inside her, just as her fingers and toes uncurled.

Later, when they were lying beside each other, sated but still out of breath, she said, "We do that pretty well."

"We do. I never expected this."

"Good sex?"

"Good sex with a woman who I find incredibly sexy and also sometimes challenging."

"Is 'challenging' your nice way of saying ridiculous?"

"Maybe. Don't hate me."

She patted his chest. "Fortunately for you, I don't."

And she really didn't. But she was starting to feel things that were troubling considering they weren't in a real relationship.

So where did that leave them? The sand was running out of the hourglass. She rolled onto her side and draped her arm around him, determined to hold on to this for as long as it lasted.

CHAPTER 17

THE WHITMAN STREET SPRING FESTIVAL was an annual harbinger of the impending spring, falling in early April when winter's clutches finally loosened. Ten blocks of Whitman Street shut down to give the space to food trucks, tables for local businesses and independent vendors, and carnival rides.

Paige manned the Cat Café's table. She'd found a bedsheet covered in cats at a discount store and used it as a tablecloth. Then she set up plastic display containers and filled them with flyers and brochures advertising the café's regular events—Paige had just started after-hours movie nights once a month with cat-themed films—and cat adoption opportunities. She'd also let Mitch come by with flyers for his own organization, and he hung out around the table to answer questions about how people could volunteer to catch and tag feral cats in Brooklyn.

Sunday had been chosen as the feline ambassador—Sadie couldn't handle outside noise and would have panicked the whole time—and she was in a huge kennel set up on the table so that people walking by could be lured in by the very cute cat. Sunday seemed very mellow now, lying on her little cat bed and occasionally yawning and stretching like this was no big deal.

Lauren walked back and forth between the table and the café. Monique was in charge inside, with Victor slinging lattes at the counter, and they were getting a fair number of customers who had indeed been lured in by the table and wanted to check out the space. Lauren struggled a little to figure out where she'd be the most useful.

When Lauren went back outside, Caleb walked out of the vet clinic with a Tupperware bin the size of a shoebox that appeared to be full of paper. He looked infuriatingly handsome today, his skin a bit flushed, his hair neat aside from one thin tuft that had escaped and draped over his forehead. He had on his white doctor's coat over his standard uniform of a button-down shirt and khakis. That Lauren knew what he looked like under all that clothing made her flush a bit.

If Caleb felt any of that, he didn't show it. "Olivia said you said we could put some pamphlets for the clinic on your table."

"You could get your own table, you know," Paige said. "All businesses on Whitman Street are allowed to put one table out on the street here. The fee is waived just for the street fair."

Caleb said, "There's no one to man it. We all have patients today. It's Saturday."

Lauren supposed the "Saturday is our busiest day" was implied. Caleb's haughty tone irritated her like a bugbite, though, so she said, "Oh, well, I didn't realize you all were so important."

He leveled his gaze at her. "Oh, you know. No big deal. Just the lives of living creatures hanging in the balance. Where should I put these?"

Paige reached over and took the box. She took some pamphlets out of it and slid them into an empty slot in her plastic display, then put the box with the remaining pamphlets under the table.

Lauren looked Caleb over. It would have been nice if they could walk around the fair together like a couple instead of playing at being adversaries. Neither seemed that offended by the mocking. It would have been nice if they didn't feel the need to be so performative in their dislike of each other, though. Or else Caleb had reverted to his bratty self, back to the man Lauren hadn't seen in a week or two as they'd had good sex and pleasant conversation a few times. Maybe he was…overcompensating now. Or Lauren was wrong in thinking he'd turned some new leaf and this was just who he always was.

Lauren saw in her peripheral vision a blond standard poodle and a harried-looking woman going into the vet clinic. Caleb must have seen it, too, because he said, "That's my next appointment." He looked around. "This is quite an operation."

"It is," said Lauren. "If you have a spare few minutes and can bear spending time among the hoi polloi later, I'll give you a tour."

"All right. Well. Uh. Break a leg?"

"Later, Caleb," said Paige, waving in a way that looked a little patronizing. He mirrored her movement and went inside. "So he's still a dick."

"Yep," said Lauren. But he was hers, wasn't he? At least for now. Something had definitely changed between them recently, at least in private.

Evan came by the table then, a plastic bag from the bookstore hooked around his wrist. "Don't look," he said, "but Pablo has a table with a mix of weird used books and new releases, and there is absolutely no more shelf space anywhere in my apartment, but he had, like, eight things I want to read."

Lauren turned to look despite Evan's warnings. Pablo was indeed a few tables down, chatting with a woman who was pointing at books in the new release display.

"These excuses for talking to Pablo are costing you quite a bit of money. You pay full cover price for those books in your bag?"

"There's a ten percent off street fair special."

"Right."

Evan frowned and looked at his bag. "He must think I'm way smarter than I am. I've only read a tiny fraction of the books I've bought from him since he started working at Stories."

"Or you could ask him out."

Evan shook his head. "When I was a teenager, I worked at a clothes store in the mall. There was this girl I worked with sometimes who thought my name was Jason. I corrected her a few times, but it never sank in, and she kept calling me Jason. Eventually, it had gone on too long, and I didn't want to embarrass her by telling her she'd been getting my name wrong for months, so I just...responded when she called me Jason. I feel like this thing with Pablo is like that. I missed the window. I should have asked him out when he left Star Café, but now so much time has gone by that it's embarrassing if I ask him out *now*."

"That's insane," said Lauren. "Why not just walk up to him and say, 'Hey, I really like you, let's get a drink sometime. There's a great bar just up the block that has amazing martinis.' Done and done."

Evan guffawed. "As if." He looked around. "Hey, can I stash this bag with you. It's heavy. That truck with the guy who makes the arepa sandwiches is just on the other side of Henry Street, and I've had dreams about his steak sandwich since the last one of these street fairs."

"I'll put your books under the table if you get me that chicken and avocado thing he sells."

"You got it."

Caleb got a break midafternoon. Rachel informed him two of his appointments had rescheduled, probably because of the street fair—a ten-block stretch of Whitman Street was closed to car traffic, and several patients had complained about the ripple effect that had on the rest of the area—so he had about an hour to kill.

He'd brought Hank with him to work that day since he knew he'd probably end up working late. He grabbed Hank's leash from the coat hooks near the desk.

"You want to walk down to the grocery store that used to be a bank at the intersection with Court Street," Rachel said as Caleb snapped Hank's leash into place. "For some reason, the best food trucks park down there. The two best ones are the one with bison burgers and the one with empanadas. The empanadas are small, though, so order one of each kind to get the full experience."

Caleb laughed. "Thanks for the tip. Is this whole street fair just an excuse to overeat?"

"Pretty much, yeah. And if you end up with any leftovers, your friendly neighborhood vet tech would be appreciative."

"I'll keep that in mind."

When Caleb walked outside, Lauren was standing near the Cat Café table, looking at her phone. "You got a few minutes?" he asked her. "You promised to show me around. Hope you don't mind if Hank comes along."

"Oh. Yeah, sure." She reached down and pet Hank's head. He licked her hand as a reward. She looked up at Caleb. "Is it Take Your Dog to Work Day?"

"That's every day at the clinic. Olivia gave me permission to bring Hank to work, so I have been when I work overnights. I did today, too, because my dogwalker wasn't feeling well."

"All right. Well, come on."

As they walked through the center of the street, she said, "Have you ever been to a street fair in New York?"

"No, I can't say I have."

"They're all kind of the same. This one is a little fancier because they get a bunch of really good food trucks and those have become kind of the draw, but every New York street fair is pretty similar. There are always a couple of trucks or booths with deep fryers, so you can get funnel cakes or falafel. There's always a table with a guy selling packages of socks or bedsheets. I don't know why. And then there are a bunch of random vendors, usually jewelry, dresses made to fit only very skinny women, and at least one table that's just random New York tourist junk. At *this* street fair, most of the vendors are businesses on Whitman Street. So each of the restaurants has, like, one dish they'll give you or samples of their popular dishes in little cups. And then all the stores are showing what they sell. Like here."

Lauren walked over to the table in front of the yarn store and gestured toward it. There was a basket on one end of the table that held colorful balls of yarn. Hank gave it a sniff, but he wasn't tall enough to do any damage. They also had stacks of knitting books and displays of knitting and sewing notions. A woman behind the table was having an intense conversation with a potential customer using a lot of jargon Caleb didn't understand: roving, spinning, weight, and other terms he assumed did not mean to these women what they meant to him.

After Lauren made some small talk with the women at the table, they moved on. As they walked, Lauren said, "I've already had lunch, but if you see something you want to eat, let me know."

"Rachel said something about a grocery store that used to be a bank."

"Oh, yeah! At Court Street. That's the biggest intersection on Whitman Street until you get to Flatbush, so it's kind of prime real estate for the food trucks."

"But...a grocery store that used to be a bank."

"That's Brooklyn. Some developer bought a bank building that has been here since the nineteenth century, and the building was landmarked, so they couldn't tear it down or renovate it, but they could add aisles. It's this really beautiful building with huge vaulted ceilings and these columns and arches that separate the space. So you go to buy meat in the area I think used to be the vault, and then you can admire the ceiling best from the frozen food aisle. There are cashiers where the tellers once sat."

"This city, man. I bet most people don't even notice the old parts of the building. Developers in New York never want to preserve, they just want to maximize profits."

"The basis of this city's economy has been commerce and money for four hundred years. What do you expect? Plus, shopping at this grocery store is kind of a novelty because the architecture is so unusual. I go there sometimes because they're the only shop in the neighborhood that sells this obscure brand of yogurt I like, plus they have an amazing cheese counter."

Caleb laughed. Lauren was never shy when talking about food. Kara had always acted in public like she never ate anything. Caleb liked trying new foods, though, and liked having someone who actually enjoyed eating to have elaborate meals with.

He wound up following Rachel's suggestion and got one of each kind of mini-empanada from the offerings available at the truck: three meat, three vegetarian. Rachel would appreciate it if he shared.

As they walked back toward the Cat Café, Caleb admired Lauren, who seemed to be in fine form today, chatty without being too effusive. Her long hair was pulled back in a no-nonsense ponytail, which showed off her pretty face and the dusting of freckles across her nose. She wore a knee-length plaid dress and a baggy black cardigan that seemed to show she cared more about warmth and comfort than style. Still, she always looked put together, even if Caleb didn't like how the baggy cardigan obscured her amazing body.

He sighed. It was nice of her to walk around with him, and he was enjoying talking with her and checking out the fair. It was a beautiful day, sunny but still too cool for short sleeves.

Contentment washed over him as he followed Lauren down the street at a slow pace. He noticed that Hank gazed at her with adoration, and his patience was rewarded when Lauren snagged a dog treat from a table in front of a pet food store and offered it to him.

"I believe you just made a lifelong friend," Caleb said.

"Aw. You're a good dog, aren't you, Hank?"

Hank barked happily.

If they were a real couple, he could take her hand. He could lend her his jacket if she were still cold. He could buy her a necklace from one of the jewelry vendors or an ice cream cone from one of the food trucks. But they weren't a couple, and none of that was appropriate.

"Has business been good at the Cat Café table?" he asked.

"We've gotten a lot of traffic. The goal is more to attract future customers than to make money on the spot. A lot of people have come into the café to check out the cats, but they aren't really buying anything."

"You could charge a couple of bucks for people to sit in the cat room, you know."

"I could, yeah. But the point is to encourage people to come meet the cats and fall in love with them. Hopefully the people stopping by today will come back some other day and spend money on food and beverages. It's about long-term business, not short-term gain."

"Makes sense."

Lauren grinned. "And I don't even have an MBA. I've learned a lot on the job, though. I may make it look haphazard and accidental, but there is actual thought that goes into keeping that place open."

Caleb chuckled. He could appreciate that she was often self-deprecating.

When they returned to the table, Paige offered a chair so Caleb could sit and eat his empanadas, but only if he was willing to answer questions about cats from random passersby. Caleb was game, so he sat and dug in. Lauren took Hank's leash and held it tight after Hank started sniffing at Sunday's crate. Hank didn't seem to be anything but curious, but Sunday retreated to the back of the crate and stared at Hank.

"You want me to bring him back inside?" Caleb asked. "Rachel can watch him while I eat."

"Nah, it's fine. He probably likes being outside."

Indeed, Hank lost interest in Sunday when a woman with a beagle walked by. Lauren let the leash out a little so that Hank and the beagle could sniff and bark at each other.

Then two familiar faces approached the table.

Caleb didn't recognize them at first, or didn't believe what he was seeing. The row of men in dark suits and sunglasses with earpieces behind them gave something away, though. Then Lauren said, "Wow, Mayor Martinez, Senator Schmidt. Thank you so much for stopping by."

So that was something significant. The mayor of New York City and one of New York's United States senators were just standing right there at the table.

Hank went looking for attention and barked at the senator. "Who is this friendly guy?" Senator Schmidt asked.

"That's Hank," said Caleb.

"Can I pet him?"

"Absolutely. I believe he would love that."

Hank's tongue rolled out of his mouth as the senator scratched his ears.

"So tell us about your business," said the senator.

"We're a café that allows customers to have coffee and pastries and then sit with cats in our back room," said Lauren. "We've found hanging out with the cats is good for bringing down your stress levels."

"We also do cat adoptions," said Paige. "Our goal is to find forever homes for all the cats in the café."

"Except Sadie," said Lauren. "She's kind of our mascot."

"What a clever idea," said Senator Schmidt. "I've heard about animal cafés in Japan."

"I went to an owl café in Tokyo once," said Mayor Martinez.

"And business is good?" asked the senator.

"Yes, very!" Lauren fidgeted like she was nervous, but it was pretty neat to be talking to high-ranking politicians about one's business. "Oh, and this is Caleb Fitch. He's one of the veterinarians at the clinic next door. We work with the vet clinic a lot."

Caleb stood and shook hands with each man. He felt a little overwhelmed.

"Hank is Caleb's dog," Lauren said.

Mayor Martinez chuckled. "So there's a bit of a cats versus dogs rivalry, huh? Which is better, cats or dogs?"

Caleb said "dogs" at the same time Lauren said "cats."

"We're very excited to see such a wide range of successful,

flourishing businesses on Whitman Street," said the Mayor, still chuckling. "Anything else on this block we should be sure to see?"

"Julie's Closet across the street," said Paige. "It's a really nice thrift store. The owner is picky about what she'll take on consignment, but you can get some amazing deals there if you're shopping for clothes."

"Stories," said Evan. "They sell new and used books."

"Bloom's is the best florist in the neighborhood," said Lauren. "And Stitches, the yarn store over there? They're very popular."

"I'm glad so many independent businesses are thriving here," said Mayor Martinez.

Caleb had to swallow the snort. The development of downtown Brooklyn meant rising rents, to the point that a lot of mom-and-pop businesses were getting pushed out of the area. Whitman Street was like a unique bubble, where these little businesses could still thrive…for now. The chain pharmacy on the corner and the fancy boutique gym across the street were signs that corporate giants were encroaching, too. Some parts of the street were populated mostly by banks and cell phone stores—the sorts of businesses that could afford the astronomical rents. Not to mention that empty café across the street that would surely be some new chain restaurant now that a big developer had gotten a hold of it.

But why burst the mayor's bubble today?

This building at least was owned by an eccentric rich woman who loved animals enough to want animal-centric businesses occupying her first-floor storefronts.

Speaking of the devil, Diane breezed outside then, floating

out from the residential entrance to the building. "Oh, Marco, it's lovely to see you." She walked right up to the mayor, and they kissed each other's cheeks. "I see you've met some of my fine young employees."

"This cat café must have been your idea," said Mayor Martinez.

"Yes, it was." Diane chuckled. "Lauren does an amazing job running it, though."

The mayor and the senator left a short time later to talk to some of the other businesses along Whitman Street, leaving Caleb feeling a bit like he'd been integrated into the fabric of the neighborhood a little. Diane even turned toward him and said, "Hanging out with the girls today instead of seeing patients?"

"We had some cancellations, so I'm checking out the festival," he said.

"The street closures are probably making it hard to get over here if you're traveling by car."

"I imagine so."

Diane nodded thoughtfully. Hank sat at her feet and let out a little "*whumpf*" to get her attention. She smiled and pet his head. "Hi, Hank. How are you, big fella? I hope you're not thinking about trying to get any of the cats?"

Sunday meowed as if to register her displeasure.

Diane laughed. "Oh, I do enjoy festivals like this, though. It feels like spring has finally arrived. That was a hell of a winter, wasn't it?"

It certainly had been. Caleb nodded. "I'm glad it's over."

Diane pat his shoulder. "Well, have a good afternoon with my girls from the Cat Café. I'm going to go find a funnel cake."

Caleb took a deep breath and shook his head as she walked away. "I should probably get back to work and give Rachel the rest of these empanadas," he said to Lauren. He reached out his hand to take Hank's leash.

Lauren handed it over. "All right. We'll be here until sundown if you get bored again. Then Pop is hosting a party for the vendors who participated in the street fair today, so Evan and I plan to get our martini on if you want to join us."

"I'll think about it, although I should probably get Hank home when my shift is over." Trying to have a conversation in a crowded bar was not really Caleb's idea of a good time. "Thanks for showing me and Hank around."

"No problem. I'll see you around, Caleb."

"Yeah." He went back inside, contemplating the fact that, had they been a couple, they might have hugged or made more concrete plans than "see you around." It felt a little wrong to just leave Lauren after they'd spent a pleasant hour together, but... They weren't a couple.

That's what Caleb kept telling himself, anyway.

CHAPTER 18

"SO, OKAY," PAIGE SAID AT the next staff meeting. "Have you heard about these services that bring puppies to offices to help employees calm down?"

Lauren and Monique glanced at each other. "That's a real thing?" asked Monique.

"Yeah. There's a pilot program in Austin. I printed out an article about it." Paige whipped a stapled printout from her folder and handed it to Lauren. "Anyway, I had a brainstorm. What if we had a kitten party at the café? Just before we adopt out Lauren's kittens, we get them all over here and have guests come play with the kittens. We can market it as a stress-relief kind of thing."

It was a cute idea. Lauren nodded. "If you want to talk to Mitch to see if he has more rescue kittens, we could also potentially have adopted, please do. I'm not sure five kittens necessarily constitutes a party."

"So you want to do it?" Paige asked, sounding eager.

"Sure, put a proposal together. We'll run it by Diane to see what she thinks."

Shortly after the meeting broke, Evan walked into the café.

"If I ordered a coffee, could you make it Irish? I'm having a day."

"Is there some astrological phenomenon at work this week?" Lauren asked. "Everyone seems totally frazzled."

"Mercury in retrograde," said Paige gravely. "We drank all the booze from the party, unfortunately. If you're nice, Monique might put an extra caramel shot in your latte, though."

Lauren cleaned up the table where her staff had just been meeting and was thinking about ordering a tea when Evan returned from the counter with a cup in hand.

"What happened?" Lauren asked.

"Mostly just stupid work stuff. There's a new clothing boutique near the Atlantic Center that wanted me to design some signage for their front window, but they don't actually want me to design so much as they want to give me a design drawn on napkins and Post-its and have me correctly interpret their chicken scratch into being exactly their vision. So there was that. But the real kick in the teeth just happened."

"Oh, no." Based on Evan's facial expression, whatever he was about to say had upset him a great deal.

"Pablo has a boyfriend."

"I'm so sorry. How do you know?"

"Well, I was walking here from the meeting with the boutique ladies, and then I thought I'd just pop into the bookstore and say hello, and then there was Pablo, making out with a beardy hipster near the romance novels in the back, which is just fucking perfect."

Lauren reached over and put her hand on Evan's. "Oh, honey, I'm so sorry."

"I'm too late, aren't I? All the queer men in Brooklyn are paired up and none are left for me."

"I don't think that's how any of this works," said Lauren.

"It's not even about Pablo per se. I mean, I think he's sex on legs, but we've never had a conversation that lasted longer than ninety seconds. So I'm disappointed, but I think it's more about the fact that it's been so hard to meet people lately."

Lauren nodded. She could relate to that. Perhaps her whole plan to swear off men and focus on herself wasn't so much about Derek getting married as it was about the fact that it was hard to meet people in New York City—despite there being eight and a half million people to meet—and she hadn't wanted to put in the effort. It was…easier not to.

And instead she'd met Caleb.

A strange thought popped into her head, probably because of all the event brainstorming they'd just done at the staff meeting. "Maybe the café should do a singles mixer."

Evan guffawed. "Are you serious?"

"No. I don't know. Just thinking aloud. Do people still meet at mixers?"

"You talk like you're eighty years old. I appreciate that you've chosen yourself, but I for one would like to have sex again before I die."

Lauren pointed at Evan's phone, which was in his hand. "Aren't there apps for that?"

"Sure, if you're twenty years old and look like an underwear model."

"You serving wine at your pity party?"

Evan rolled his eyes. "Shut up. I just mean…well, of course Pablo has a boyfriend. And Derek is married. And you and I are still single because there is no justice in the world."

"Our cases are not that terminal. It's just…a dry spell. A rough patch. You're a good-looking guy, Evan. There's gotta be an out-of-work actor or adjunct faculty member or someone out there waiting to be with you." And it was true. Evan had dark hair and olive skin—he was half Colombian on his father's side—and went to the gym with more regularity than some nuns went to mass, and he probably could have passed for a guy five years younger. He ran a successful graphic design business, he had a nice apartment, and just like Lauren, he had a lot going for him as a potential mate for someone. Lauren knew she wasn't a lost cause, but it was hard sometimes to venture out of her comfort zone, and dating hadn't been a major priority lately.

Except that she did have someone.

"Well, thank you," said Evan. "You're not so shabby yourself. Actually, you're the best person I know, and if I were even a little attracted to women, I'd marry you tomorrow so we could be a Brooklyn power couple and have our perfectly designed penthouse in one of those new high-rise buildings close to the Manhattan Bridge. I like the peen a little too much, though."

Lauren laughed, but it bothered her that she couldn't explain what had been happening with Caleb. She had a regular fuck buddy, but they had no future.

On the other hand, neither she nor Caleb was seeing anybody else, and they'd spent three of the last seven nights together, and it sure seemed like they were in a relationship, albeit a secret one.

They still bickered sometimes and disagreed about everything from what to watch on television to if they liked rainy days to whether or not bagels should be toasted. She was afraid to ask his opinions on political issues, because she'd probably find out he had opinions she couldn't stomach.

Still, they had *something* between them, and they got along more than they fought lately, and it would be nice to be able to tell her friends she was seeing someone, or at least be able to explain what was happening in her life. She didn't like keeping things from Evan. But she didn't feel like she could say anything, either.

"There's no way you're the last single gay man in Brooklyn," Lauren said to deflect attention off herself.

"Don't say things like that out loud. You'll jinx me."

"I'm just saying, the man you'll end up with is still out there somewhere. So it's not Pablo. That doesn't mean there are no other men in the world. And also, maybe what you saw isn't what you think you saw."

"You think Pablo makes out with random customers at the bookstore on a regular basis?" Evan raised an eyebrow.

"Probably not. But maybe the hipster guy is just the man of the moment. He'll be old news by next week."

Evan sighed. "Well, like I said, my current malaise is not really about Pablo. I just worry sometimes that life is passing me by when I'm not looking. Maybe I need to be more aggressive."

Lauren's heart sank. What was it about her current situation that made her feel this way? Her secret boyfriend, probably.

Maybe she should ask Caleb to go public. But that would, of course, be asking him to acknowledge they had a relationship, which he'd seemed reluctant to do. He may not have thought they had a relationship, but they did, however untraditional it was.

She let out a breath. "This seems like a conversation we should be having over drinks."

"Hence the Irish coffee request."

"Well, let me see if I can wrap up my time here for the day. We can drown our sorrows at Pop instead."

"Am I having my quarter-life crisis late? Is there such a thing as a third-life crisis?"

"You must know you're handsome, Evan. And you're kind and smart and funny. Any man would be lucky to have you."

"I appreciate that, but I have to meet other single men to make said man lucky."

Lauren could tell from the expression on his face that Evan was about to get maudlin, so she told him to stay where he was while she checked in with her staff and made sure she was good to leave for the day. Monique assured her about eight times that she and Paige could take care of closing, so Lauren went back to her office and grabbed her things. On the way back toward the front door, she grabbed Evan.

"Come on, Mr. Sad Sack. Let's go have fruity martinis."

"Yes, please!"

There'd probably been some protocol broken when Lauren and Caleb exchanged phone numbers. It felt like a step toward actually contacting each other on purpose instead of only getting together through happenstance and coincidence and a well-timed argument.

But Caleb further broke protocol when he actually texted Lauren on his day off and invited her to come over.

It was a move that broke through the artifice. He'd been kidding himself if he thought whatever was between them would be limited to them stumbling into each other. He'd stopped himself from texting her a few times, but ultimately, he realized he wanted to see her.

She'd shown up at his door with a brown paper bag with the Shake Shack logo on it, so they'd had burgers for dinner and sex for dessert.

And now Lauren was in the bathroom while Caleb sat in his bedroom, fretting about whether he'd crossed some line from this being something vague and ephemeral to this being something concrete and real.

He still wasn't ready. He couldn't fall in love. He wouldn't get married. He just wanted sex and companionship, not for this to be a whole thing. Because Lauren was...Lauren. The cat café manager with her head in the clouds. They were unsuited for each other. It didn't matter that he enjoyed her company now. It was likely only a matter of months before they wouldn't be able to stand each other anymore.

When Lauren walked back into the bedroom, Caleb was sitting on the bed, flipping through channels on his television. He tried to push all thoughts of this being a relationship out of his head.

"I only own one TV," she said. "Having one in the bedroom seems luxurious."

"I put the TV on to help me fall asleep sometimes."

"Yeah? What do you watch?"

"Well, for one thing, there's this forensic investigation show on one of the upper dial cable channels that airs all night. They solve crime with science." Caleb paused on an ad for a personal injury lawyer. "I love this guy's accent."

It was a pretty aggressive Brooklyn accent; the guy looked Italian and had probably grown up in Carroll Gardens or Bensonhurst. Not only did he have the "*cawffee tawk*" vowels down, but he hit his consonants hard.

"Better or worse than the Boston accent?" Lauren asked.

"Dunno. More of a novelty, maybe. When I lived in Boston, one of our vet techs had a hard-core Southie accent, so I heard it every day and got used to it. Plus I grew up in Maine, where nobody pronounces Rs, either. Still, the first time the tech told me a canine patient had parvo, I had no idea what he was talking about. He kept saying '*pah-vo*.'"

"Parvo?"

"Canine parvovirus. It's a virus we see in dogs sometimes. Anyway, my point was that the New York accents are new and different."

She looked at the TV for a long moment. "It's perfectly in character for you to be into a forensic investigation show."

He shrugged. He'd done enough necropsies in his career that not much turned his stomach, but he could admit that someone with a weaker constitution might not like the content of the show. But he liked that they could solve the puzzle of these crimes with hard science and logic.

And speaking of logic, if Lauren noticed he'd broken protocol, she hadn't said anything.

He looked over at her. She had on a pair of lacy pink panties and one of his old T-shirts. She climbed onto the bed, where he sat in a pair of boxers, and snuggled up beside him.

Were they about to...watch TV in bed together? It seemed like such an established-couple thing to do. Certainly not what two people only seeing each other for sex would do.

"Can I ask you a question?" Lauren said.

Caleb's chest tightened in anticipation. "Yeah."

"I just... Well, I had drinks with Evan the other night, and we were talking about dating, and it felt very strange I couldn't tell him about you and me."

"What about you and me?"

Lauren leveled her gaze at him and patted his knee. "I hate to break this to you, but we have a relationship. It's secret and undefined, but it's still a relationship."

He sighed, unable to deny that.

"So at some point," Lauren said, "you and I transitioned from people who hate each other to people who sometimes have sex to people who are basically having a secret affair. We've spent more nights together the last few weeks than some real couples do. But... It is a secret, isn't it?"

Going public, for lack of a better way to explain it, would be like advertising to the world that they were in a relationship, and Caleb didn't feel he could do that. He wanted to keep seeing Lauren, especially like this when she was half naked in his bed, but he didn't want to make a commitment. He didn't know *that* much about her, did he? They got along well in bed but less so out of it. It wasn't like they were going to end up together. Caleb had no intention of marrying again. He'd trusted love once. He wouldn't make that mistake twice.

"Do we have to label things?" he asked.

"No, not this minute. I'm okay with the way things are. I just feel weird about this all being a secret."

"I know women talk, but do you really have to talk about *this*? It's no one's business. I'd really rather it not be public knowledge."

Lauren leaned back and stared at him, her expression surprised. "Women *talk*?"

"You know. You go for drinks and gossip and stuff."

"I don't live in an episode of *Sex and the City*. I would just like to be able to tell my friends about something significant happening in my life. But maybe what we have is fleeting and not significant and doesn't matter."

Oh, here it was. "It's…fun. I enjoy spending time with you like this. Does it have to be anything more than that?"

"No, it doesn't have to be." She sat back against the headboard and crossed her arms. "This thing between us may become something you don't want, though."

"What do you mean by that?"

She rolled her eyes. "How long do you think this can just… be the way it is? How long before one of us gets emotionally invested? How long until one of us meets someone else? I mean, maybe none of those things will happen, especially to you since you have no feelings, but I have a hard time believing this can just go on forever. And neither of us wants it to."

"But if it's working for us, why change it? Why not just…let it work this way for as long as it does."

She closed her eyes for a long moment. "All right. And then the minute it isn't working, it's over?"

"I guess so." Which was all he could offer, but Caleb still felt a little twinge. Did he want this to be a big thing? No. Did he want it to end? No.

She seemed dissatisfied with his answer, too, and turned toward the TV. Caleb looked at what appeared to be an episode of *Law & Order* from the '90s.

"We talked about this. This right here is all I'm capable of right now," he said.

"Fine."

"You're mad."

She grunted. "I'm not... Okay, I'm a little mad. Do you even like me?"

"Yeah, of course I do."

"As more than a body?"

He had to think a little harder about that. He wouldn't have broken protocol if he didn't though, would he? "Yes."

"Am I wasting my time here?"

"Is there somewhere else you need to be?"

"No."

"Then..."

She sighed again. "Status quo it is, then."

CHAPTER 19

THE CRACK OF THUNDER OUTSIDE ensured a slow afternoon at the café. Lauren tidied up the cat room, lamenting the weather interrupting her business.

"I went on a Tinder date last night," Paige said. "This guy Brandon who lives not far from here."

"Okay." Lauren picked up a series of cat toys off the floor while Paige draped herself in a chair to tell her story.

"So, first of all, we ate at this upscale Mexican restaurant near Smith and Bergen, and the food was delicious. I think it was maybe the best Mexican food I've had in New York."

"Low bar," said Lauren. Any cuisine from around the world was available somewhere in New York City, but Mexican food was decidedly mediocre if one didn't know the right places to find it. The popular Mexican restaurants in midtown Manhattan could provide a serviceable burrito, but for Lauren's money, the best Mexican food she'd had come off a food truck she'd found in Red Hook one time when she got lost trying to get to Ikea. Which meant she'd never find it again.

"I mean, it's probably not *authentic*," Paige said. "It was tasty, though. But get this. When I was walking there from the subway, I walked past a store that only repairs those fancy trendy strollers all the rich parents have."

"Are you serious?"

"Yeah. Can you imagine? A whole business whose only job is to repair one brand of stroller, and there's enough business in the neighborhood for it to stay open."

"That's wild." Lauren shook her head. "I mean, we're clearly part of the problem, but it's amazing what gentrification brings to Brooklyn. A cat café is one thing, but a stroller repair shop?"

"The Mexican restaurant is a block from that new indie bookstore, so I made Brandon take me there after dinner so I could check it out. Compare it to Stories."

"And?"

"It's more open and modern. It's a huge space and they've got a good variety of books, but I always thought Stories has old-school charm. Also, they sell T-shirts. I should tell Pablo to let the owners at Stories know that they should sell T-shirts."

"Maybe *we* should sell T-shirts."

Paige's whole face lit up. "We *definitely* should. You should hire Evan to design them. I bet he'd give you the best friend discount."

It was a sound idea, Lauren thought, and another potential income stream for the business. She filed that away in her mind and grabbed a broom to start sweeping the floor. "How was the date otherwise?" she asked.

"It was...fine. Brandon seems like a nice guy. He's *young* though. Only twenty-five."

"That's only, like, two years younger than you are."

"Yeah, but there's a wide gulf of difference in life experience. He lives in an apartment over a pizza place on Nevins with, not kidding, four roommates."

"Did you see the inside of this apartment?"

"Not yet. The potential of all those people overhearing us was daunting, and then I chickened out about inviting him back to my place because I thought having to ride the subway together would be awkward and might spoil the mood and I didn't know how to break it to him that my place is kind of fancy. We're seeing each other again next week, though."

"That seems promising."

Paige shrugged. "We'll see. I want to keep my options open. I kind of think I might be the oldest person on Tinder, though."

"That can't be true. But that is also why *I'm* not on Tinder."

"Nobody meets in person anymore. We're all too busy looking at our phones. I want to meet a great guy and fall in love, so I might as well give this a shot."

"What about all the frogs?"

Paige smiled. "There's got to be a prince in there somewhere."

"I admire your optimism. I wish I shared it."

Paige sighed and looked at the table.

"What?" Lauren asked.

"I just… Please don't be mad, but Evan and I talked recently about you. Like, maybe this whole choosing-yourself thing is just because you don't want to put any effort into dating."

Lauren didn't want to have this conversation. Part of her did believe strongly that she had to see to her own happiness before she could commit to anyone else, but this thing with Caleb was throwing her off her plans. She'd forgotten how nice it was to spend time with a man in a sexual and romantic context. She loved her friends, she loved spending time with them, but it felt like Caleb had fallen into a hole in her life.

But her life was not complete. Not while things with Caleb were secretive. Their relationship felt unreal at times.

"Maybe," she said, trying to sound noncommittal. "Although I was serious when I said I wanted to work on myself before anything else. If I don't date, why does it matter? If I'm happy and single, I'm not hurting anyone."

"Sure, but...are you happy?"

Lauren smiled to show she was. It probably wasn't convincing. "I'm getting there."

"Are you?"

Lauren was frustrated her friends didn't really get this or thought she was lying. She wasn't; she'd meant it when she'd said she wanted to find her own happiness. "Look, it wasn't a hollow sentiment. I could probably walk into Pop right now and find some guy to go home with. That's not the point. The point is to focus on myself, to find a way to be happy with my life even if I never end up meeting the man of my dreams. Evan's been freaking out about Brooklyn being out of eligible men, and although I think his fears are unfounded, there is a real possibility that I will never meet a man I want to spend the rest of my life with. I don't want my future happiness to hinge on whether or not I get married. Maybe I will, maybe I won't, but it shouldn't matter."

Paige held up her hands. "All right."

"I'm just saying. And that's not a knock on you and Evan either. If finding the right person and getting married and having babies makes you happy, then you should do that. If being in a relationship makes you happy, then I hope you find the best guy in New York to be with. I personally have some other priorities, and I want to be successful in my work here more than anything else right now. I like my life as it is. If the right man wandered in here one day, well, that would be one thing, but since he hasn't walked into my life yet, then I want to work to make my life amazing, man or not."

Paige frowned for a moment. "Okay. I mean, I get it. I believe you. I just wanted to be sure that you were swearing off romance willingly and not because you feel hopeless or whatever."

"I haven't sworn off romance. It's just not a priority."

"All right. Well. I think I'll give Brandon another chance."

"Good. I hope that works out." And now things were awkward between them. Lauren sat on the sofa and rubbed her forehead. "I'm sorry for speechifying."

"It's okay. I do understand what you're saying. We women kind of grow up molded into thinking our job is to please a man, when our goal should be to please ourselves. Uh, pun intended, I suppose. If you're not dating, I hope you own a good vibrator."

Lauren laughed, which seemed to break whatever tension had arisen between them.

Paige stood, so Lauren did, too. Paige walked over and gave Lauren a tight hug. "You're a great friend and I love you. I want you to be happy."

"Thanks," said Lauren. "Same for you." She sank into the hug and felt some tension drain from her body.

When they pulled apart, Paige said, "I need to get going whenever this weather passes. I'm crashing a book club meeting at a café near the courthouses to try to talk them into switching locations." She winked. "Plus I read the book. It's this wacky novel that takes place in parallel universe New York Cities, and there's this old man and a teenage girl, and I can't really explain it, but it was excellent."

Thunder roared outside again.

"Or maybe I'll stay here for a bit. I think I'll test the new barista's latte skills. You want anything?"

"Sure, I'd drink a vanilla latte, while we're testing him."

"Cool. Be right back."

Lauren went back to sweeping. She mulled over the conversation she'd just had with Paige. Caleb had been on her mind, but of course she couldn't say anything aloud. His wish had been for whatever was between them to remain secret and undefined. That would continue for as long as they both wanted it to. So did Lauren want it to?

She didn't know. How did she feel about him?

Well, she liked Caleb, despite everything. She liked spending time with him. The sex was mind-bending, but she liked just hanging around and watching TV with him, too, or eating takeout Asian food with him, or even just talking with him. They still argued, sure, but the arguments were fun. She enjoyed riling him up, frustrating him, and he enjoyed doing the same to her. At first, fighting had been acrimonious, and she still thought he could be arrogant, but she understood what his whole deal was better now.

What she wanted was for them to be in a real relationship.

Would they get married? Who knew? Who cared? Right now, she just wanted to see what would happen if they explored what they had.

When Lauren was a kid, her mother had owned an antique candle snuffer shaped like a deer. Lauren and her brother would fight at the end of every big meal over who got to be the one to snuff the candles. The way Caleb wanted to frame their relationship felt a lot like that candle snuffer. It had been a heavy thing, made of some kind of metal, and it could douse a flame in half a second. In a way, Caleb hovered over his relationship with Lauren like a candle snuffer: heavy, unwavering, and ready to put out the flame at any moment.

That was unworkable. Back when their relationship was just sex, the impending end of the relationship hadn't felt like a big deal. But now they'd crossed some threshold and had grown fond of each other, or at least Lauren really liked Caleb. The impending end of the relationship was not something Lauren wanted or looked forward to, though it still felt inevitable.

Maybe it was time to put an end to it, then. If Caleb wouldn't commit to anything, why bother keeping it up?

Doug Francis ran into the vet clinic, drenched. Caleb had been conferring with Rachel at the front desk when the thunderstorm started, so he wasn't surprised to see Doug had been a victim of the storm.

"That's some rain out there," said Doug.

"You all right?" Caleb asked.

"Fine. Just…wet."

"There are clean scrubs in the storage room," said Rachel.

"Bless you. If I stand here in wet clothes in this air conditioning I will freeze. Is it always so cold in here?"

Doug headed into the back of the clinic. Caleb glanced at Rachel. Rachel shrugged. "With rain this bad, all our afternoon appointments will be late."

"I only have one more today I think. Then I'm out."

"Oooh, hot plans tonight?"

"Hardly."

Rachel laughed. "Really?"

"When you say it like that, you make me feel like a bridge troll. Can't a guy go home after a long workday to eat leftovers and watch a baseball game?"

Rachel raised an eyebrow, then laughed. "I mean, look, you're a handsome man. You probably own a mirror and already know that. I know you just got divorced, but Brooklyn is not a terrible place to be single."

Caleb did not want to have this conversation. "I'm good, really."

"Last weekend, my boyfriend and I went to this barbecue restaurant over by the Gowanus. Which is, by the way, like two blocks from another barbecue place. Why are there so many places in Brooklyn that sell smoked meat?"

Caleb laughed. "I don't know."

"Well, anyway, we were at this restaurant, and this place is a total meat market. In *all* senses. It's all open-air, which means it's probably quite hot in the summer, and there are bars all over the seating areas and then a counter where you order food. Huge crowd this weekend, though. People everywhere. I got hit on by a guy at the bar who was, like, fresh out of college, and I turned him down of course, but I admired his nerve."

"Is there a moral to this story?"

"I'm just illustrating that there are lots of places like that in Brooklyn to meet people if you wanted to, you know, rebound from your divorce."

"Thanks. I'll keep that in mind."

"Unless you're already seeing someone?" Rachel raised her eyebrows.

"No," Caleb said, mostly to see how the lie tasted.

He didn't like it. Saying he wasn't seeing anyone felt like a betrayal of Lauren. But why should it? He had just had this discussion with Lauren. They didn't have any kind of commitment to each other. They had no future together. They were just fooling around. It would end soon, probably.

But if it was really fleeting, he wouldn't feel so sad by the prospect of it ending.

He shook his head, trying to push the thoughts aside. Doug emerged in a clean pair of bright blue scrubs looking ready to conquer the day. "All right. I'm ready for the sick dogs and cats of Brooklyn now."

Rachel looked toward the front window. "Well, the rain seems to be slowing down. Hopefully that means patients will come in soon."

But instead of dogs or cats, the next people who came into the vet clinic were a pair of men in boxy suits. The sleeker one extended a hand toward Caleb, probably because he happened to be standing near the door.

"Hello, I'm Brian Randolph," the man said, "and this is my assistant Mr. Newton. We own the building across the street."

"Uh-huh," said Caleb. He could sense that both Rachel and Doug had tensed.

"I've been speaking with the owner of *this* building about a possible sale. She hasn't said yes yet, but I can play hardball. I just wanted to take a look at the clinic here, since I'd be your new landlord. I understand it is one of the busier ones in the neighborhood."

Rachel put her hands on her hips. "We're one of only two vet clinics in all of Brooklyn with emergency hours. The other one is in Midwood."

"Yes, quite a distance from here," said Randolph, nodding. "You folks have nothing to worry about, at least not in the short-term. A business like this provides a valuable service to the neighborhood."

The use of the word *business* made the hair on the back of Caleb's neck stand up. Even when he'd owned a clinic and had to deal with its finances, he still thought of it as a clinic more than a for-profit business. Caleb and Kara had opted not to pay themselves during the early lean months, for example, because the patients were more important than their bank balance. Luckily, that period of their lives hadn't lasted long, and they had turned a profit, but Caleb still didn't quite think of it that way.

Lauren had mentioned this slimeball had taken an interest in the building, but Diane didn't seem interested in selling. So why was this Randolph guy sniffing around the vet clinic?

"Does that mean in the long-term that you might close the clinic?" Rachel asked. "If you buy the building, I mean."

"No, not at first."

Right.

"Let me guess," said Caleb. "You're buying up buildings on the block so you can level it and replace everything with some eyesore of a glass tower, so you can have a bank and a Starbucks on the first floor and luxury condos upstairs, thereby stamping out all the personality from the neighborhood."

Randolph balked. "I'm interested in investing in real estate on this block, yes, but not for nefarious purposes. I'd like to find businesses that best serve this neighborhood. More housing, better restaurants, and yes, a veterinary clinic, are all a part of that. But wouldn't you all prefer to practice your craft in a state-of-the-art facility? Better technology, newer equipment, nicer facilities? This waiting room is quite dark, don't you think?"

A woman and a German shepherd came in then. Rachel ran to the door and held up a trash can for the woman's umbrella. Caleb was grateful to the dog, his next appointment, for getting him out of this conversation. Doug busied himself looking at the schedule on Rachel's desk.

"We've got patients," said Rachel, gesturing at the dog. "Nice of you to stop by, though."

The assistant, who had said nothing while inside, looked visibly uncomfortable in the presence of a wet dog. He stepped toward the door, clearly intending to flee, and the German shepherd chose that moment to shake the water out of his fur. The Newton guy was covered in little droplets and looked ready to crawl out of his skin.

"Yes, let's go," Newton said to Randolph.

"Indeed." Randolph took one last look around, clearly sizing the place up. "Hopefully I've given you something to think about. The current owner of this building can't afford to pay for many upgrades, but I can." Then they left.

Rachel told the woman with the German shepherd to take the dog to Exam 1. When they had passed through the door, Rachel shivered in an exaggerated way. "Ugh, that guy is skeevy. Gave me the willies."

"Olivia said there was a real estate developer sniffing around the building," said Doug. "Guess that was him."

"You don't think Diane would sell, do you?" asked Rachel.

Doug shrugged. "I don't, but a huge pile of money will make people act out of character. And that looks like a guy who's got a vault full of cash that he swims in like Scrooge McDuck."

"Diane is eccentric, but I'd much prefer her as a landlord than that guy. Good gravy." Rachel shook her head. "And what was all that about better facilities? Is he trying to get us to talk Diane into selling? Or to moving to some other fancier building so he can tear this one down? What is his end game?"

"Unclear," said Doug. "He's like a cartoon villain."

"I like this job," Caleb said before he thought about it too much. Rachel and Doug both turned toward him with questioning looks on their faces. He sighed and said, "Just saying. I like working here. I'd like to keep working here. It would be a real shame if some dickhead developer bought the building and tore it down."

"Amen," said Doug.

"I'd better go see to..." Caleb grabbed the chart from the desk. "Captain von Trapp."

Doug sang, "The hills are alive with the sound of barking..."

Caleb laughed and walked back to the exam room.

CHAPTER 20

LAUREN STOOD IN A CROWDED hotel ballroom with theater seating, looking for an empty seat. She'd come to a symposium about new science regarding feline behavior because Diane encouraged this kind of professional development. It was being held at a hotel in Midtown. Since moving to Brooklyn, Lauren spent far less time in this high-traffic tourist area around Times Square, mostly by design. She was already stressed from having to push through the slow-moving crowds of tourist families gawking at the buildings and lights around them, worried she'd be late because people needed to walk five-abreast on the sidewalk.

When Lauren had first seen the website for the symposium, she'd thought learning more about how cats behaved might better inform some of the decisions she made for how the café was run, but now that she was here, she felt outclassed by the audience. Nearly everyone around her had *Dr.* or *DVM* on their badges, and she was here as just the manager of a cat café.

She hadn't felt this silly or out of place in a while.

"There's an empty seat over there," said a voice to her right.

She turned and saw a handsome man—a veterinarian named Michael, according to his name badge—and smiled. "Thanks."

"Here, come with me."

So Lauren followed Michael to a pair of empty seats at the end of one row about eight rows back from the dais.

"Thank you for helping me find a seat. I was a little overwhelmed."

"No problem. I'm Mike, by the way. I work at a vet clinic uptown."

"Oh. Nice to meet you. I'm Lauren." She deliberately withheld her credentials, because he would likely mock her, the way Caleb had when they'd first met.

Caleb had some grudging respect for her work now and he'd probably be impressed she was attending this symposium. But she didn't want to push it too far with this stranger.

"Did you know," said Michael, pointing to the program in his hand, "that in ancient Greece, a symposium was an event at which a bunch of men sat around drinking and talking. I guess we've evolved if a woman as pretty as you is allowed in."

Lauren didn't know what to do with that. He'd found her a seat; she didn't owe him more than her thanks. So now he was hitting on her? Okay. She smiled, hoping the lecture would start soon. "I didn't know that," she said. "About the word *symposium*, I mean."

"I was a classics major in college for a semester before I decided to switch to biology so I could find a job after I graduated that didn't involve asking if you want fries with that."

"So not only did you switch majors, but you did many years of extra schooling to get that job?"

Mike shrugged. "I liked school, what can I say?"

Well, he was annoying her now. Caleb had his faults, but his arrogance didn't approach the smug look on Mike's face as he grinned at Lauren.

Ugh. What the hell was up with this guy? And why couldn't she get Caleb out of her head?

Thankfully, some music began to play and the panel for tonight's discussion walked out onto the dais and sat behind a table. Lauren kept her gaze forward, focusing on the speakers, trying to ignore Mike.

He behaved until the talk ended.

She stood and was about to make a beeline out of the ballroom when Mike said, "This hotel has a really nice lounge on the top floor. It rotates, actually. Excellent view of the city. Can I interest you in a drink?"

It wasn't even that Mike had behaved poorly. She just got a vibe from him she didn't like. She opened her mouth to tell him she was seeing someone, but was she? She hated having this secret, ill-defined relationship with Caleb. On the other hand, there was no reason Mike deserved the truth, and Lauren's thoughts were clearly tied up with another man, even if they weren't officially seeing each other.

"You okay there?" Mike asked. "Just a drink. Not a marriage proposal."

"Listen, Mike, it was great talking with you, but—"

"Lauren?"

Lauren turned and, as if she'd conjured him, here was Caleb. "Oh. Hi," she said.

"I thought that was you." Caleb planted himself beside her

and thrust his hand toward Mike. "I'm Dr. Caleb Fitch. I'm a veterinarian in Brooklyn."

"Right. Nice to meet you." Mike shook Caleb's hand.

"What are you doing here?" Lauren asked.

"Jenny Cartwright was a classmate of mine in vet school," Caleb said, hooking his thumb back toward the dais. Dr. Cartwright had been one of the panelists. "I came to see her and offer moral support. You?"

"Professional development," Lauren said, feeling a little embarrassed. She definitely didn't belong here.

"Yeah, Jenny's research on feline behavior is really interesting. And good for her. I wanted no part of more academia when we graduated, but she thought research was more interesting than actually practicing veterinary medicine."

"Are you guys friends?" Mike asked.

"Neighbors, in a way," said Caleb.

Lauren tried to mentally transmit to Caleb that she didn't want him to say she managed a cat café, and then she felt stupid because she should take pride in her work and not feel like she didn't belong here. She did belong. She'd understood every word of the presentation and also found the research interesting.

"So, about that drink," Mike said.

Caleb put an arm around her, which surprised her. It felt heavy around her shoulders.

"She's going to have to give you a rain check," Caleb said. "She's coming out with me now."

Caleb's tone was forceful and a bit possessive, leaving no room for argument.

Mike held up his hands, likely recognizing he'd just lost this territorial dispute. "All right. See you around, Lauren. Nice to meet you both."

Once Mike took off in another direction and Caleb started to steer her toward the exit, she said, "Well, that was beastly of you."

Caleb frowned. "Was that inappropriate? I just thought—"

"I was working out how to politely turn him down, so it's fine, but you might as well have just peed on me for how much you acted like a caveman there."

Caleb took his arm away. "Oh. I'm sorry. I wasn't even thinking. You know I don't think I *own* you or anything, right? I just didn't like that guy."

"I know. Me neither. Let's just get out of here."

The spike of jealousy that had pierced Caleb's chest when he'd seen Lauren talking to that Mike guy in the ballroom had surprised Caleb, even though it shouldn't have. He should really face facts that he was developing feelings for this woman.

So he'd swept in there to get her attention and prevent her from going out with that guy, who could have been perfectly nice. And it would have been within her rights to go out with him, because it wasn't like she had any kind of commitment to Caleb. And yet.

"Well, now what?" she asked when they were outside.

"Uh, well. You want to get a drink?"

Lauren scrunched up her nose, clearly displeased with that suggestion. "Can we just walk for a bit? Get out of the Times Square area?"

"All right. Lead the way."

Caleb still didn't know the city well, but he recognized they were walking east, toward Sixth Avenue. It wasn't very late, only just after eight o'clock, but once they were outside of the Times Square bubble, the streets were fairly empty, the office workers all gone home.

"Did you have dinner?" Lauren asked.

"Yeah, I ate with Jenny before the presentation."

"This Jenny. Is she—"

"Happily married to a high school math teacher. We're just old friends."

"Not that it's any of my business."

Caleb didn't want to pursue that. Likely the thought process in Lauren's head was similar to the one he'd just worked through. "Did you eat?"

"Yeah, I had a sandwich before I came here. I could use a snack or something, though." She looked around. "Oh, it's one of those frozen yogurt places that has a zillion flavors. Let's go there."

Caleb laughed. "Okay."

"Unless you don't like frozen yogurt."

"Who doesn't like frozen yogurt?"

"Monsters. All right, let's go."

The yogurt place was self-serve, with twenty-one flavors to choose from and an extensive toppings bar. Caleb looked at all the options, sampled a few, and settled on a bit of strawberry and a bit of vanilla yogurt, with fresh berries on top. When he convened with Lauren at the checkout, she had a cup with at least five different flavors and a flurry of toppings: crushed cookies, chocolate chips, rainbow sprinkles, marshmallows, and a dab of whipped cream.

"That's some sundae you've got there," Caleb said.

Lauren peered into his cup. "Fresh fruit? Do you know how to let loose at all?"

"Just put your cup on the counter." He pulled out his wallet. "Dessert's on me."

"All right."

"You're not going to fight me? Protest that this isn't a date? That you are a modern woman who can pay for her own frozen yogurt?"

Lauren grinned and put her cup next to his on the scale next to the register. "All those things are true. But also, you offered, and you make more money than I do."

Caleb handed the cashier his credit card. "Fair enough."

They settled into a booth with bright red seats, sitting across from each other. Lauren dug in. Caleb watched her eat for a moment before taking his first bite.

He said, "So what's a dame like you doing in a place like that?"

"Huh?"

"What brought you to the symposium?"

"Oh. Diane encourages me to do professional development, so she's got me on every mailing list for every organization in the city relating to pets or animal rescues or veterinary anything. When I got the invitation to this thing in the mail, Diane encouraged me to go. She thought maybe learning more about feline behavior would help me better manage the cats at the café."

"Did you learn anything useful?"

"Yeah, the discussion of observed behaviors in feral colonies was especially interesting. I didn't know that cat tails could tell you anything, but I've seen the cats at the café greet each other with their tails up all the time. If that really means they are approaching in a friendly way, that seems like good news."

"Also that purring could be a way to lure prey into a false sense of security."

Lauren laughed. "That I knew. And I totally believe it. I've been attacked by enough cats at the café to know that purring is not always a sign of contentment."

"Attacked?"

"Nothing major. Scratches, mostly." She held out her arm. There were a few red slashes across it, all minor.

"You ever get bitten?"

"Every now and then. Not often. We've got a procedure in place for when that happens, at Olivia's suggestion. There are several full first aid kits and antibacterial ointment in the staff restroom."

"Okay. Just curious. I get bitten every now and then, too. Usually when I'm giving cats shots."

"Yeah, I learned that lesson the hard way. I brought one of the first café cats to the clinic to get her shots, and as soon as the needle hit her skin, she turned her head and sank her teeth into my hand. My whole hand was red and puffy for week. I had to get prescription-strength antibiotic ointment."

"Fun."

"Yeah, not so much."

They both laughed.

"I guess it was good you were there tonight," Lauren said.

"You guess?"

"Something about that guy Mike rubbed me the wrong way. And I'm not sad to see you."

"I'm not sad to see you, either." In fact, he'd had a whole cycle of emotions once he'd spotted her. He'd been surprised to see her, but happy about it. He'd considered maybe just ducking out of the auditorium until he saw Mike, at which point his feet carried him right to her. Because he wanted her to himself. Which was not at all a fair way to view the situation.

As they ate and chatted about some of the finer points of the symposium, it occurred to Caleb that they'd crossed some other threshold, and now they were the sort of people who had casual dates to eat frozen yogurt like they were in some fantasy of the fifties. He also much preferred this to trying to hear each other in a noisy bar if they'd gone for that drink, because he quite liked listening to her.

But was that enough? He didn't want a long-term relationship. He wasn't sure he could trust love to last longer than a dog's attention span. And he wasn't sure that he and Lauren even had enough in common to sustain anything worthwhile.

He just liked her.

So they ate yogurt. And when they were finished, they sat in the booth with their empty cups and kept laughing and talking. And when the staff kicked them out because the store was closing, they walked back outside, and Caleb wanted to take Lauren's hand. Except, no, they weren't in that kind of relationship.

"What train do you take home?" Lauren asked.

"I can take almost anything. The 4/5 or the 2/3 or anything that goes to Jay Street."

"Let's get the F, then. That's the train that stops nearest my building."

"All right. Lead the way."

Lauren's knowledge of the city streets was clearly much better than Caleb's. She confidently led him south toward Bryant Park. On the way, they chatted about new building developments— Lauren pointed at a skyscraper a few blocks away that hadn't existed a couple of years before—and how the city changed. Caleb found the amount of construction in Manhattan and Brooklyn to be puzzling at times, wondering where there was even room for new developments, but New York was a forward-facing city, constantly sloughing off the old to replace it with the new.

Then he said, "Oh, that Randolph guy you mentioned stopped by the clinic the other day. He seems like a scumbag."

Lauren laughed. "Yeah, he's pretty slick. Diane told him she wasn't selling in no uncertain terms, but I guess he's not taking no for an answer."

"He assured us he'd keep the vet clinic in the short-term, at least until he rips down all the buildings on the block to put in some phallic high-rise."

Lauren scrunched up her nose. "That wormy little assistant of his asks a lot of questions about health department regulations. The law is clear that I can serve food as long as the animals are kept in a separate room. I'm worried he still might file a complaint in an attempt to shut us down and give Diane an incentive to sell."

"Really? Not much of an incentive. Diane could just rent the space to someone else."

"Diane is both the owner of the space and the business, so maybe they think the financial hit if the business goes under will persuade her to sell. Maybe that fear is irrational, but I asked Diane to talk to her lawyer. Apparently, we're in the clear, but... I don't know. Randolph could cause a lot of trouble for us."

"Or Diane will turn him down a few more times and he'll give up. There are plenty of other blocks in Brooklyn for him to conquer. Hell, he already owns that one building across the street."

"True. Evan and I have been speculating about what he'll build there. But honestly, I'd be pretty angry if he shut down the Italian restaurant or the thrift store. Or if he changed anything. I don't know. Since I live there, I feel a sense of ownership for that block."

"I get it. When I lived in Boston, they tore out this charming row of little shops near our house to put in a weird little mall. It totally upended the neighborhood. And for what? So some real estate developer could make a fortune building a thing that nobody shopped in. It took them forever to get tenants. I hope he lost money. My favorite pet food store was in that row of shops."

Lauren laughed. "You're not bitter or anything."

When they got to the park, they found it full of people. A massive movie screen was set up on one end. It took Caleb a moment to recognize the movie was *Big*.

"Aw, I love this movie," said Lauren. "Too bad it's almost over."

Caleb laughed. "You don't want to watch it, do you? There's no room in the park." It looked like people were sitting on every conceivable bit of available space.

"No, it's fine. I own it on DVD, actually." Lauren sighed. "Okay, so is it strange I find it romantic? Like, Tom Hanks and Elizabeth Perkins have this sweet romance, but it's not meant to be because, you know, he's actually thirteen."

"Romantic and not creepy?"

"The way it's acted, it's not creepy. Elizabeth Perkins isn't, like, a pedophile. She thinks Tom Hanks is a normal thirty-year-old man. And you kind of get the feeling she doesn't meet a lot of good men, so it's really sad when it turns out they can't be together." She paused. "What?"

"What?"

"You're doing a thing with your face."

"What am I doing?"

"Like… I don't know. You think I'm silly, but you're indulging me."

"Maybe I am a little." Caleb felt the grin pull at his mouth.

"Would I be wrong to guess you find my silliness charming instead of frustrating now?"

"You're not wrong," he said.

"It's a star-crossed romance. The movie, I mean." She stepped closer to Caleb. "Two people who really like each other, but the timing is terrible, so it won't work out."

Caleb met her gaze. She looked at him with an earnestness he'd never seen on her face before. Was she implying that, had the timing been different, she and Caleb could have been a good match?

Maybe they would have been. But all he had was right now. And right now, he wanted to kiss her.

So he did. First, he said, "Timing's a bitch." Then he leaned in and met her lips. She put her hands around his shoulders and pressed into him. He'd intended it to be a sweet indulgence, like all the toppings she put on her frozen yogurt. But instead, it became charged.

He *really* liked her.

But the timing was impossible, so he pulled away.

She smiled. "What as that for?"

"You're cute."

"You just kissed me in public."

"No one was watching."

She raised an eyebrow. "Right. Well, let's go, lover boy. Your place or mine?"

"Mine. I gotta take Hank out."

"I'm not presumptuous in inviting myself over, am I?"

"Nope. I want you to come home with me. Will Molly be okay?"

"I fed her before I left for the symposium."

"Then let's go."

They rode the subway back to Brooklyn across from a couple that was apparently very into each other. Lauren was talking about some customer at the Cat Café, and Caleb wasn't really listening, but he was satisfied when she faltered in her speech as he put his arm around her.

"I thought we weren't a couple."

"Let's pretend for a few hours."

She looked at him with a furrowed brow as if this confused her, but then she shrugged and said, "Okay."

CHAPTER 21

CALEB LIKED TO SLEEP LATE on his days off. Often he felt like he needed it, especially after an overnight shift. The last overnight had been particularly harrowing. A dog had been hit by a car. The dog, miraculously, hadn't sustained any life-threatening injuries, just a broken leg, but the stress of having to test for internal bleeding coupled with the frantic owner who blamed herself for the dog bolting out into the street had left Caleb feeling wrecked when he finally got home.

So the doorbell pulled him out of a deep sleep. He was a little startled to see it was nearly noon. He hastily threw on a robe and went to the door, expecting it to be a package, probably some clothes he'd ordered a few days before.

But, no, it was Lauren.

Caleb rubbed his eyes. "What are you doing here?"

"I'm sorry. I'm on a Diane-mandated day off and I got bored so I thought I'd come over to say hi. So, hi."

"Hi. Um. Come in?"

Caleb stepped out of the way to let her in. As wakefulness came over him in waves, he realized he was somewhat uncomfortable to have her here. They weren't the sort of couple who just popped over to each other's apartments. They weren't even really a couple. Well, okay, they *were*, it was hard to deny that now, but he did not like her showing up unannounced.

"I brought lunch," she said. "Sandwiches from that Italian deli on Joralemon."

"Oh. Um. Let me just put on a pot of coffee."

He went to the kitchen and tried to shake off the sleepiness as he got the coffee maker going, mostly through muscle memory. He was curious what Lauren had brought, mostly because he was hungry, but he wondered how she knew what to get him.

Well, they had eaten a lot of meals together, hadn't they?

When he returned to the table, there were two heroes wrapped in white deli paper. "Meatball parm," Lauren said pointing to one, "and prosciutto, mozzarella, and roasted red peppers. Pick one, or we can each have half of each."

Both sounded good. But Caleb was still uncomfortable with Lauren in his space. He decided to keep the peace while he got some food and caffeine into his bloodstream. They wound up sharing both sandwiches, and the meatball was particularly delicious. Lauren pulled some of the prosciutto off her half of the other sub, declaring it too salty.

He liked this woman. A lot. But this was not the sort of relationship they had.

As if reading his thoughts, Lauren said, "What is it?"

"What?"

"Something is clearly bothering you. You've been fidgety and looked uncomfortable since you sat down."

He should really just tell her. No sense in putting himself through this anytime she got a notion to see him. "You're gonna think I'm a dick."

"Just tell me."

He sighed. "Okay, I don't love that you just showed up without calling or texting first."

"Oh. All right. I'll text next time."

"Well, no, that's not precisely the issue. It's just that... This is not the relationship we have."

She sat back in her chair. "Oh."

"We had fun the other night, but nothing has really changed for me. I don't want to get married again, not that we're anywhere near that, but still, I wouldn't want to mislead you. Nothing has changed."

Lauren swallowed and nodded slowly. "I'm not... I'm not asking you to marry me. I don't even need some big commitment. But I like you. I just want a chance to see where this goes, and I feel like you've basically made a fort out of your baggage and you will not be budged."

Caleb put a hand over his mouth so as not to laugh at the image, which was apt. "I do have some baggage. My divorce was... Well, if not traumatic, it was awful, all the way through. Not just the fact that Kara cheated on me and left me, but the fact that this thing I had put so much faith and work into turned out to be flimsy instead of solid. And it's not that I don't trust *you*, but I don't trust...life."

And that was basically true. He wasn't sure what he'd done to piss off the universe, but this whole year had been shitty. And the worst of it had been, when he'd been fighting with Kara over every last penny in their clinic, he'd felt like the biggest idiot. Why hadn't he seen how doomed their relationship was? Why hadn't he seen Kara was unhappy? Had he really been so committed to his life plan that he hadn't seen the ways it could be turned upside down?

It wasn't that he didn't trust Lauren. He did. But he didn't trust himself. He didn't trust his own judgment.

"That's kind of fucked up," Lauren said softly. "How do you even function if you don't trust life?"

Caleb looked away because his chest hurt with…weakness? Embarrassment? He wasn't really sure, but he didn't like it. He didn't want to feel this way in front of Lauren. He wanted to live in the magical bubble where he was just ill-tempered and they had good sex and talked about TV over takeout food and took long walks where she pointed out interesting things about the city. He didn't want her to know how deeply fucked up he was, how he felt.

"It's a challenge," he said.

"Right. So this is your nice way of saying, 'It's not you, it's me.'"

"I don't…this isn't a breakup. I don't want to stop seeing you."

Lauren frowned. "But you also don't want anything to change."

"I'm sorry. I like you, too, but this…" He gestured between them. "Some of this, anyway, makes me uncomfortable. I don't have my sea legs yet where dating is concerned. So this cutesy, spontaneous thing makes me nervous."

"No, I get it. You got burned, you don't want to try again, that's natural. I don't think any human can get to their thirties without accumulating some baggage. But to just cut this off—"

"You knew what this was, too. We talked about it."

"Fine. You don't have to tell me twice. I'll go."

"No, Lauren, that's not what I—"

"You can't have it both ways, Caleb."

Lauren didn't like the idea of ultimatums. Often they were unfair or set up impossible choices. But "take me or leave me" was starting to feel like something she should say aloud.

Instead, she said, "All right, I'm sorry for barging in here. I thought after the other night, something had changed between us, but I'm clearly wrong."

"Lauren, don't—"

"Or, you know, you could just interpret the fact that I came over with sandwiches as me wanting to have lunch with you on my day off and not like I'm trying to trap you into marriage."

Caleb frowned. "I didn't accuse you of—"

"We all have baggage! I've been in good relationships and bad relationships and had my heart broken a time or two. I get that you're skittish. Hell, I'm skittish. My ex just announced on Facebook that his first child is on the way, and I still haven't figured out how to process my feelings about that." She paused to rub her forehead. She'd just seen that particular post this morning and was still reeling from it. There'd been a time in her life when she'd imagined making such announcements with Derek. Watching him put out this announcement today was like looking at some kind of alternate universe. But she focused back on the more immediate issue. "Let's not cut off our noses to spite our faces."

"We probably spend more time arguing about our relationship than being in our relationship," Caleb said.

"So...what? Do you even want to be with me?"

"Of course I want to be with you!"

Lauren had half expected him to say no, so the conviction in his words was enough of a surprise she couldn't speak for a moment. He looked just as surprised he'd said it out loud. She rubbed her forehead.

"Just in a naked way, or..."

Caleb frowned. "I'm not an idiot. I'm not blind to the fact that we've done lots of non-naked things together, like watching TV and eating frozen yogurt. I'm enjoying our time together. I don't want to lose you."

"But you also don't even want to be in a relationship. You don't want to tell anyone we've been seeing each other. You just want whatever is between us to exist in a little bubble."

"What do you want me to say?"

Part of Lauren wanted to run screaming. There was no way to win this argument, no way to walk away without getting some part of her heart trod on, no way to mold this into some happily ever after. So she said, "I need you to trust I'm not trying to trick you. I need you to trust that all I want from you is your company. I want to be able to be with you in public and not feel like a dirty secret. I just want us to be able to figure out what we could be instead of fearing the future."

Caleb stared into the distance for a long moment, his lips pursed. He never looked more handsome than when he was thinking hard about something, and the fact that she'd caught him this morning just out of bed, with his usually neat hair a mess and sticking up on one side, in only old sweats and a threadbare robe, made her feel like she was seeing the real him and not the Caleb he presented to the world. And because she sometimes got glimpses of *that* man, the man she got to be with sometimes, she thought she had him figured out.

Maybe he'd agree to at least give them a shot.

But what he said was, "I don't feel ready."

This was probably the moment when Lauren should have shut it all down. He was never going to agree to be in any kind of non-secret relationship with her. He was holding onto his divorce and his fear and he wasn't ready to move on yet.

But what Lauren said was, "If you don't feel ready soon, there's only so long this can go on."

"I know. I've always known that."

"So what do we do?"

Caleb took a deep breath, his chest expanding and contracting. He said, "We're together. Or we're not."

"Yes, but what does that mean?"

Caleb shrugged, which annoyed Lauren so much she almost yelled at him, but she bit her tongue.

He said, "It means that, for right now, we finish lunch. Maybe we come up with something to do this afternoon to make the most of us both having today off. Maybe we go see a movie or take a walk, I don't know. I've got enough stuff in my kitchen to make us dinner tonight, probably some kind of pasta thing. If the mood is right, we have sex and you spend the night, or we don't and you spend the night, or we do and you go home, or whatever it is you want to do tonight. And if at any time this doesn't feel good or doesn't feel right, that's it, we both walk away."

"That's it?" Lauren found it extremely dissatisfying that he was being so casual about this. Did he not feel what she felt? Did he not feel his heart squeeze when she was nearby? Did he not feel his pulse race when she stood near him? Did he not feel giddy when he thought of her, did he not warm when he first saw her walk into a room, did he not think about what they were like in bed together when he was alone?

"That's all I can give you right now," said Caleb.

She should have left. What he was offering was not enough, not after everything she'd felt with him, everything they'd done together. But she said, "Then let's make the most of it."

CHAPTER 22

WHEN CATS CAME TO THE Cat Café without names, which sometimes happened when they were rescues, the staff picked a theme and chose names based on it. Monique had suggested names from antiquity, so the new group of cats had been named Caesar, Ramses, Boudicca, Antony, and Cleopatra. The last two were inseparable and often slept curled together on one of the sofas, so Lauren thought the names were apt. She'd taken to calling them Tony and Cleo and hoped to find a forever home that would take them both.

She was sitting on the sofa beside Tony and Cleo with her laptop balanced on her thighs, updating the Cat Café's website, when Caleb walked into the cat area. Paige also sat nearby, finishing some paperwork, and Evan was in a corner, working. There were a smattering of customers at the café tables, chatting, so it wasn't quiet, but it was pleasant, and Lauren was enjoying the afternoon in her domain.

Caleb carried a sack of cat food. "Courtesy of the clinic," he said, shifting it in his arms.

"All right. Come on back."

Lauren put her laptop aside and escorted Caleb to the storage room. After directing him where to put the food, they stood there smiling at each other for a moment.

"How are you?" Lauren asked.

"All right. Wondering again why these huge sacks of food can't be delivered to you directly."

"The clinic gets a discount the café is not eligible for."

"Maybe the better question is why I always get appointed to carry these bags over here."

"You're still the new guy. Maybe it's hazing."

Caleb grunted.

One of the cats, a calico named Chester, wandered in through the open door and rubbed up against Caleb. He knelt on the floor and pet the cat, who immediately presented his backend to Caleb's face.

"Why do cats do that?" Caleb asked, sounding like the question was rhetorical. "You're cool. Smell my butt."

"Your friend the cat behavioral specialist said it's to show they trust you. Cats expose vulnerable parts of their body to humans they trust not to hurt them. Did you not listen to the lecture?"

"I listened. That was my poor attempt at a joke."

"Right. This cat has only known you about thirty seconds, so he doesn't know you're a vet. If he knew, he'd probably run from the room."

"Ah. Thanks for portraying me as the root of all evil. I should get back to torturing animals."

"I didn't say that. Cats are generally distrusting of vets, though."

"Sure. I really do need to get back, though. I'm on a tight schedule today."

"Now, wait a second. I don't get so much as a hello? You just come over here, grunt a few times, and dump a big bag of cat food here?"

"What is it you want here? I have appointments all afternoon."

"Right, I forgot. We're not a couple."

Lauren didn't mean to throw a fit, but she was suddenly so mad she didn't want to look at Caleb, so she turned on her heel and walked back into the main room.

Caleb ran after her. "Now, come on. I didn't mean anything by that. Don't be offended."

Conscious of the audience, she turned toward him and said under her breath, "You can't have it both ways."

"Is this about the other night?" he asked.

Lauren glanced toward the other people in the room. The customers were mostly ignoring them, but Paige and Evan had both picked their heads up and were watching Caleb.

"I can't do this here," Lauren said.

Caleb rolled his eyes. "So like a woman to not just say what you mean."

Lauren took a step back, surprised. "Are you serious right now? What the hell is that supposed to mean?"

"We keep talking around things without saying them."

"All right. I refuse to argue with you in my place of business, so I am telling you we can talk directly about anything you want at another time and in another place. Satisfied?"

"No. Why are you mad at me? What did I do this time?"

What had he done? Why was she so mad? He'd been rude and had refused to acknowledge their relationship, but that wasn't new. The truth was, this *was* about the discussion of the other night, about how they had no future, and Lauren was pretty sure they were both wasting time investing in something that would never go anywhere.

But her friends and several customers—who had taken notice now—were in the room and she would not have this conversation here, with this many witnesses.

"Fine," she said, lowering her voice. "I'm sorry for getting mad. You didn't do anything. I guess it's just your face."

He sighed. "Gee, thanks."

"I didn't mean that the way I said it. What I meant was seeing you reminded me of our...discussion the other night, and I guess I'm still upset about it, but this is *not* the place to discuss that, so I'm calling a truce."

"Fine. Then I'm going back to work."

"But you *were* rude."

"Well, I'm sorry, *sweetheart*, but I wasn't aware I had to be overly polite when interacting with you."

"That's not what I'm saying. Come on, Caleb."

He looked at his watch. "I really do have to go. My shift ends at six if you want to yell at me more then."

He left, which was essentially what she'd told him to do, so she shouldn't have felt as angry as she did. In the early days of this...thing with Caleb, whenever she'd felt this worked up, they threw themselves at each other, but maybe whatever had happened between them had matured.

No, it definitely had matured. But Caleb wouldn't admit that, which was the central problem. They had a relationship or they didn't, was basically what he'd said the day before, and it was becoming increasingly clear they didn't have much of anything.

She turned to go back to her laptop on the sofa, but Evan was now standing beside her. "So that's going well."

"Shut up."

"What happened the other night that has you so upset?"

"Nothing. It was nothing. Just something he said that I disagreed with. Which is basically everything he says, actually."

"It's not more than that?"

She hated lying, but she felt like she had to adhere to Caleb's wishes, at least until they really hashed this out. Caleb wanted this to be their secret. So Lauren said, "I don't want to talk about this right now."

"All right. But if he said something that offended you, I will totally go kick his ass."

"Not necessary. Thank you, though."

"All right. Well. I guess I was wrong about you two. You really don't get along."

"I tried."

"Yeah. Well. If you need to get back to work, I'll let you. But before you do, I want to show you something."

"All right."

Lauren followed Evan back over to his laptop. He sat and said, "Paige let it be known that you were thinking about potentially selling some merch, and I think that is an excellent idea. I mocked up some T-shirt ideas. Tell me what you think."

Evan had already designed the logo for the Cat Café that appeared on the website, but he'd enhanced it a bit for the T-shirts. He'd also made a few designs with punny phrases, like *I spent a purr-fect afternoon at the Whitman Street Cat Café!*

"Cute!"

"I thought we could make also make stickers with cartoony representations of some of the cats with their names on them. We could even put Sadie on things, like mugs or shirts. You can get these produced for a reasonable price and mark them up to make a profit."

"Email me these. I'll run them by Diane."

"I'm still making some tweaks, but I definitely will when I'm satisfied."

"You do so much work for us; Diane's going to have to put you on salary."

"I'd settle for getting paid for a few hours' work."

"Of course. I'll see what I can do. Thanks, Evan. Maybe the profits from this will make Diane less nervous about hiring more people."

"You're rocking this, you know. If Diane can't see you're making this space fun and profitable, she's crazy."

"Thanks. I think she does see that, or I wouldn't still have a job. But once she gives me a budget, it's hard to get her to part with more money sometimes. This whole place was a gamble in a way her other businesses aren't. It seems like such a flash-in-the-pan idea, you know? But I think we can make it something that becomes a neighborhood institution, or, like Paige thinks, the hub for pet lovers in the area. That gives us all longevity and job security."

"Yeah, definitely. Keep killing it, girl."

Evan held up his hand, so Lauren gave him a high five. "Thanks for your help."

"Now if we could just sort out your love life…"

"Oh, please. That will never happen."

At five minutes before six o'clock, Lauren burst into the veterinary clinic and said, "I'm checking on my kittens," without so much as greeting or acknowledging Caleb, who was manning the front desk.

He stayed at the desk, finishing up the chart for his last patient that day, an Angora rabbit who really had no business living in an apartment, despite the owner's protestations that she had set up a huge rabbit habitat. He listened carefully, but the back room, where the kitten kennel was located, was too far away for Caleb to really hear anything. At any rate, all five kittens were close to the age at which they'd be adopted. All five were thriving and, fine, pretty dang cute. Giant still occasionally had trouble holding food down, but for the most part, he was doing just fine. He was smaller than his siblings, but he was scrappy and playful.

Caleb signed the chart, filed it away, and checked his email. Olivia came in, ready for her overnight shift. She and Caleb chatted until Lauren emerged.

"The kittens look good," said Lauren.

"They're all doing well," said Olivia. "We've gotten some potential interest for them. And I think Diane has fallen for Giant."

"Oh, good! It'll be good to have someone we trust taking him home."

"Well, I'm just going to pack up for the day," Caleb said, a little awkward in his delivery. Both women basically ignored him, so he got up and went to the back to get his bag without further ado.

When he emerged, Lauren was making a show of smiling and laughing with Olivia, but there wasn't much joy in Lauren's eyes. Which Caleb could tell now, because they'd gotten to know each other quite well.

"Well," he said. "Good night, ladies."

"I should get going, too," said Lauren. "Have a good night, Olivia."

Lauren followed Caleb out of the clinic. Once they were outside, she said, "Let's go to my place."

"Okay."

Without saying much, Caleb followed Lauren through the building's residential entrance and up the three flights of stairs to Lauren's apartment. She didn't really speak until they were both through the door and it was shut. Then she threw her handbag at the sofa and swung around to face him.

"Let's have it out," she said.

"All right." Caleb took a deep breath, steeling himself. They weren't even going to sit, he supposed. She'd picked her apartment because it was private enough for them to yell at each other, not because she wanted anything sexual to happen. Caleb suspected the days of them fighting and fucking were over.

The first thing Lauren said was, "Are you so determined for us to *not* be in a relationship that you can't even extend some courtesies to me when we work together? Are you really that paranoid?"

"So was ignoring me just now your revenge?"

"No, I… Well, maybe a little. But you were rude to me earlier."

Caleb rubbed his forehead. He hadn't made any conscious thought, in fact, paranoid or otherwise. "I brought you some cat food. It wasn't a social visit."

"I can't exist in this limbo. I hate it. I like you, I want to spend time with you, but I want to do it in the light of day. I don't want to feel like I have to be careful when I run into you in public. I want to greet you with a hug or something, like a girlfriend would, and not like we barely know each other. It feels like a betrayal of everything we've done together, and honestly, I don't understand why we're being secretive."

Because acting like they were in a relationship in public made it a real relationship, and Caleb wasn't ready for any such thing. "Public means commitment, doesn't it?"

"It can. I'm not saying love me forever. I don't know why you keep going to this weird place where us acting like we actually like each other means we have to get married. I know the ink on your divorce papers is still drying. I'm not trying to push you into anything. I just want to, like, have a drink with you at the bar I like down the street and not worry that if we laugh at something together and Evan sees it, you aren't going to freak out because he knows about us."

"Going public implies commitment. I don't like commitment. Commitments end. They crash and burn."

"Sure. Or you're throwing roadblocks in our way to sabotage us without giving us a chance."

"I thought you didn't want me to love you forever."

Lauren angry-hissed and spun in a circle. He hadn't seen her this genuinely angry in a while. Playfully angry, yes, but she was upset here. He felt a little bad about pissing her off, but this was also well-trod ground. Did she not understand him?

"I know you have some baggage," she said, frustration in her voice. "I know your divorce made you wary of trusting people. But if you don't want to be in a relationship, don't be in one."

Caleb opened his mouth to say he wasn't, but he recognized that was a lie. He and Lauren had definitely crossed a line into being in some kind of relationship. He couldn't deny that anymore. So the question now was whether it was a relationship he wanted to be in or one he should walk away from.

He didn't know.

"It's a risk," he said, trying to sound calm. "If we decide this is a real relationship, that *is* a commitment. It's a commitment to being with each other and seeing where it goes. And I don't trust commitment. I once stood in front of my friends and family and committed to love Kara forever, and she still left me."

"You can't let that rule the rest of your life."

"It's not that I want to! It's been less than a year, though, and I need more time. I can't do a big commitment right now. I hear what you're saying, but I can't."

He watched the emotion play out on her face. She looked disappointed and angry and maybe a little relieved. Then she said, "Then what are we even doing?"

"What are you saying?"

"The limbo? It doesn't work for me. We're either going to be together in public, or we aren't going to be together at all. Otherwise, it's too strange. I don't want to be your dirty secret, and I don't want you to be mine. If I'm going to be in a relation-ship, I want it to be one I can talk about with my friends. I want it to be with someone who I can greet without worrying about giving something away. I want it to be with someone I can exchange PDAs with, someone who wants to get drinks at Pop and dinner at Elizabeth's and be affectionate with me in those places. I don't want to just eat takeout at each other's apart-ments and have sex. That was fun for a bit, but it's not fulfilling to me now."

Caleb understood where she was going with this. He didn't want things to end, though. He just wanted more time to make up his mind. To see if there was the kind of potential between him and Lauren to make this into something that might be worth risking his heart on. Right now, he still didn't know if the risk would be worth it.

"I can't give you what you want," he said softly.

"Well, then here's where we are. Either you're with me all the way, or you're not with me at all."

That hung in the air for a moment. Being with Lauren might make him happy…until she met someone else. Until she grew frustrated with him. Until she dumped him. Given that they worked in close enough proximity to each other for things to get awkward, it would probably be better to end things cordially, so they could get along when they had to.

Although they didn't do a great job of getting along as it was.

"I've enjoyed spending time with you," he said. "We're great in bed together, and we've had some fun. But we hardly get along out of bed at all. We still have dumb fights all the time. How can we possibly have a strong relationship if we're barely friends outside of a bedroom?"

"So that's it then. You want to end things."

He sighed. "I don't *want* to end things. I want things to stay as they are. But if that's not enough for you, then maybe I should just go."

"You should just go then."

But he didn't want to. His feet felt glued to the floor. "Why now?"

"You really think we can just go on doing whatever it was what we were doing indefinitely? Having sex because we're attracted to each other even though we clearly can't stand each other?"

"Is that still true, though? Seems to me we get along more often than we don't."

"Except here we are, fighting again. A relationship shouldn't be this...acrimonious."

"A relationship can be whatever we make it."

"Except a private affair." Lauren sighed. "That's not working for me. Was it working for you?"

"It worked fine."

Lauren sat on the sofa finally. She rubbed her forehead. "You told me you didn't used to be such a jerk. That you were jaded because of your divorce. And the last couple of weeks, I thought I saw some of the old you. We had fun together. You even seemed happy sometimes. But maybe I was wrong. Maybe you really are this cold, stoic jerk. You wanted to get your rocks off and nothing more."

"Come on, Lauren. It was more than that."

"But you're not willing to give me much more than that. So just...whatever it was we had? You didn't want it to be a relationship, so it isn't. We're done here. Please leave."

"Lauren..."

"Don't try to argue that this is anything more than it is. We had a good run. I had fun. No hard feelings. But get out."

"So you're giving me an ultimatum. A real relationship or nothing at all."

"That's exactly what I'm doing. And I hate to give you an ultimatum like that, but I can't keep pretending the in-between is working. So I'm calling it off. We'll each go off on our merry ways. You can go be bitter somewhere else."

"It's over."

"If it ever even started."

Caleb nodded once. They got along great between the sheets but not out of them. That wasn't something to stake a future on. Especially not when he couldn't trust that Lauren wouldn't one day break his heart just as Kara had. "Fine. Nice knowing you."

Then he let himself out.

CHAPTER 23

CALEB WOKE UP TO HANK licking his face. He laughed for a moment, then pushed Hank aside. "That's enough, boy."

A quick glance at the clock told Caleb his alarm wasn't set to go off for another fifteen minutes, but attempts at falling back to sleep proved futile.

Lauren's words from the day before echoed in his head. He'd made the right decision, though. She wanted to change the terms of their relationship, and he hadn't been ready for that. He didn't want to be in a relationship at all.

Then why was he so sad?

He got up and tried to shake it off. He went for a run with Hank, taking his usual route through the neighborhood, then around Cadman Plaza near the courthouses, then back home. He passed a lot of the same joggers he saw every morning, and in a lot of ways, the morning felt routine. But also totally different.

After his shower, he got dressed in his typical work uniform of khakis and an oxford shirt. He slipped into his comfortable loafers—comfy shoes were a must for any veterinarian, since he spent so much time on his feet—gave Hank a few more pets, snapped the leash on, and then he and Hank walked out the door.

He followed his usual route to work. He walked this way three or four mornings a week, and often passed the same people. He tended not to register people's faces, but he knew all the dogs along this route. There was a black Lab mix with white feet that pulled an old lady in a housecoat around the neighborhood. There was a huge brown chow chow that looked like a bear; Caleb never saw the owner because he was always so startled by the dog. A teenage girl walked a Shiba Inu around Borough Hall every morning and a middle-aged guy who always looked tired walked a German shepherd closer to Whitman Street. Vet clinic patients stopped him on the street sometimes to say good morning.

When he got to Whitman Street, he paused near the café entrance. He'd been getting coffee there the last few mornings so he could say hello to Lauren in the mornings, which seemed silly in retrospect. Since Hank was with him, he decided to take his chances with the coffee in the vet clinic waiting room.

Hank made himself at home in the lobby. He nagged Rachel and the other vet tech on duty to pet him and entertained patients as they came in.

"I used to work at a vet clinic that had a cat who lived in the lobby," Rachel told him. "It's kind of fun having a dog. You should bring him more often. He could be, like, our mascot."

"I might just do that," said Caleb. He hadn't thought through the decision to bring Hank today, he'd just done it, but he supposed he needed a little companionship.

His morning included a cat with behavioral issues and a dog

with a splinter in his paw. Everything felt very routine, except it didn't, because he wouldn't be seeing Lauren today and there was no potential for them to hook up tonight and he was quite disappointed by that.

Well, more than disappointed, if he was honest.

It was a cat-heavy day. He was giving a booster shot to a tabby cat that afternoon when the thought entered his head that maybe he'd been hasty with Lauren. Maybe he should have just done what she wanted and seen where their relationship might have gone. But, no, he'd been right, he wasn't ready for that.

This was verified later when a woman came in with an orange cat. Caleb didn't recognize her at first, until she said, "I'm so glad I found you. You were the only vet Stanley could tolerate."

"You were a patient at the old clinic in Manhattan?"

"Yes. Coincidentally, I just moved to Park Slope, and this is not so far from there. I was sorry to hear you closed. What happened?"

"Ah, well, my wife and I got divorced. My wife-slash-business partner."

"Oh, right, the other Dr. Fitch. I never liked her. Stanley used to hiss at her something awful."

Caleb peered at Stanley. He sat with his paws tucked under him on the stainless-steel table, his eyes half-closed, looking perfectly calm. Caleb stroked his back.

"I like this practice, though," Caleb said, and he meant it. "The other vets here are all very nice and good to work with. Because this is a bigger practice, they have more resources."

"And you're right next to the Cat Café. My friend, Nancy,

and I have been going there once a week. It's delightful. Have you been there?"

"I have."

"The manager is super cute. What's her name? Lola?"

"Lauren."

"Yes. Lovely woman. Loves cats almost as much as I do." The woman laughed.

After that appointment, Caleb retreated to Olivia's office for a few minutes to gather his thoughts before his next patient. He sat on the sofa. Hank trotted in after him and rested his chin on Caleb's thigh. Caleb petted his head and took a deep breath. This was all a reminder how much better off he was now. He hadn't heard from Kara since she'd left town, aside from one call from her lawyer because she was looking for her grandmother's china, which he didn't have. The china was, in fact, in a storage unit that was still in Kara's name, a quick investigation turned up. And Caleb had decided if the woman he once loved with his whole heart was going to communicate with him only via her lawyer, well, it was well and truly over.

And maybe there'd been a lot he hadn't seen, warning signs he hadn't paid attention to, things he hadn't wanted to know about Kara. He hadn't noticed her unhappiness, just like he didn't notice the faces of the people who walked their dogs by him in the morning. And maybe she hadn't been the person he'd thought she was, because that person never would have just left him.

And really, it wasn't that he didn't trust commitment. He didn't trust himself and his own judgment. He'd chosen poorly with Kara. How could he be sure he wasn't choosing poorly again with Lauren?

Caleb took Hank back to the lobby, where he immediately made friends with a huge mastiff who let out a heavy "*woof*" before he and Hank sat beside each other, their tails wagging wildly. Caleb walked to the back room to check on the animals being housed there. Olivia had tacked up a list on the kennel where Lauren's kittens frolicked, each cat next to a person interested in adopting them. Caleb recognized most of the names as patients at the clinic, and of course, there was Diane listed next to Giant. In another week or so, these adoptive pet parents could come pick up their kittens, all of whom would likely grow into happy cats. Giant walked over to the edge of the pen and stuck his paw through the slats, as if he were trying to swipe at Caleb.

Caleb probably deserved it. He knew he'd hurt Lauren. He hadn't wanted to. He'd liked things being loose and easy. Why had she needed to qualify it?

He walked over to a dog who'd had to have surgery to remove a benign tumor from his leg; currently he was snoozing in a kennel off to the side. He checked the wound, which was healing well. Poor guy had a cone of shame around his neck, though, since as soon as anyone took it off, the first thing he did was chew on his stitches. There was also a young cat who had just been spayed who was sleeping off the rest of her anesthesia before the owners came to pick her up.

As Caleb updated the animals' charts to show he'd checked on them, Rachel knocked on the doorframe. "Your four o'clock is here."

"Remind me what it is again?"

"Elderly cat who has been vomiting a lot."

"Lovely." He sighed. "Feels like a metaphor for my whole day."

"At least you didn't have to hear about it from the panicked pet owner in excruciating detail this morning."

Caleb laughed. "I love my job."

Rachel smiled. "I know. Good luck!"

The morning rush wasn't enough of a distraction for Lauren not to notice Caleb pause outside the front window on his way to work. He didn't stop in, though.

Because they were no longer seeing each other.

The rest of the morning played out the way many did. Lauren helped out at the counter by bagging pastries while Monique and Trevor, one of the new baristas, made espresso drinks and handled the cash register. The crowd petered out a little after ten, at which point Lauren went to check on the cats. A few customers drifted in through lunchtime. A few of the freelancers from the neighborhood had taken to working out of the café a few days a week, and a woman who lived up the block took over one of the sofas to read with a cat in her lap. Boudicca, the brave warrior cat, escaped the cat room, and Paige had to chase her past the counter but caught her just before she got to the other door.

In other words, it was a typical day, but it felt atypical, because she had nothing to look forward to after work.

And that was something that had somehow happened over the

last few weeks. She either caught Caleb and invited him over, or she walked home with him after work, or they texted each other during the day and made plans to meet later, and she'd grown to really look forward to the time they spent together. Not just the sexy parts, although those were very good, but also the time they just spent talking over takeout.

Caleb protested too much when he'd pointed out that they didn't get along well outside of bed. They did, actually, or had been lately. They got along just fine. They sometimes got into arguments about things they were both passionate about, but she'd thought they both understood the arguments were playful at times, a kind of foreplay. They'd had the argument the day before about Caleb being rude, but that was part of the bigger issue, wasn't it? She'd been upset because, had they been a normal couple, he would have come in, they would have greeted each other fondly, maybe exchanged hugs or quick kisses, and he would have done more than essentially dumping some food in the storage room before brushing her off to go back to work. The whole interaction had rubbed her the wrong way. That was why she'd been upset.

But it wasn't that she didn't *like* Caleb. She liked him a great deal. She wanted to be with him.

And that was the kicker, wasn't it? She'd sent him away, but she still wanted him.

She was sitting at a café table and staring into space when Sunday hopped up on the table and lifted a paw to get Lauren's attention.

"Hi, little girl," Lauren said, giving Sunday a few pets on the head. "Did you know I was sad? Did you come to cheer me up?"

Sunday rubbed her head against Lauren's chin, so Lauren took that as a yes. Cats were intuitive, in her experience. When she was home and not feeling well, either physically or emotionally, Molly would come out of hiding to sit with her, or snooze on top of her as she lay on her couch. And now that Sunday was giving Lauren attention, Sadie must have felt left out, and she showed up to rub against Lauren's legs.

"Thanks, ladies. I appreciate all the love."

Lauren laughed as Caesar walked over, his whiskers twitching as he sniffed and tried to suss out the situation.

"You cats are not doing a very good job of keeping up your reputation for being snooty and rude."

Paige walked over. "Did you bathe in tuna today?"

Lauren laughed. "You would think. Not sure what merited all this attention."

Paige sat and reached over to pet Sunday. "Monique wanted me to pass on that we broke some kind of record this morning. A hundred and fifty more dollars than yesterday, plus we sold out of nearly every pastry."

"Excellent. Not sure what we're going to feed people this afternoon, but that's very good news." And it was. Lauren was buoyed somewhat by the business she ran doing well.

"I can run over to Little Red Bird and buy them out of some of their cookies or something."

"Good plan."

"You doing okay, boss? You've seemed a little down today."

"Yeah, I'm fine."

"Okay. I'll go see what Little Red Bird has."

"Take some cash from the till. Maybe sixty bucks. Leave a note explaining how much you took and why so I remember when I'm counting it later."

"No problem."

When Paige was gone, Lauren sat with the cats. Sunday was purring hard as she rubbed against Lauren. Her thoughts, of course, drifted back toward Caleb.

She really liked him. Maybe issuing the ultimatum had been a mistake. They could have worked something out. Or if she'd given him the time he wanted, he might have come around. Because she felt happy when they were together, and there was always a little bit of magic in the air, and she wanted to spend more time with him, and...

Oh, shit, she was in love with him.

Well, okay, maybe it wasn't love exactly, but she'd definitely developed stronger feelings than she'd been willing to acknowledge. She liked him. She *really* liked him.

She sighed. This was exactly what she had not wanted to happen. She was supposed to be focusing on herself, first of all, but the fact that she'd fallen in love or something like it with a grouchy veterinarian who wasn't interested in a relationship seemed like exactly the wrong thing to do. And yet, she'd done it anyway, and then she'd told him to leave.

Because it was very likely he never would have come around. Because of some stupid ideas he had about commitment, he never would have wanted to be with her in any way except behind closed doors. And that was a good reason to break up with him, if "break up" was even the right term for ending something that hadn't ever really started. They didn't want the same things out of life, out of their relationship. They liked each other a lot, but Caleb didn't care about her, not the way she cared about him. Otherwise, he would have fought for her. Right?

Or he didn't think he was worthy of love, maybe. That moment a few nights ago when he'd mumbled he was fucked up, maybe that meant he'd taken the wrong lesson from his divorce. His ex-wife had hurt him. Maybe part of him thought he'd deserve that. But why?

Well, it wasn't Lauren's job to get to the bottom of that—a mental health professional would have been more qualified—but she also didn't want to keep having the same fight. If he didn't want to be with her, then fine. They wouldn't be together.

Ugh, what a mess. Lauren leaned back in the chair a little and pet the cats that surrounded her, trying to take solace in the fact that many other things in her life were going very well.

But it was a truism of city life that the three most important things were career, housing, and love, and at any given time, one of those things would not work. Lauren couldn't remember who had told her that—Evan, probably—but it had long been true for her. During the Derek years, she'd had a good apartment and a good boyfriend but a crappy job. And now, she had a job she loved and was good at and a great apartment she paid so little for it was practically a crime, but her love life was a mess. So this was all in order.

She grunted. Well, if things with Caleb wouldn't work out, she could at least devote herself to the cats. She gently moved Sunday away and then stood up. "Which of you cats wants a treat?" As if they all understood English, they followed her like she was the pied piper toward the storage bin where the treats were kept.

CHAPTER 24

THAT FRIDAY, LAUREN, EVAN, PAIGE, and Lindsay convened for end-of-the-week drinks at Pop.

"So," said Lindsay, "a friend of mine is starting a website for Brooklyn pet owners and is trying to get me to work for her full time. Since you guys are the cat people, I figured I'd get your opinions."

"Because web start-ups are always cash cows," said Evan, "you're of course going to turn her down."

"I mean...yeah. I think so. But it might also be interesting. I like writing about food, but it might be refreshing to write about something else. Plus she wants some help with research and marketing."

"I would never tell you not to go to work for a friend," Paige said, "but that sounds a little sketchy. Does the website have income?"

"From ads, I assume."

"How long has she been in business?"

"A few months." Lindsay sighed. "That's what's giving me

pause. I should probably stick with writing restaurant reviews for now. I don't think my friend is making enough to pay me much. She has implied that the per-article fee could go up when she starts making money, but right now she wants me to work for a low fee and 'exposure,' and I can't afford to work for that. At least restaurant reviews pay really well."

"That's something. Anything good coming up?" asked Evan.

Lindsay shrugged. "My boss at *Dine Out NY* wants me to go to that new hipster food court on Nevins and try all the offerings there."

"Hipster food court?" said Lauren.

"Yeah. You know. It's a fancy food court. Someone bought a store that used to be a laundromat and converted it into a big open space that looks like a warehouse, and there are a half-dozen food booths around the inside perimeter. And it's not, like, normal food court food. No soft pretzels or fast food or any of that. If I remember correctly, there's a ramen restaurant, a sushi place, a taqueria, a Filipino place, and a couple of other things."

"Oh," said Evan. "Is it the Filipino chain with the ramen burger? I can't remember what it's called. They have one over by my apartment."

Lauren laughed. "I feel like I'm on a different planet. Ramen burger?"

"They make the bun out of ramen noodles, then instead of ground beef, the meat in the middle is pork belly, and there's also some kind of secret sauce. It's a sodium bomb with I'm sure, like, seven thousand calories, but it's *so* good."

"Anyway…" said Lindsay. "The food court just opened on

Nevins near the intersection with Whitman Street, so I've been assigned to try one thing from each restaurant and write it up."

"Uh, if you need any help with that, I'm your man," said Evan.

"Noted."

"Well, this makes me feel better about everything," said Evan.

"What's going on with you?" Lauren asked.

"Absolutely nothing, which is kind of the problem. I met a nice fellow at the library last week, of all places. We got to talking about our mutual love of this esoteric book I read last month. I thought it was going well. Then his girlfriend came by to pick him up."

Everyone groaned.

"I'm sorry, honey," Lauren said, patting his arm.

"And what about you, Lauren. You're a few martinis into the evening. You feel up to sharing anything?"

Lauren wanted to talk about what happened, but she didn't even know how to start. To stall, she said, "What do you mean?"

"You think you're pulling a fast one over on old Evan, but let me tell you, things have been super weird between you and Caleb all week, and I want to know why. He referenced some conversation you had when he came by the other day, and I want to know what you talked about."

"Wow," said Paige. "That's bossy of you."

"You have to admit, you must be curious."

Lauren sighed. Caleb was right, she was a little tipsy. There was just enough vodka in her system to make her think telling the truth was a good idea. "Okay, I'll tell you everything, but don't be mad."

Evan crossed his arms over his chest, like he felt vindicated.

So she gave them the *Reader's Digest* version: She and Caleb had been secretly sleeping with each other for nearly six weeks now, and they'd been spending a ton of free time together, Lauren thought they were finally getting somewhere and thought he'd be willing to go public with their relationship, but he'd balked, so she'd ended it.

"I'm so sorry for not telling you guys," she concluded, "but I was trying to follow Caleb's wishes and he wasn't ready for us to go public."

Evan, Paige, and Lindsay were silent. Evan and Paige glanced at each other.

"Well, that wasn't what I expected," Evan said.

"Are you mad?"

"No, of course not," said Paige. "It's up to you what you feel comfortable telling your friends."

"I mean, I'm a little mad," said Evan. "We usually share these kinds of things."

"Just because you're an oversharer doesn't mean Lauren has to be," said Lindsay.

"Fine. I'll forgive you, Lauren, if you buy the next round."

Lauren laughed, despite feeling tense. "All right. But the thing is, I wonder if I made a mistake."

"In what way?" asked Evan.

"I mean, I really like him. I think I was most of the way toward falling in love with him. And I gave him an ultimatum, which is so unlike me. But I needed him to make a decision about whether we were going to be together for real or not. I guess I got my answer."

"Yeah," said Paige.

"But I keep wondering if we could have worked things out if I'd just given him more time, or if I had been more understanding. I mean, he did *just* get divorced. Like, maybe we would have been something really great if I hadn't pushed him away."

Everyone appeared to think on that for a moment.

"No," said Paige. "He doesn't deserve you."

Lauren sighed. "Really?"

"If he can't see how amazing you are, then he's a fool, and you should not be with a fool."

"I agree," said Lindsay. "It sounds like he was never going to commit. You can't wait around forever for him to figure things out. You were together for all those weeks. Shit or get off the pot, man."

Lauren laughed. "Gross, but thanks?"

Evan looked at them all, his head tilted as if he was thinking hard.

"Well?" Lauren asked.

"I don't want to say I told you so, but… I did tell you so. All those times we saw you fighting, you were really fighting and then finding a closet to fuck in, weren't you?"

Lauren felt heat flood her face. "Maybe."

"I don't need details. This just goes to prove my larger theory that the two of you were basically meant for each other."

"This is not helpful, Evan. You want me to go back to him?"

"No. Not at all. He's an idiot if he can't see that you're the right woman for him. But maybe this is an absence-makes-the-heart-grow-fonder thing. In fact, I hereby predict our dear Caleb will realize how dumb he was to let you go and come back with some big romantic gesture, and you, my dear, will swoon, and then marry him so hard, and I will expect my ten dollars paid in cash."

"Evan, that's insane." Lauren didn't see Caleb coming around. Because keeping his distance would have been the easy thing. Relationships were hard. They took effort and commitment and time. They were wonderful, too, or Lauren wouldn't be mourning the (non-)relationship with Caleb as much as she was, but likely Caleb was guilty of the same thing. It was easier not to get involved, not to put oneself out there, not to risk anything.

Caleb was right. Commitment was a risk. But it was a risk that had the potential to pay off in a wonderful way. Lauren was willing to take that risk, but if Caleb wasn't, they were at an impasse.

"So what do you think I should do?" Lauren asked.

"Nothing," the other three said in unison.

"Even you, Ev? You think I should do nothing."

"Wait for him to come to you. Which he totally will. Because destiny."

"You're so full of shit," said Lindsay. "The world doesn't work that way."

"All right. I want ten bucks from you when I'm right, too."

Paige rolled her eyes. "How are you doing?" she asked Lauren, putting a comforting hand on Lauren's arm.

"I'm all right. Sad that it's over. More time to focus on the café, though."

"It's not over," said Evan.

"We're definitely going to need more drinks," said Lindsay as she flagged down a waitress.

Caleb's thoughts unraveled in the shower.

He did his best thinking there, probably because there weren't many distractions and he could autopilot through the process.

So after his morning run, he stood under the spray and let his mind wander. At first, he was just planning his day. His shift today would end at five, and after that, maybe he could grab Lauren and get dinner somewhere...

Well, no, he couldn't do that.

And he was doing the overnight the following day, so he should probably just come home and rest in preparation.

Why did he want to see Lauren so much anyway? They weren't together anymore. He'd made the right decision to end things because he couldn't do a commitment.

Maybe there was someone else he could go out for drinks with tonight. Maybe Rachel would want to...or whichever other vet was working today...

But he hadn't really reached out to this community much, had he? Because the block of Whitman Street that held the vet clinic was its own ecosystem, in a way. Most of the vets seemed to know everyone on the block. The Cat Café was doing collaborative events with the yarn store and the bookstore. Lauren did her laundry at the big laundromat up the block and he'd spotted Paige going in and out of the high-end thrift store quite a bit. Caleb got lunch at the corner bodega all the time because the deli counter made a pretty solid sandwich.

He was friendly with the other vets, but they didn't socialize much outside of work. He could probably invite Doug or Olivia for a post-work drink as an overture—Lauren liked that bar Pop, right?—and he could develop those friendships.

But the person he most wanted to spend more time with was Lauren.

He sighed and shampooed his hair.

He had some regrets. Lauren really hadn't been asking him for more than just the opportunity to explore where their relationship went. He didn't trust his own judgment where romance was concerned, but he did really like Lauren. She was beautiful and passionate and she cared a lot about all those cats.

What did his gut tell him?

As he got out of the shower, he realized he wanted Lauren. He could fall in love with Lauren.

And wasn't that a kick in the teeth? All these weeks of trying to keep her at arm's length, and at some point, she'd worked her way under his skin, to the point where he couldn't stop thinking about her, couldn't stop imagining what their next encounter might be like. She was on his brain all through his morning run, through the shower, and now as he got dressed. She was always on his mind.

He was an idiot.

As he walked to work that morning with Hank, he tried to think of what to do. Let her go? Take the fact that he'd been so reluctant to say *yes* as a sign he wasn't ready for a relationship and he'd made the right decision? Or should he try to fight for her?

He knew better than to think he could just walk up to her and say he'd changed his mind, though. Or could he?

She was, in fact, standing outside the Cat Café when he got

to Whitman Street. She didn't see him at first because she was intently focused on her phone. But Hank started barking as soon as he saw her, and she looked up.

"Oh. Hi," she said.

"Hi. How are you?"

"I've been better." She focused back on her phone and tapped at it angrily a couple of times.

"So, uh…" he tried.

"Sorry, I'm dealing with a pastry crisis right now. One of our vendors is super late with their delivery and we're not going to have anything to feed people soon if I can't track them down. My contact says the delivery guy left twenty minutes ago, which is clearly a lie, because the bakery is only a ten-minute drive, tops."

"All right. Good luck."

Caleb shifted toward the door to the vet clinic. Lauren brought her phone to her ear as he slipped through the door.

He couldn't tell if she'd been short with him because she didn't want to see him or because of the pastry crisis, so he decided to drop by the Cat Café on his lunch break to clear the air. It was probably the wrong thing to do; he'd rarely stopped by the café when they'd actually been seeing each other.

But he couldn't help himself.

She was standing near the counter, talking to Monique, both of them all smiles. Apparently the pastry crisis had been solved. But Lauren frowned when she saw Caleb.

"Hi," he said. "Uh, regular coffee?"

"Sure," said Monique, going into action and grabbing a cup.

"What are you doing here?" Lauren asked.

"Getting a cup of coffee. And saying hello. You were a little preoccupied when I walked by this morning, so I just wanted to make sure you were okay."

"I'm fine." Lauren's tone was short and direct.

"Two dollars," said Monique, placing his coffee on the counter.

The pastry display was pretty stark, with only a single plain bagel and a couple of cookies.

"I'll take that last bagel. Toasted with cream cheese."

"Sure. That's another two-seventy-five."

"No problem." Caleb pulled a five from his wallet. The whole time he moved, Lauren stared at him like he'd grown a tail. While Monique dropped his bagel into the toaster, Caleb turned to Lauren and said, "Did your pastry delivery arrive?"

"Yeah. Later than I would have liked, but as you can see, we sold out."

"Glad that worked out."

"Who *are* you?" Lauren asked. "Do you want something?"

"No, I just came by because it's my lunch break. I'm trying to be sociable."

"But...why?"

So it wouldn't be easy to slip back into her life. She was wary of him, with good reason.

"Can we be friends, at least?" he asked.

Lauren glanced at Monique, who was now smearing cream cheese on Caleb's bagel. "I don't know," she said softly. "Probably not."

Well, that was an answer. If Caleb wanted to be with Lauren, he'd have to undo some of the damage he'd done. If that was what he wanted.

They stood there in awkward silence until Monique finished the bagel, wrapped it in deli paper, and put it next to Caleb's coffee on the counter. He handed her six dollars and told her to keep the change.

The thing was, Caleb still wanted Lauren. It was like his body was full of iron filings and Lauren was a big magnet. He wanted to touch her, hold her, kiss her right here with all the customers watching, but he also knew she would shiv him if he tried any of that now.

And that was all she'd wanted the whole time. For him to come in here on his lunch break and greet her as if they were dating, and to be a solid couple. And he'd fucked it up by telling her no.

"I'd better get back," Caleb said.

Lauren frowned at him. "You come in *now*?"

"I just wanted to say hi."

"Right. Well, don't let the door hit you on the way out."

So she was pissed. Would she even take him back?

Part of him wanted to find out.

He doctored his coffee and grabbed the bagel and walked back to the vet clinic. He should probably let it go. Avoid Lauren for a bit while the awkwardness subsided so they could work together again. Move on with his life and try to forget any of this ever happened. The timing was terrible, he wasn't ready, and he couldn't give Lauren what she wanted. He was doing the right thing here and resented Lauren a little for making him choose between something good and nothing.

Better to get out before they both got in deeper.

Even if it felt like agony to walk away.

CHAPTER 25

DIANE COOED OVER THE KITTEN pen. All but Giant had been brought to their forever homes, and Giant had been merely waiting for Diane to return from a quick jaunt out of town.

"This little guy grew fast!" Diane said.

"Kittens do that," Caleb said. "They eat like teenage boys, too."

"I got that kitten food you recommended."

"Good. Let me know if he has any trouble with it. We've been feeding him that food here and he's been doing okay, but if he stops eating or otherwise acts strangely, let me know. He may have grown out of his digestive issues, but if he hasn't, we've got some options."

Diane picked Giant up. He rubbed his little head against her chin. "Aw. Don't worry, Dr. Fitch. I'll take very good care of this little guy."

Caleb was surprised to feel a swell of protectiveness over this little cat. Lauren would probably tell him he was a marshmallow after all, because he felt a little squishy inside as he pet the kitten's head. He supposed he'd grown attached to Giant that night he and

Lauren had saved him, and he was glad Diane was adopting him and could give regular updates.

A cell phone rang. Diane said, "Here, hold him." She shoved Giant into Caleb's hands, so Caleb pet the kitten while Diane answered his phone. "Hello? Oh, hi, Lauren."

Caleb's heart rate spiked. He didn't want to feel this. He wanted to push it aside and move on with his life. Instead, he held his breath and leaned forward a little, hoping he could hear Lauren's voice on the other end of the call.

She sounded distressed. He couldn't really make out more than a few words here and there, but he did hear, "...trying to shut down the café."

"I'm just next door at the vet clinic," said Diane. "I'll be right there."

And because he couldn't help himself, when Diane hung up the phone, Caleb said, "What's going on?"

"You know that real estate developer who has been sniffing around here? Well, his squirmy little germophobe of an assistant has decided to bring an inspector from the health department to look at the Cat Café." Diane sighed and pocketed her phone. "He's trying to get the place shut down. I can't tell if this is some ill-thought-out ploy to make me lose income and sell the building, or if that squirrelly little assistant is just doing this for spite. I'm sure Randolph has pulled stunts like this with a dozen other landlords. But this asshole has never had to deal with me before."

Without giving it much thought, Caleb put Giant back in the kitten pen and followed Diane back out to the waiting room. Rachel stood and asked what was going on, so Caleb said, "Something's up at the Cat Café. I'm just going to make sure everything is okay. Be right back."

He and Diane walked next door. In front of the café counter, Lauren stood with her arms crossed as Newton stood right in front of her, his posture equally authoritative. Neither was speaking.

Diane hurried to Lauren's side. "What's happening here?"

Lauren gestured toward the counter. "Mr. Newton brought a health inspector. I keep telling him the cats are confined to the cat room and we're following the letter of the law here."

Caleb could see through the glass that a man in a suit was kneeling behind the counter, examining the pastry case.

"I'll call the lawyer," said Diane. She took a step away from Lauren and got out her phone. While she placed the call, Caleb looked over at Lauren, who was clearly distressed. She chewed on her thumbnail and watched the health inspector look through the pastry case.

"Looks clean here," said the inspector.

"There's no way they can have this many animals and not have a sanitary issue," said Newton. "There's a reason people can't bring their dogs into restaurants. It creates unsanitary conditions."

"My lawyer's on speaker," Diane said, placing her phone on the counter.

The inspector seemed disinterested in all of this. "I'm going to take a look at the cat room."

Lauren rubbed her forehead.

"The law says no animals in places that serve food," said Newton.

"We worked with the city to make sure everything was up to

code," said a male voice from the phone. "Because, actually, you can bring your dog into some bars. The law that passed last year allows for animals in places that serve food as long as the animals are kept away from where the food is prepared. The Whitman Street Cat Café goes a step further to keep the cats separate from where the food is served. And given that the café brings in food from outside and doesn't prepare anything except for coffee, there's no violation."

Caleb looked around for Sadie and saw no evidence of her, not even the cat bed that usually sat in the corner. Lauren had probably recognized Newton was out to shut down the Cat Café and had made sure they were in compliance with the law. Not that he was bothered by Sadie having free rein of the café space as long as she stayed away from the food. But that didn't appear to be the case here.

The inspector walked back into the café space.

"How frequently do the café tables get bussed?" he asked, hooking his thumb back toward the cat room.

"Often, but everyone is up here dealing with this right now," said Lauren.

"Er, if I may," said Caleb. "I'm a veterinarian from next door."

Everyone turned to look at him. Lauren look startled, like she hadn't known he was there.

Caleb took a deep breath. "Look, I'd be the first one to tell you there's something a little crazy about a cat café, but I can tell you in the two months I've worked next door, I've never known Lauren to do anything but keep this place clean and adhere to the letter of the law. Mr. Newton may not like the idea of animals living in the same building as a business that sells food, but he doesn't have to dine here if that's the case. There's nothing illegal happening here."

"I own this business," said Diane. "And I concur. If I thought Lauren was doing anything less than keeping the safety of both the cats and her customers paramount, I'd shut this place down myself."

"All right," said the inspector. He pulled a tablet from his bag and started tapping at the screen.

When Caleb turned to look at Lauren, she was staring at him.

Lauren assumed Caleb had come in with Diane from the vet clinic, but it was still alarming to see him standing there. How had she not noticed him walk into the café? And was he defending her?

"Do the cats ever walk around up front here?" asked the inspector.

"Not on purpose."

She glanced at Caleb. It would be just like him to tell the inspector that Sadie hung out up front sometimes. After the first time Mr. Newton had threatened to bring in health inspectors, Lauren had put Sadie's bed in the cat room and was better about keeping her in the cat room during regular business hours. It was the sort of bending of the law that was fairly common in the neighborhood, from what Lauren could tell. A lot of the restaurants let customers bring their dogs if they sat outside. There was a bar a few blocks away that let dogs in regularly. It was a law no one enforced as long as the customers were happy.

"What does that mean?" asked the inspector.

"Every now and then a cat gets out," said Paige. "You've met cats, I assume. You can't really tell them what to do. We always catch them and put them back in the cat room."

"Again," said the lawyer. "Strictly speaking, the only thing the law requires of us is keeping the cats out of the area where the food is prepared."

The inspector tapped at his tablet screen a few more times. Lauren looked at Newton, who looked irritated, but Lauren didn't think they were out of the woods. The inspector could still shut them down if he decided further investigation was warranted, or he could put them on probation and do random checks to make sure they were complying. A lot of outcomes could cause big problems for the café, especially if the morning rush crowd found another business while they were closed. That would be a hard thing to recover from.

But she knew she was in the right here, that she hadn't violated any laws. She'd be vindicated. Just maybe not with this Newton guy standing here.

The inspector looked up. "You're not using that kitchen in back?"

"No," said Lauren.

"If you decide to, we'll need to inspect again."

"Noted," said Diane.

"There's no violation here, is there?" asked Caleb. "I'd be willing to vouch for—"

"That's not necessary," said the inspector. "I don't see any violations here. Know that we can inspect again at any time, but I'm signing off on keeping your A rating from the health department and keeping this place open."

"Thank you," said Lauren.

"I'll send a copy of this to the email on file," said the inspector. "I think I'm done here. Have a nice day, everyone."

"Are you serious?" said Newton. "There's no way this is a safe situation. If a cat gets out and gets in the pastry case—"

"That won't happen if the café staff keeps the case closed." The inspector leveled his gaze at Monique.

"We always do," she said.

"You may not like it, Mr. Newton," the inspector said, "but the lawyer on the phone is right. They're adhering to the letter of the law here." He slid his table into his bag. "I've got other inspections today, so if you'll excuse me. Have a good day, everyone."

The inspector left the café. Newton looked furious. "If you think this is over—"

"Let me stop you right there," Caleb said calmly. Lauren looked at him, still astonished he was here.

"We all see what your game is here," Caleb went on. "You want to shut down the café so Diane has a financial incentive to sell. I think what you just learned is no one here is interested in selling and you can't shut down the café as easily as you think. So go back to your boss and tell him nice try, but this building is not for sale."

Diane laughed, sounding delighted. "What he said. Please leave, Mr. Newton. You are no longer welcome here."

Newton fumed for a moment, and then stormed out of the café.

Once he was gone, everyone cheered. Lauren pressed a hand over her chest, still not relaxed but feeling a bit relieved. "Thanks, everyone. I'm glad we got through that. For the record, we reserve the right to refuse service to Mr. Newton, should he come here again."

She took a step to go back toward her office so she could collect herself, but Caleb hooked his hand around her elbow. "Hey. Are you okay?"

She looked him over. Given how foolish he thought the café was, it was strange for him to defend it. He was probably defending his own livelihood; he'd mentioned that, if Randolph bought the building, he could very well level it and put the vet clinic out of business.

Except the singular thought in Lauren's head was, *What the hell is he doing here?*

"I'm fine," she said. "A little shaken up. If he had been able to shut us down just temporarily, the losses would be very hard to recover from." She realized his hand was still on her arm, and she looked at it, not sure how to process what was happening.

He pulled his hand away. "Diane and I were checking on Giant when you called. I overheard that the inspector was here so I thought I'd try to help."

"And I appreciate that, but Caleb, we're not—"

"No, I know." He smiled ruefully. "We're not even friends right now. That doesn't mean I can't worry about what's happening to you."

It wasn't that Lauren wanted Caleb to leave. She found his presence somewhat comforting and she was touched that he'd defended her. But now that the dust was settling, she felt awkward, and if Caleb didn't want a relationship, they had nothing to talk about.

Softly, she said, "Nothing has changed, has it?"

Caleb pressed his lips together. "I don't—"

"Right. You probably have patients."

"Yeah. Diane, should I put Giant in that carrier you brought down?"

Diane was on the phone, but she said, "Many thanks, Stuart," and hung up. "Yes, get Giant ready to go, but let him play for a few more minutes. I want to chat with the café staff. Then I'll be right over."

"All right."

Caleb left. Monique went back behind the counter and busied herself with wiping down everything. The customers had cleared out when the health inspector came in, so the only other people in the café were Paige and Diane. With a sigh, Laurén dropped into the nearest chair and put her head in her hands.

Diane reached over and pet her head, then sat in the chair across from her. "You did great, Lauren. And I told you guys I'm not selling. I meant it."

Lauren sat up. "Thanks. I know. Just... I worried that inspector would shut us down. I knew intellectually we've done nothing wrong, but all it would take is that one inspector who is allergic to cats and having a bad day. You know?"

"I do." Diane smiled. "That man cares about you a lot."

"Who, Caleb?"

"Really?" said Paige.

"Think about it. As soon as he heard you might be in trouble, he came right over. He defended you against the people who want to shut this place down. And he checked to make sure you were okay. He cares. A lot."

"What the hell is happening, then?" asked Lauren. He had defended her, even though he thought the café itself was silly. "Last week, he told me he didn't want a relationship. If he cares about me so much, why doesn't he want to be with me?" And then Lauren put a hand over her mouth because she couldn't believe she was saying all this to her boss.

But Diane was no ordinary boss. "Honey, I've been through this before. My relationship with Winnie got off to a rocky start. Why doesn't he want a relationship? A lot of reasons. He just got divorced, for one."

"So he keeps saying."

"Maybe he doesn't feel ready to commit. He's still too hurt from the divorce. Maybe he doesn't trust you. Maybe he doesn't believe he's worthy of you."

"That arrogant bastard?" Paige said. "Ha."

"I'm serious. I think that's a man who views his divorce as punishment. He may think he did something or he is a certain way that makes him unworthy of love. I mean, I'm just spitballing, I don't really know. I do know you were right: When he first started here, he was grumpy and closed off, but I've seen him soften in the last few weeks. He even smiles sometimes now. And he's very protective of that little kitten, Giant. It's like he doesn't want to let him go. It's very cute. Surely you agree."

Lauren rubbed her head. She didn't know what to believe anymore. She just knew the facts at hand. She and Caleb were great together, but he didn't want a relationship. He'd just told her nothing had changed. For her own sanity, she had to assume that was true.

Page shook her head. "He broke her heart. We don't like Caleb."

Diane laughed. "I wouldn't rule him out just yet. That's all I'm saying." She stood up. "Now I'm going to take that little kitten home. Assuming no one else tries to shut us down today, I'll see you all at the staff meeting tomorrow. Hang in there, Lauren."

What Diane said rang in Lauren's head long after Diane left. A little later, when she was bussing the tables in the cat room, Paige said, "I hate to say it, but I think Diane is wrong. There's no point in waiting around for Caleb if he doesn't want a relationship."

"I'm not waiting around."

"No, I know. Just... I don't know why he was here today, but he's a bigger scumbag than I thought if he's going to jerk around your heart like that."

Lauren laughed. "Thanks, Paige. I appreciate it. I'm just... ugh. I don't know what's going on with him. But I'm not going to sit around pining for him if he's not interested in me. So don't worry about that."

The words sounded more confident than Lauren felt. The more she thought about it, the more puzzling she found Caleb's behavior. It was likely he did care, but he thought he couldn't be in a relationship for whatever reason.

None of this mattered. If he didn't want to be with her, he didn't want to be with her.

With a sigh, she carried her bin full of dirty dishes back to the kitchen to run them through the dishwasher.

It wasn't her job to worry about Caleb.

CHAPTER 26

CALEB HAD A RARE TWO days off in a row. He spent the first one basically just bumming around his apartment, alternately napping and catching up on his DVR. On the second, he went to an exhibit about early color photography at the Brooklyn Museum that he and Lauren had talked about checking out together before they broke up. Caleb didn't know a lot about photography, but he thought the exhibit was interesting. As he walked around the rest of the museum, he couldn't help but think this would have been more fun to do with Lauren. She probably knew a lot about art that he didn't.

Everything went sideways shortly after he got home, when Kara called.

Without much preamble, she said, "I have a tax issue. I need some information from you."

Without putting up much of a fight, Caleb went to his computer and looked up the information she needed. When he was done, he said, "If that's all..."

"You've never been the type to easily forgive," said Kara.

"You want me to forgive you? To what end? You're in California, I'm in New York, we never speak anymore. You've got young Peter. What do you need me to forgive you for?"

"We were married for five years. Doesn't that mean something?"

"Apparently not. It didn't stop you from breaking your vows."

She grunted. "Could you not see how incompatible we were? Not at first, but... I changed. We both did. We had so much fun in the early days, but then we grew apart. You wanted your carefully detailed plan of work, kids, the perfect little house in the suburbs. I wanted travel and adventure."

"You could have talked to me about that."

"Would you have listened? The things I wanted weren't a part of your plan."

"You didn't give me a chance to revise the plan!"

"I didn't call you to fight."

It hit Caleb quite suddenly that Kara had made assumptions. She'd assumed Caleb was immovable. He might have resisted, but he would have listened to Kara. Maybe he wasn't the most flexible, but she hadn't even given him a chance to try.

Just like he hadn't given Lauren a chance.

He sighed. "Maybe there's some magical future where we can talk civilly again, but that time is not now. You *had an affair* and *left me* and destroyed the clinic we ran together. In what universe is that something I should just get over quickly? More to the point, you haven't been in touch with me at all except through your lawyers in eight months, and you're only getting in touch with me now because you need something. So don't pretend like this is some friendly overture. I can't talk to you right now."

"Just like Caleb. So fucking stubborn. Are you really so hurt you can't even talk to me?"

"Kara. It's not even that you left me. That alone is something I shouldn't forgive you for. It's that you didn't trust or respect me enough to come to me to talk to me about why you were unhappy. We never had a conversation. You made a decision without involving me. But I was your *husband*, Kara. You should have come to talk to me. You should have *trusted* me."

"Well, that's all over now. And if you're just going to yell at me, I have better uses for my time."

She hung up, which seemed right. Caleb sighed and put down his phone.

Was he just playing old tapes? Had Kara tried to tell him, but he'd just been too stubborn to hear it? Was he being too stubborn now?

Well...yes. He'd closed himself off from any kind of love or romance. He didn't trust anything. But was that fair? He was right to guard his heart, but he hadn't realized the degree to which he'd locked himself up.

Lauren had tried to pry him back open, and he hadn't let her.

But he wanted to. Was he really denying himself happiness because of some principle? Wouldn't it be better to see how things with Lauren went? Maybe it would implode, but wasn't it better to try than to become some hermit who cut himself off from everything? Because that wasn't working. He was lonely.

He went to sleep that night feeling resolved. Lauren was

unlikely to just forgive him after everything he'd said and done, but he wouldn't be able to live with himself if he didn't try to win her back. To give her a real chance this time. To trust her in a way Kara hadn't trusted him.

When Caleb rounded the corner to go to work the following Monday, Evan was leaning against the café window talking to a guy with dark hair. Evan appeared to be flirting heavily. It occurred to Caleb that, of Lauren's friends, Evan was the one she talked about the most and was probably closest to, so if anyone knew how to win her back, it was this man.

Caleb stalled in front of the yarn store and pretended to look at the display in the window, which, now that he looked at it, was pretty interesting. Someone had knit little dolls in sweaters who were settled on an orange sofa. It seemed to be a diorama showing a scene from *Friends*. And, okay, that was pretty darn cute.

When Caleb turned back, the dark-haired guy was walking away and Evan was watching him go. When the guy went into the bookstore, Evan sighed and looked around. His gaze settled on Caleb approaching.

"Hi," Caleb said.

"Hello. You should know, I'm contractually obligated to hate you. It's part of the best friend agreement."

Caleb's heart sank. This would be a challenge. "So she told you what happened."

"She did."

"That does put me at a disadvantage."

"You broke her heart, you know."

That was something Caleb had been afraid of. Even though

she'd been surprisingly glib about it, her anger every time they ran into each other indicated that he'd hurt her more than he'd initially realized. This might mean she wasn't reachable anymore, that she was too angry to forgive him. "I do know. I regret that."

Evan narrowed his eyes at Caleb. "Why are you talking to me?"

His tone wasn't accusatory so much as curious. Caleb decided to interpret that as a door opening.

"Well, you were standing here, for one thing," said Caleb. "But I do want to talk to you."

"All right. About?"

"I think I made a mistake."

"A mistake?"

"I shouldn't have let her go."

A smile spread slowly across Evan's lips. He looked like a child who just caught on that his mother had bought him that candy bar after all. "So what I hear you saying is you want to make a big romantic gesture to win back Lauren's heart, and you would like my help to do it."

Evan's enthusiasm was startling. "Yes. But if you're contractually obligated to hate me, why are you being so nice?"

Evan waved his hand dismissively. "You and Lauren are meant to be. I could tell all along. I would be happy to help you. Do you have time right now?"

"Well...I am a little early for work. I can give you maybe twenty minutes."

"That's not much time. Hmm." Evan looked up and down the block. "Obviously, we can't do our plotting in the Cat Café. But there's an evil chain coffee place on Bergen, a few blocks south of here, if you don't mind walking a little."

"Lead the way."

After he had a rough plan, Caleb walked back to work, swinging by the big chain pharmacy on the corner down the block from the vet clinic. He was full of caffeine, but he wanted some candy or something, a high-calorie way to calm his nerves.

He mulled over his choices and thought about what Evan had said. The trick would be for Caleb to demonstrate he'd been an idiot, and that he cared for Lauren and wanted to be with her and was willing to see where this led.

There'd been a moment early in his relationship with Kara, back in vet school. They'd had to spend the day at a horse farm, tending to a horse whose owner was convinced the horse had colic and would need to be put down. Caleb was quickly able to determine it was just indigestion because the owner's kids had been feeding the poor horse all manner of junk when the owner wasn't looking. And once that puzzle was solved and Caleb had saved the day, he and Kara had waited in the stall for the bad food to pass to make sure he was right.

Sitting around a stall waiting for a horse to poop was not exactly the most romantic of settings, but they'd gotten to talking.

"What do you see yourself doing after graduation?" Caleb had asked.

"Not sure. What do you see yourself doing?"

"I figured I'd open a practice somewhere. Maybe in Boston, or in the suburbs. Or I could go back to Maine. Lots of retirees are moving into the area outside Portland where my parents live, I bet a lot of them have pets."

Kara had given him a scathing look. "Really? Taking care of the pets of the elderly? Gee, that sounds exciting."

"What would you do?"

"Oh, I don't know. I could see myself opening a practice in Manhattan and taking care of the purse dogs of the rich and famous. Or I'd travel. I don't want kids, just so you know, but I would like to see the world."

It was an odd thing to think about. Kara had been right on the phone the other day. Part of him hadn't heard her when she'd said she didn't want kids. Or he'd told himself he didn't need them even though he'd always pictured himself as a father. As long as he and Kara were happy, he could revise his life plan, because he knew as well as anyone that plans were not predictions.

Did Lauren want kids? Did she have plans? Caleb wanted to know. And he'd listen this time. He'd learn from his mistakes instead of letting his mistakes rule him.

Now, as Caleb stared at a display of chocolate from around the world, he realized there had been a fundamental incompatibility from the beginning. Caleb liked to travel...on vacation. He'd rather have stability. He'd rather have family nearby. Instead, following Kara around like a lovesick puppy had stranded him in Brooklyn, three hundred miles from his family, working at an urban practice. It wasn't how he saw his life going. He wasn't upset about it per se; he did really like the Whitman Street Clinic and the other vets who worked there. And Brooklyn was charming in a way he hadn't expected. He could see himself potentially having a life like the one he'd once envisioned here in Brooklyn.

But he'd been too jaded to see that, too upset at Kara for ending everything, too angry to see Lauren was perhaps willing to give him the family he'd wanted once upon a time.

He hadn't thought about that conversation in years. A family and a practice taking care of the pets in a community. If he was willing to get over himself and trust in the potential for something great with Lauren on Whitman Street, he could have that.

He grabbed a bag of gummy bears and headed back toward the counter, cutting through an aisle of travel size products. Then something colorful caught his attention.

It was a display of luggage tags and keychains with tags cut into unusual shapes. The luggage tags were shaped like dresses or sunglasses or flip-flops. The keychains were mostly shaped like New York landmarks. But there was one keychain that had a tag shaped like a suitcase.

And he heard Lauren's voice in his head, yelling at him about his baggage.

He took the keychain from its hook and headed for the register.

CHAPTER 27

LAUREN SAT IN HER OFFICE, staring at a computer monitor and trying to balance the account books to put together a report for Diane. She wasn't ready to let go of the idea of possibly hiring a pastry chef, even though actually using the kitchen to prepare food was probably asking for Randolph and Newton to try to shut them down again. Still, a girl could dream.

Paige stuck her head in the door. "There's someone here who is interested in adopting a cat. I thought you might want to talk to him."

"You can't handle it?" Lauren slid away from her desk and opened a drawer. She pulled out a manila envelope. "All the forms are in here."

"You aren't curious about which cat he's interested in?"

"I mean, I am, but my numbers aren't adding up right for some reason. I think I mistyped a digit somewhere. It's only off by a few dollars, but..."

"Lauren? Boss lady? Please take a break. I think you'll want to talk to this customer."

Paige smiled in a way that made the dimple on her left cheek prominent, which made Lauren think she was up to something. Was the customer a celebrity? That had happened a couple of times. There were a few pretty big actors who lived in the neighborhood, and sometimes they popped in to check out the Cat Café. Lauren had seen the hot young star of a popular HBO show on the street a number of times in the last couple of weeks, and it was plausible he wanted a cat.

"Yeah, all right. Give me one second."

Lauren scanned the column of numbers again, finally found where she'd made a mistake, and fixed the error. When the formula recalculated the numbers, the balance came out correctly. She let out a breath.

"We're still in the black for this month," she said to Paige.

"I'm glad. Come on."

Lauren followed Paige out to the cat room. On the way, she tried to remember all of the famous people who lived in the neighborhood to narrow down who this might be. Maybe it was the mayor. Or a popular writer; there were a few of those in the neighborhood, too.

But, Lauren saw when she arrived in the cat room, it was actually Caleb.

Paige stepped away. Lauren looked around the room and noticed Lindsay and Evan were there, too, standing off to the side and grinning.

"What is happening?" Lauren asked. "There's no way on earth Caleb is going to adopt a cat, and the way you all are smiling makes me think I've been betrayed."

Monique walked over. "Dr. Fitch has filled out the paperwork for cat adoption," she said, handing over a form.

"*Et tu*, Monique?" Lauren took the form and scanned it.

The top part contained Caleb's name, address, and contact information. But in the box under *Why are you interested in adopting a cat?*, he'd written, *Because I made a terrible mistake and I want Lauren to know I'm sorry and I want her back.*

"Are you kidding me with this?" she asked, holding up the form. It felt like a cruel joke. She'd been trying so hard for the last week to push Caleb from her mind, because it was clear nothing would happen between them, and here he was with some jokey cat adoption form.

Caleb frowned. "All right, you got me, I'm not really here to adopt a cat."

Lauren cursed and crumpled up the form. She tossed it at a trash can. Caleb watched the ball of paper sail through the air. Then he turned his attention back to Lauren.

"Did you read it? I meant what I wrote."

"So, wait, I'm supposed to believe you, a man who told me just a couple of weeks ago that he couldn't give me what I wanted, who has told me more than once he couldn't be in a relationship with me, who has decided to come to my place of business and pretend to adopt a cat as a way to win me back?"

The smile that had been playing across Caleb's lips fell. He glanced toward Evan, who moved his hand in a circular *keep going* gesture.

Caleb sighed. "This was supposed to be my big romantic gesture. See, isn't it cute? Caleb's adopting a cat. But he'd never adopt a cat because he's a dog person. Ha, ha."

Lauren rolled her eyes. Her stomach churned. She felt like she was the butt of some April Fools' joke. "How gullible do you think I am?"

"No, I..." Caleb frowned and rubbed his forehead. "I'm fucking this up. This was supposed to be a cute gesture where I get you to laugh long enough for me to tell you I made a huge mistake. You were right, I put up walls and didn't give us a chance to see where things could go. I thought I didn't want to be in a relationship, and I still think relationships are scary and risky generally, but I want to be with you enough that I'm willing to take the risk. I've missed you like crazy since we ended things."

Wasn't this what Lauren had wanted to hear? Hadn't she fantasized about the moment Caleb realized he was stupid to let her go and came groveling back? Well, here he was. He was telling her he'd made a mistake and he wanted to be with her. But something still wasn't right.

"How do I trust this?" she asked. "How do I know you won't change your mind in a week and send me packing again?"

"Well, speaking of packing, I thought this could help." He reached into his pocket and pulled out a keychain with two keys on it. The tag was shaped like an old-fashioned suitcase. He handed it to Lauren.

Lauren held it and examined it. "What is this?" she asked, her pulse kicking up.

"Well, we talked a lot about our baggage, about how it was in the way. I thought this could be a peace offering. Those are the keys to my apartment. The square one is the deadbolt and the round one is the main lock."

"You're...giving me keys to your place?"

He took a step toward her. "I want us to be a couple for real. To go over each other's places when we feel like it, because we trust each other and are comfortable around each other. In a way, I guess I'm sharing my baggage with you, too. My past experience is part of who I am now and I can't just get rid of it, but maybe with you, I won't let it hold me back anymore."

Lauren looked down at the keychain in her hand, feeling mystified. He... He was really telling her he wanted them to be a couple. Giving her keys felt like a tangible commitment. He was trying to tell her he'd heard her and what she'd asked of him and was trying to give it to her now.

What did she want? She looked up at Caleb and met his gaze. Well, she cared about him. She loved him, in fact. She'd been miserable the last few weeks since they'd ended things.

What about the whole focusing on herself thing? She was pretty happy about her job. It was going well, even though she was losing sleep over a pending discussion about money with Diane. Still, she liked the challenge of demonstrating that she could expand the business in a viable way. And she loved her apartment, she loved the cats, she loved her friends. And she loved Caleb. Being with him would make her happy. And if the ultimate goal was to be happy, shouldn't she go for it?

"You're not talking," said Caleb. "Please say something. What do you think? Am I too late, or..."

"No, you're not too late," Lauren said, the words coming out a little watery. "This is..." She held up the keychain. "You're really serious. You want us to be together."

"Yes. It was wrong of me to end things without really trying to make it work. I've regretted that since the moment I walked out of your apartment. I just didn't know how to give you what you wanted. But now I do. So, yes, I do want to be with you. And, hey, all your closest friends are here to bear witness to it."

"You invited them?"

"Well, I invited Evan. He took some liberties."

"You're welcome!" Evan shouted from across the room.

Lauren laughed. "Well... I mean, I can't believe you..."

"Lauren. Letting you go was a stupid thing for me to do. I was wrong about us. Yeah, we argue about dumb things sometimes, but that just means we're both passionate people with strong opinions, and the truth is, toward the end we agreed more often than we didn't. Anything we disagree on is something we can work on together. I mean, I may even come around on the whole keeping-a-cat-as-a-pet thing."

Sadie wandered over then and rubbed up against Caleb's leg. Caleb bent to give her scritches on her head.

"Well. I'll believe that when I see it." Lauren took a deep breath and looked at the keychain again. Could she deal with Caleb's baggage? Yeah, she probably could. "You mean it. You want to be with me?" Every time she repeated it, it felt truer.

Caleb opened his mouth to say something, then snapped his jaw shut, then shook his head like he'd made a decision. "Yes," he said. "I want to be with you. I love you."

Well, there it was. They loved each other. And hopefully that was enough. They could work together on everything else.

"Please say it's not too late," Caleb said. "You want to be with me too, right? I'm not just embarrassing myself in front of all your friends so you can kick me to the curb, am I?"

"No, I…" Warmth spread across Lauren's chest. This was really happening. Caleb was standing here telling her he wanted to be with her, he loved her, and they could have what she'd wanted for them since the first time she'd realized she liked him more than she hated him.

That line between love and hate really was thin, wasn't it? Or was it a coin that was easy to flip around?

She smiled. "You're not too late. I'll take you back. I love you, too."

His whole face lit up. "Really?"

"Yeah."

"Kiss her!" yelled Evan.

Caleb laughed. Then he closed the distance between them, cupped her face, and placed a perfect kiss against her lips.

Lauren parted her lips to let him in more deeply, putting her hands on his shoulders, then behind his head to pull him closer, and he put his hands on her waist to hold her there. And they kissed right there, in the middle of the cat room, with the whole crowd of friends and customers looking on. Their relationship was secret no longer.

Lauren eased away and took a step back. Everyone was staring at them with giddy expressions on their faces.

"You know," Lauren said to Caleb, "normal boyfriends bring their girlfriends flowers. Not cheap keychains."

"Sure, but I also know a lot of flowers contain toxins that are bad for cats."

Lauren laughed.

Paige stepped forward. "I'd offer you privacy, but, well, this is a place of business and it's the middle of the day."

Lauren was tired of having an audience anyway. To Paige and Monique, she said, "You guys have got the rest of the day handled, right?"

"Absolutely," said Monique, smiling.

"Cool. Come on, Caleb, we'll go to my place."

She grabbed his hand and started leading him toward the door. There were some hoots and hollers from the peanut gallery.

"You...consulted with Evan to do all this?" Lauren asked.

"Yeah. Was that the wrong thing to do? The cat application thing was his idea."

"It was probably exactly the right thing to do. Evan has been rooting for us all along."

"Really?"

"He's a smart guy."

He was so smart, in fact, that he'd run into the back and returned with Lauren's handbag. He handed it to her and then said, "You crazy kids get out of here."

Lauren squeezed Caleb's hand. "All right. Let's go, Caleb."

───────────

As he crossed the threshold, Caleb realized the last time he'd been in Lauren's apartment was the day he'd left her. It felt a little strange to be walking back into it now.

"Pardon the mess," said Lauren. "I wasn't expecting anyone to come over today."

Caleb looked around. The apartment wasn't messy so much as a little cluttered. The blanket on the sofa was askew, there was an empty coffee cup on the table, and she busied herself now with picking some errant pieces of mail off the floor.

"Molly can't abide my leaving mail on this table," Lauren said. "I'm forever picking it up. Anyway."

And now it was awkward. Where should Caleb stand? What should he say?

Lauren pulled the keychain he'd given her out of her pocket and hung it on a hook next to the door. "This is really a key to your apartment? It's not just some old key you put on here to make a point?"

"Those are real keys. I meant everything I said. That's why I got witnesses."

"You didn't have to go that far."

"Yes, I did. I had to do something to prove I'm serious. I do trust you, you know. I mean, maybe text before you come over, but you really are welcome at any time."

Lauren laughed while rolling her eyes. "Text first. Of course."

"If I don't answer, I'm probably sleeping. I do that on my day off a lot."

Lauren shook her head. Caleb couldn't interpret the look.

"What?" he asked.

"I'm not asking for free and open access to your apartment, but you're already putting restrictions on this."

He was about to protest that this had not been his intention, even though he was still a little nervous about her just barging right into his space, but then Molly darted out from under the sofa and streaked across his path, which startled him so much he tripped backward. He caught himself on the arm of the sofa, but he cursed.

Lauren rolled her eyes. "You afraid of my cat?"

Her tone was adversarial, and Caleb couldn't exactly blame her. She'd agreed to take him back, but he still had a little work to do to make her trust him "I'm sorry," he said. He sat on the sofa. "This is going all wrong. I was joking. I mean, I do trust you, but—"

Lauren sat beside him and put her hand over his where it rested on his thigh. "It's okay. We haven't been dating very long. I never even needed that much from you, not this soon. I just wanted you to open up a little and accept that something had changed between us. That we were starting to mean more to each other than just sex. Now you and I can be together and see where it goes."

"I know. I understand that. That's what I was trying to show you. Did I bungle it?"

"No." She smiled.

"Because I've changed. You changed me."

She blinked a couple of times. "Are we having a romantic comedy ending? Is this like every other Julia Roberts movie?"

He laughed. "I'm just a boy...sitting next to a girl...asking her to love him."

She smiled. Her eyes looked a little watery. "*Have* you changed?"

He took a deep breath. "If I haven't, I want to. I'm tired of feeling the way I have since Kara left. Putting on armor may keep me safe, but it sure is lonely in there. And I honestly don't know if you and I will work out. I just know my life is better with you in it. The more time we spent together, the more I started to feel like myself again, and not the jaded asshole I'd become. I will probably never be the old Caleb again, but I am this man now, and I want to be open. Unlocked. Not closed."

She smiled, definitely teary now. She leaned forward, cupped his chin, and pressed her lips against his.

That was when he knew they might be all right. If he remained open to Lauren, they would figure the rest out.

He slid his fingers into her hair. He'd missed this hair, missed the silky feel of it between his fingers. He'd missed her voice, he'd missed the freckles across her nose, he'd missed how heartfelt and genuine she was. He'd missed this woman, period. He deepened the kiss and pulled her into his arms, and before he even knew what was really happening, she was straddling him on the sofa.

"Are we doing this?" he asked, her hair hanging down around his head like a curtain.

"Yeah, we are."

He laughed, encouraged by the growl in her voice. "This is the easy part, you know."

"What, the sexy bits?" She grinned. "I know. We'll have to work at the other stuff. As long as you're willing, I am, too."

"For you? Anything."

They kissed again. Caleb settled back into the sofa and took Lauren into his arms. And he felt...content. Right. Like everything was falling into places. Why had he been fighting so hard to accept this in his life? He'd been so sure Lauren would betray him the way Kara had, but this felt different. He'd learned things in the decade since he and Kara had made a commitment to each other. He'd changed. Things would be different this time. And rather than be afraid of what the future might hold, he'd be open to it.

"So, ah..." Lauren said with a smile, running her hands down Caleb's chest. "Should we, um, seal the deal?"

"Are you making a sexy double entendre?"

"I am."

She waggled her eyebrows, which made him laugh. Had he laughed this much with Kara? No, he didn't think so. And he would stop comparing Lauren to Kara, because this was a different relationship with an entirely different woman, and the potential was there for this to be something really amazing, as long as he stayed open to it.

EPILOGUE

LAUREN WAS PUTTING HER EARRINGS in as she walked out of the bedroom. Hank was asleep on the living room rug, with Molly curled up in a ball against him.

Lauren shook her head. Of all the developments of the last few months, the fact that Hank and Molly got along was the strangest. When Diane had agreed to lease them this place—a two-bedroom up a floor from Lauren's old one-bedroom—Lauren had been convinced putting the animals together would end with Molly scratching Hank's face off, but they'd become fast friends instead.

Caleb was in the kitchen pouring himself a bowl of cereal. He was still in his gym clothes, beads of sweat standing out against his hairline. His one complaint about the building was that it wasn't near any good places to run, so he'd taken to running on the treadmills at the gym across the street instead. Lauren felt a little bad about that, but not enough to give up her discount on the apartment. There were New Yorkers who would have killed to get the kind of deal they had.

"We still on for dinner tonight?" he asked, his mouth half-full of cereal.

"Elizabeth's at six, yes. See, I'm getting better at letting go and delegating. The Cat Café is open until eight today. Paige is closing."

"I'm very proud of you."

"Uh-huh."

He grinned at shoveled another spoonful of cereal into his mouth. "I like how those earrings go with the new ring."

"Yeah?"

He smiled again.

"All right, buddy. Calm down. You look like a cat who just caught a mouse."

"I'd say more like...a dog...who caught a cat?" Caleb laughed. "That metaphor doesn't work at all, does it?" He set his now-empty cereal bowl aside.

"Nope."

Caleb hooked his arm around Lauren and pulled her close. He gave her a quick kiss and said, "I love you. That's all that matters, right?"

"Yeah. I didn't know you'd end up being this sentimental, though. Kind of makes me want old jerk Caleb back."

"Really? That guy's a dick."

Lauren laughed. "Yeah, yeah. Go shower, big guy. We've both got to get to work."

A half hour later, Lauren walked into the Cat Café, the morning rush already in full swing. After ascertaining that the counter crew had things under control, she walked into the cat room and spotted Evan sitting at a table in the corner. He'd been working out of the Cat Café for the last few months, finally having given up on finding a good café from which to freelance. Working from home didn't seem to be ideal, since he'd recently acquired new neighbors in the apartment next door, a lesbian couple who had quite loud, passionate arguments, based on Evan's descriptions.

Lauren knew a little about that.

Although she and Caleb argued hardly ever these days, they still had the occasional dumb arguments over who forgot to pick up milk or whose turn it was to clean Molly's litter box. Caleb got grumpy on rainy days because Hank was sometimes a little too precious about getting wet and there wasn't much in the way of good park space within a ten-block radius, especially as all the new high-rises were eating up downtown Brooklyn. They could both get worked up about their interpretation of a newspaper article or an episode of television, but more often than not, arguments like that ended with them making out on the couch, so it wasn't all bad.

In fact, they were pretty happy these days. And Lauren was about to make Evan happy, too.

Lauren walked up to Evan now and placed a ten-dollar bill on the table.

"What's this for?" asked Evan.

"You told me when he proposed, I owed you ten dollars. I never welch on a bet. So, there you are. Ten dollars."

"He *proposed*? Are you kidding?"

"Nope." She held out her hand to show the ring.

"Holy shit!"

"He proposed last night. In the most Caleb way possible. On the pretense of needing to help Hank stretch his legs, we walked up to the Brooklyn Heights Promenade, and he proposed right there, with the skyline and everything, under the stars. It was pretty romantic."

"Aw. I knew that guy had it in him. Are you guys over the moon or what? You picked a date yet? Can I be your best man?"

"Yes, I'm very happy. No, we haven't picked a date. And yes, you can be my…man of honor."

Evan grinned. "I'll take it." He clapped a few times. "Oh, girl, this is going to be the most fun."

"Really? I never would have guessed you'd get much into wedding planning."

"Hey, my love life is DOA right now. Work is a little slow. I need a project." Evan shrugged. "Also, I told you so."

"I know, I know. I should listen to you more often."

"I *am* usually correct. Oh, speaking of, there's your man."

Lauren looked through the glass door. Caleb had just gotten in the coffee line, as was part of his pre-work routine. He looked up and saw her standing next to Evan. He waved. Evan waved back.

"Am I the first person you told?" Evan asked.

"Yup. Before Facebook, even."

"Wow. I'm flattered."

"Is Paige here? I didn't see her at the counter?"

"Do you not know your own employees' schedules? I know them and I don't even work here."

"What?"

Evan laughed. "Paige had some big date last night. I'm betting it was a disaster, just like all her other dates have been lately. Either way, she took today off. I haven't heard from her yet, though, so maybe it was fine."

"A big date? Do you know who with? Was it that fussy chef Lindsay has been trying to set her up with?"

Evan shrugged. "She didn't say."

As Lauren moved to go tell Caleb to have a good day, Evan called out, "If you're going up there, can you get me a blueberry muffin?"

"Yes, fine."

Lauren walked through the door. She slid into the line with Caleb and took his hand. "Good morning again," she said.

"Morning. Everything here looks under control."

"Yeah, it seems to be. Although I can't wait until we finally find the right pastry chef, because we're already down to the last bagel, and it would be nice if we had someone in back who could, like, whip up another batch."

"Are bagels really the sort of thing you just whip up?"

"I dunno. I don't know how to make bagels. I'm just saying."

"Did you figure out the health inspector situation?"

"Diane's lawyer is supposed to come by tomorrow."

They got to the front of the line then. Caleb ordered his regular coffee to go and Lauren asked for a couple of muffins.

After Caleb doctored his coffee, he gave Lauren a kiss on the cheek. "I gotta go take care of some animals."

"My hero."

"I'll check on that kitten Mitch brought in for you and let you know at lunchtime if I can. If not, I'll see you at dinner. Fiancée."

Lauren smiled broadly. She liked the sound of that. "All right. Fiancé. Have a good day."

He smiled. "I will. Love you."

"Love you, too."

Lauren watched him go. Then she turned back to the cats.

HEAD BACK TO WHITMAN STREET FOR
MORE ROMANCE AND ANIMAL
HIJINKS IN BOOK TWO OF THE
WHITMAN STREET CAT CAFÉ SERIES

Coming soon from Sourcebooks Casablanca

CHAPTER 1

LANDING A JOB AT A high-powered corporate law firm was not all it was cracked up to be.

At eight o'clock, Mr. Provost's paralegal carried a stack of files into Josh Harlow's office. Josh glanced outside. He had an office, at least. The internship he'd finished at Davis, Cash, and Lee the summer between his second and third years had ensured that he'd be offered a good job at a great salary upon graduating from law school and passing the Bar, which he'd done last summer. Josh certainly couldn't complain on that front; his salary was adding a lot of padding to his bank account right now. Unfortunately, he never got to spend any of it because he spent every waking hour at this very desk.

"Mr. Provost wants a summary of the Donaldson depositions before he has to be in court at ten on Thursday."

"Yeah, no problem. I'll just squeeze that in between the Appleton case and the O'Dwyer paperwork."

The paralegal winced and left the office.

Josh sighed and gazed out the window. His office faced Sixth

Avenue, about three blocks south of Rockefeller Center. He could see roving bands of tourists walking up and down the street, the lights on the signs of the bodegas and souvenir stores and clothing shops and grab-and-go lunch spots across the street. He'd been so absorbed in what he'd been working on that day that he hadn't noticed the sun setting.

New York City had a lot of lawyers, but it also had a lot of ex-lawyers, and Josh was starting to understand why.

When he finally left the office close to midnight, he took advantage of the company car service account and got a ride home. His apartment was in a massive high rise in downtown Brooklyn, and given that he'd started work at DCL about a week after he'd moved to the city, he hadn't had time to decorate or, well, furnish the apartment yet, despite living there for almost six months. The bed, the old sofa, and the kitchen stuff had come from his apartment in Georgetown, but most of his books were still in boxes, his refrigerator was empty except for energy drinks and an expired bottle of milk, and the desk he intended to set up was still packed in a long, slim box, waiting to be assembled.

On the way into the building, he stopped to say hello to Bill, the doorman. He'd picked this building because it was about eight blocks down Whitman Street from the cat café where his sister worked and had an upstairs apartment. When he'd signed the lease, he had a vision of popping down there on weekends to say hi and hang out. He spent his weekends now mostly sleeping or working.

Something had to give. Josh was fucking tired.

As he brushed his teeth, he thought idly about Megan and

what she might be up to now. Was she just as busy at her new firm in Chicago? Although he still felt a pang in his chest whenever he thought of her, maybe it was just as well that they'd broken up. Working a schedule like this, he'd never see her anyway.

He finished the summary of the Donaldson deposition and brought it to Greg Provost the next morning. Provost was a bit of a snake, but he was a partner in the firm, a widely respected attorney, and Josh's boss. He spent the bulk of his time defending the firm's corporate clients against accusations of fraud and other financial crimes. Since Josh had spent the better part of the last twelve hours reading through depositions, he felt confident concluding that the fraud charge in this particular case was bullshit. So he handed over the summary and was getting ready to leave again when Provost gestured toward an empty chair and said, "Have a seat."

Provost had a corner office on the fifty-fourth story of the sleek high-rise the law firm occupied. He wore expensive suits and worked reasonable hours and Josh had to remind himself that paying his dues now was how he himself would eventually get to this place. He took a deep breath and waited for Provost to speak. Provost asked for an assessment of what he'd put together, so Josh gave him the bottom line.

Provost smiled. "Good work. I had a hunch, but I'm glad the rest of the evidence bears that out. Hopefully this stays out of court." Provost set Josh's summary aside. "You got that done rather quickly. I just gave that to Allison last night."

"I worked quite late."

"And I appreciate that. You show a lot of promise, Mr. Harlow. I want to give you some additional help on the Appleton case. Let's get another associate on it and a couple of paralegals. Would that help?"

"Yes, sir. That would be a huge help."

"Great. Hopefully that will free up time for one of the firm's other initiatives."

Oh, great. Just when Josh could almost taste free time, Provost was going to pull him into something else. He knew he had no right to complain; based on all the venting that went on in the private Facebook group for his law school class, his classmates were all going through the same thing right now. This was paying his dues and being rewarded handsomely for it. But at the same time...he missed sleep. And reading novels and watching garbage television and eating home cooked meals. He missed going for runs in the park and going on dates and having art on the walls of his apartment.

"All right," he said.

"We at Davis, Cash, and Lee believe that giving back to the community is something every employee should be a part of. As such, we ask all of our associates to volunteer for something."

Right, of course. Someone had mentioned this to Josh when he interviewed for the job. The associates had to volunteer a set number of hours per quarter. Most of the partners just donated money to good causes, which could be translated into volunteer hours via some elaborate equation. Josh nodded to seem game.

"I'm not picky about what you volunteer for, although my assistant Jane has a list she keeps of organizations we've done work for in the past if you want some suggestions. I only ask it be a long-term project and not just a charity event that takes place once a year."

"No problem. My sister works with a lot of animal shelters. She probably knows of some good volunteer opportunities."

The words were out of Josh's mouth before he realized what he was saying, although it was true that his sister Lauren managed a cat café that did a lot of work with local animal shelters in Brooklyn. It was the path of least resistance—if he just asked Lauren, he could find a project easily and wouldn't have to waste a lot of time researching it.

"Splendid!" said Provost. "Jane's got a form for you to fill out."

Josh arrived back at his own office fifteen minutes later with a form to fill out recording his volunteer hours. He added it to the mound of paper on his desk and wondered if all law firms killed this many trees.

CHAPTER 2

AS PAIGE DANVERS WIPED DOWN the tables after the Whitman Street Cat Café's monthly book club meeting, she heard the bell ring. Startled, she dropped the cleaning cloth, and as she bent to pick it up, she heard her friend and boss Lauren, who'd been cleaning up front, hit the buzzer to let in whoever was at the door. Paige set the cloth aside and left the cat room to investigate.

Mitch walked in. Mitch was an old friend of Lauren's who ran an organization that captured and spayed feral cats.

"Hi, sorry I'm so late," he said to Lauren with a bashful nod toward Paige. Paige didn't like to assume, but she was fairly certain Mitch had a crush on her. He was a nice enough guy, but a good fifteen years older than Paige and really not her type.

"It's fine, Paige and I were just cleaning up after book club. You have flyers for me?"

"Yeah." Mitch carried a medium-size box to the table closest to the counter and put it down. He opened it to show rows of brochures. "A buddy of mine just opened a copy shop in my neighborhood. He let me print these in color for free."

Lauren took one out and looked it over. "Wow, these are nice."

Sadie, the feline café manager, hopped up on the table and sniffed the box. Occasionally, Mitch brought by boxes that had cats or kittens in them, and Sadie was clearly deeply skeptical of this box.

"Not everything needs to be inspected by you," Lauren said.

Sadie meowed in response.

Paige walked over. "Are these for the next rescue night?"

"Yes," said Mitch. "We heard from the mayor's office that there's been something of a cat population explosion in certain Brooklyn neighborhoods, so we're trying to hold these events more often. I updated the brochure to show we're meeting every other week instead of once a month for now. Our next one is next Thursday. You should come."

It was an idle invitation, one Mitch made every time he saw her, but Paige had been meaning to say yes one of these days. As the cat café's events manager, she'd made it a point to get to know all of the animal rescue organizations in the region, because many of them worked with the café to help cats find forever homes. Paige periodically volunteered at a no-kill shelter in Park Slope, but she hadn't done a shift with Mitch's group yet. She was free next Thursday—she was certainly done trying to fill her off hours by dating guys she had no future with—so maybe it was time.

"If I decided to help out next week," Paige said, "what would happen exactly? Because I'm a little worried about a feral cat scratching my eyes out."

Rather than laugh, which Paige had expected, Mitch nodded gravely. "These cats can be dangerous. Some are more skittish than aggressive, but some bite. All volunteers work in groups of two or three, and we recommend wearing long sleeves and pants, heavy clothing if possible. I know it's summer, but better safe than sorry. We provide gloves and will do a workshop on how to trap the cats safely. We're usually out there a couple of hours. Sound good?"

"Yeah, that seems reasonable." Still a little scary. The cats at the café could get hostile if they got riled up enough, and they were all tame, domesticated cats. Paige was a little afraid of the feral ones.

"Cool. We meet in front of the Brooklyn Museum, on the Botanic Garden side. The regulars usually congregate near the subway entrance. Do you know it?"

"Yes. Sounds good. I'll try to make it next week. I've been meaning to, but schedule conflicts." Paige shrugged in a "what can you do" way.

"You should come too, Lauren," said Mitch.

"Not next week, unfortunately. Caleb has a few days off in a row, so we're taking a little vacation. His cousin has a place upstate. We're gonna bring the dog and savor the peace and quiet in the woods. I've been looking forward to this for a month, so I will not be canceling it. Sorry, Mitch."

"Hey, I get it. Spend quality time with your husband." Mitch glanced at his watch. "I just wanted to drop these off. I didn't mean to keep you from closing. I'll get out of your hair. But I hope to see you next Thursday, Paige!"

"Yeah, okay. I'll be there."

Josh could walk to Lauren's place from his downtown Brooklyn high rise easily enough. So the first evening that he actually made it to Brooklyn in time for dinner, he'd texted Lauren, thinking he'd get a cup of coffee and pet some cats, and she invited him to dinner.

Now he sat at a small table off the kitchen in Lauren and Caleb's apartment, three people crammed onto a table that was really only big enough for two.

"Good to see that law firm hasn't killed you yet," said Lauren's husband, Caleb, as he poured wine for everyone.

"It's a near thing," said Josh. "I still haven't decorated my apartment. I miss sports. I miss reading novels and watching shitty television. I miss sex. And bless you for the home cooking, because I've been living off takeout, and it's nice to eat something on a plate instead of out of a plastic container." He surveyed his plate. A nicely seared steak was nestled next to a scoop of rice pilaf and a garlicky vegetable medley. "I didn't know you could cook like this, Lauren."

"Caleb helped. And by helped, I mean he did most of it."

"One of our wedding gifts was a certificate for some cooking classes with a chef one of Lauren's friends knows," said Caleb. "Lauren was busy, so I took the classes."

"Well, that explains a lot." Josh cut off a piece of steak. It melted on his tongue. "Man, that's good. Money well spent on those classes."

Caleb chuckled. "Lauren cooked the rice."

"I boiled the water," Lauren said.

"You did it very well, honey," said Caleb, reaching over to rub her arm.

"Better than Mom," said Josh.

Lauren rolled her eyes. "That's not saying much." To Caleb, she added, "You're still new to the family. Mom is not the best cook."

"The chicken she made the last time we visited was good," said Caleb.

"She's not here," said Josh. "You don't have to be nice."

"Also, that totally came from a store," said Lauren.

"Ah, that checks out." Josh ate a few more bites and said, "Well, anyway. How's business?"

"Good. Diane, the café's owner, is still resisting my plan to hire our own pastry chef, and there's some nonsense with the health department we still have to negotiate to do that, but I think if I find the right person, she'll have to hire them."

"Fond as I am of cat hair in my pastries, that seems like something you should be careful about," said Josh.

"Yeah, yeah. I am very careful."

"What's going on with the health department?"

Lauren sighed. "New York has a bunch of rules about animals and food service. This slimy real estate developer guy who has been buying up buildings in the neighborhood tried to shut us down last year by ratting us out to the health department. We were in compliance, so nothing happened." She narrowed her eyes. "Are you trying to lawyer me?"

"Hey, I was just curious. Don't you bring in all your food from outside vendors? Would hiring a pastry chef put you out of compliance?"

"No. Not if we rearrange some things in the cat café. There's a way to do it."

"Uh-huh."

"We have our own lawyer, by the way."

"Okay, okay."

An alarm went off on Lauren's phone. "Hang on, I gotta call Paige."

"Paige?" Josh asked.

As Lauren held the phone to her ear, Caleb explained, "Lauren's friend. She must have had a date tonight. This is the fake emergency call in case Paige needs to bail."

"Huh. I thought they only did that on TV."

"Paige doesn't have...the best judgment. I don't know if she only dates guys who are all wrong for her or if she hasn't quite learned that men are not exactly at their most truthful when filling out their online dating profiles. Either way, she goes on a lot of bad dates."

"Yikes."

"Don't get me wrong, Paige is great. One of the sweetest, nicest people you'll ever meet. She was one of Lauren's brides-maids at the wedding, actually."

Josh frowned. He had missed the wedding and was still upset about it. He'd flown to Chicago two days before to interview at one of the big law firms there, figuring he and Megan could save their relationship if he moved with her, even though he had the job at DCL waiting for him in New York. Not only had he completely bombed in the interview and not gotten the job, but a massive storm had blown through the Midwest and grounded a bunch of flights, and Josh couldn't get anywhere near the East Coast until the day after the wedding. So he'd missed his own sister's wedding and had not gotten the job or the girl in the end.

Caleb shrugged. "She's smart and together most of the time. Just not when it comes to her love life."

Lauren put her phone on the table. "No fake emergency needed. He stood her up."

"Wow," said Caleb.

Josh laughed, a little surprised at all this. He and Lauren had always been close, but many years of living in different cities meant they weren't up to date with each other's friends or personal lives. This was also quite different from life at the law firm, but in a refreshing way. Nice to talk about friends' misguided dating decisions instead of depositions and briefs. "Anyway, you were saying about the pastry chef?"

Lauren waved her hand. "It's all boring work stuff. Not important. How's the job going?"

Josh would rather have gossiped about strangers than talk about work, but he said, "It's pretty interesting. I just wish I didn't keep getting stuck at the office after hours to get everything done. On the other hand, I just made a huge student loan payment. So, silver lining."

"Oof," said Lauren.

"But actually, there is something you can help me with. My boss is urging all the associates to do some kind of volunteer work, because DCL gives back to the community." Josh added some sarcasm, which made Lauren chuckle. "You work with a lot of animal rescue organizations, right? Can you think of any opportunities?"

Lauren nodded. "My friend Mitch runs an organization that traps, neuters, and returns feral cats. He's doing an event next

Thursday. He dropped off brochures at the café yesterday. I can email you the details."

"Isn't that dangerous?"

"It can be, but he trains everyone before he puts them to work."

"Have you ever done it?"

Lauren shook her head.

"I did events like that a few times when I lived in Boston," said Caleb. "A lot of it is just setting up traps and waiting around for the cats to walk into them."

"Well, that doesn't sound too hard."

"Then I'm one of the vets who actually neuters them and has to deal with them when they come out of anesthesia. So you have the easy job."

Caleb's tone was light, but Josh took his point. "Fair enough."

"The feral cats don't usually bite too hard," said Lauren, a twinkle in her eye.

"Gee, thanks."

Acknowledgments

This book would not have happened without Cat Clyne, who was the first to suggest a cat café as the setting for a romance series and start my brain down the path that led to Whitman Street. I also want to thank Deb Werksman for her guidance and enthusiasm when she took over this project in Cat's stead. And thank you to my agent, Moe Ferrara, for her feedback and help getting this series out into the world.

The Whitman Street Cat Café is very loosely based on the Brooklyn Cat Café on Montague Street in Brooklyn Heights. I invented a lot of the details in my cat café, but I drew inspiration from the real-life café's mission to rescue and find forever homes for the city's cats. As of this writing, the Brooklyn Cat Café is the only cat café in the city run by an animal rescue organization. And as the pet parent of two shelter cats myself, it's a mission I believe in strongly. Please consider donating or volunteering at an animal shelter near you!

And finally, I want to thank my Writing Gals: Rayna, Tere, Libby, Sabrina, and Holly. You guys are all amazing, your support and encouragement mean the world to me, and you have kept me sane through some truly difficult times. Go team!

About the Author

Kate McMurray writes smart, savvy romantic fiction. She likes creating stories that are brainy, funny, and of course, sexy, with regular guy characters and urban sensibilities. She advocates for romance stories by and for everyone. When she's not writing, Kate edits textbooks, watches baseball, plays violin, crafts things out of yarn, and wears a lot of cute dresses. Kate's gay romances have won or finaled several times in the Rainbow Awards for LGBT fiction and nonfiction. She also served in the leadership of Romance Writers of America. Kate lives in Brooklyn, New York, with two cats and too many books.

Website: katemcmurray.com

Facebook: facebook.com/katemcmurraywriter

Twitter: @katemcmwriter

Pinterest: pinterest.com/katem1738

Instagram: @katemcmurraygram